The Road Home

LAURA TONWE

For Arthur.

I'd also like to acknowledge Jensen Beach for all his help in coaching me through the many drafts of this book.

PART ONE

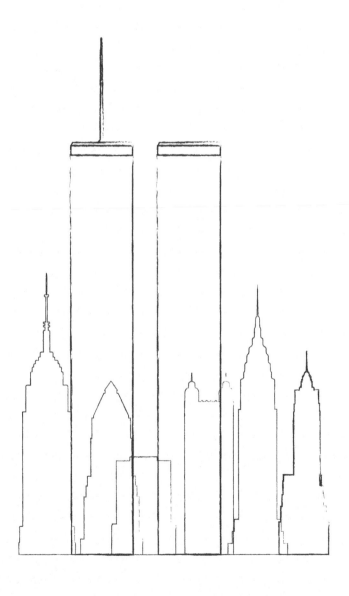

CHAPTER 1

My walk from the subway was subdued. The ghost of Rose from the movie *Titanic* was traipsing a step behind me. An older man wearing a New York Yankees windbreaker was selling snow globes for five dollars with the World Trade Center still part of the skyline. I bought one. We resumed walking. I yawned. I looked over at Rose to see if she had noticed, but she was looking around Midtown with the interest of a tourist on her first trip to New York.

I had stayed up too late last night watching old VCR movies. In an attempt to avoid the news, I had been watching a lot of movies lately. It was my first day back to an office since our headquarters downtown had disintegrated into dust.

As I walked from the Grand Central 4/5 train stop to our temporary office building on 53st and Lexington, I tried not to look at the numerous "Missing" posters covering every street light and pole.

When I got to the Citibank Building, I checked in with security and posed for a new badge. Normally I would have had to go down into a dark corner of the basement to get an employee identification photo taken, but there were so many Sun Microtek employees showing up to the new offices that they were making IDs right at the front security desk.

Badge in hand, I took the elevator to the sixth floor and tentatively opened the glass doors to our temporary suite. The borrowed office space smelled of fresh paint and carpet fibers. There was no assigned seating, so I looked for an empty desk.

People were in small groups talking quietly with each other or in solitary cubes hunched over their laptops. I didn't know the new office's floor plan, so I ended up going around in circles before I found an empty desk near some file cabinets. I set out a loose-leaf notebook on the desk. I hadn't gotten my new laptop yet, my old one having been lost in the fire and dust.

"This place looks so sterile. It needs some art to liven the walls." Rose wrinkled her nose in distaste as she looked around the office.

"It looks like an opportunity to me!" The ghost of Tess from *Working Girl* had joined us. She was in an expensive grey suit that she had borrowed from her boss in the movie, Katherine Parker. The cut of Tess's suit was tailored, with giant shoulder pads. She was wearing her own shoes, patent leather pumps that did not quite match the conservative suit. The whole outfit looked like it was from 1986, which didn't surprise me since "Working Girl" was released in 1988. I remembered the first time I saw the movie, my freshman year of college. I had sympathized with Tess back then and had cheered her on as she risked everything for a better career.

Rose looked skeptically at Tess before taking my arm as she said to me, "Don't let others distract you. It's your first day back."

I had some time before the 1 pm meeting with MV1's Chief Technology Officer. He was an expert in digital content, a new and growing field. I had read an interview last year that he had given *Wired* magazine on the topic. I had never met him before. Although I had been with Sun Microtek for five years as a solutions engineer, I had just recently asked to be switched to media accounts.

My manager Chris had declined my request to transfer from the financial vertical to media accounts at first. But I had gone over his head and had asked his boss Brett to be reassigned. Brett had agreed to my request and had assigned me to work on the MediaCom account, which was comprised of the MV1(a popular music video channel), NBS (a traditional broadcast TV channel), and the other MediaCom brands such as KidsNetwork, and Comedy Network. I hoped that being a solutions engineer for the MediaCom account would prove more interesting than working on the stock trading portals that I had been assigned to before the Towers had fallen.

Chris had reluctantly given me the name of the MediaCom account manager, Michael Jennings. I was supposed to meet him at the reception desk here and walk or take a cab to Times Square with him for the 1 pm meeting. It was only 9:30 am, and I had time to kill. I decided to get up and try to find someone I knew or at least a cup of coffee.

"Excuse me, is this seat taken?"

I looked up, startled by the polite British accent. Standing over my desk was one of the most gorgeous men I had ever seen in person. He was impeccably dressed in a highly tailored, European-cut black suit with a purple tie. He had on stylish short boots. His hair was over his ears but also slicked back, with well-trimmed sideburns. He had pale skin and grey eyes that slanted slightly at the corners, giving him a glamorous, European look. If I had seen him on the street, I would have assumed he was a British rock star.

"No, I don't think so." I stammered.

"What a hunk!" Tess whistled.

"I'm Michael Jennings."

"Stephanie Willis."

"Are you the new engineer on the MV1 account? "

I nodded.

"Great. I was hoping we'd be able to sync up before the meeting."

Michael imparted this in a low-key manner, but there was something about the intense focus in his eyes that let me know this account was important to him. I didn't share his enthusiasm. The only meaningful aspect of this account to me was that it wasn't downtown amidst the ruins.

"Would you like to grab some coffee and go over the agenda for the meeting?"

Michael was standing very close to me. I looked up at him and saw that he had an almost imperceptible black shadow under each eye, shadows that looked like he might have covered them up with makeup. This made him somehow more human to me. I smiled.

"Sure."

Instead of grabbing coffee at the deli downstairs, I was surprised when Michael walked us to the bar across the street.

"We'll have more room to go over our notes there."

The bar was empty and dark. Michael led us to a booth in the back.

"Your expression reminds me of how I felt when I first boarded the Titanic."

Rose squeezed my hand, quoting one of her lines from the movie.

I gave Rose a tight smile to let her know I was fine.

An older Russian waiter with a buzz-cut and thick eyebrows brought us menus. He gave us a look of weary patience as he stood at the side of the booth, waiting to take our order. I paused to see what Michael was going to do. I didn't want to be preoccupied with eating if he was deeply focused on work.

"I'll have a Bloody Mary, double vodka."

Michael turned to me to see if I also wanted a drink. It was 9:30.

"Coffee, please, cream and sugar."

"Would you like something to eat?" Michael looked at me politely, gesturing to the menu with his eyes.

"OK. One drink, but I'm buying." Tess gave Michael a grin as she quoted her line from *Working Girl*. Rose gave Tess a withering look. Michael motioned to the waiter, who was standing over our booth, his pencil poised.

"She'll have two scrambled eggs, bacon and wheat toast."

I was relieved that the decision had been made for me.

4

When the waiter left the table, Michael turned to me, his tone professional.

"Here are some ground rules of how I'd like to conduct the meeting. I'll broker all communication with the CTO. If he has a question, please look to me before you answer. I may want to check with our lead engineers at corporate before we give him an official response."

Michael took a big gulp of his drink, which the waiter had silently set before him a moment earlier. I put some cream in my coffee and took a sip. It was lukewarm.

"The goal is to become a trusted advisor to the CTO," he added.

"What's a CTO?" Rose asked this as she watched Michael with curiosity.

"It's a technical executive, usually one who sets technical strategy for a company," said Tess, answering the question for me. Rose looked like she wanted to ask more questions, but she just nodded.

Michael took another gulp of his Bloody Mary. The phrase "trusted advisor" was such a cliché that when Michael used the term, I thought he was joking. Yet his look was dead serious.

"I'll take your lead, Michael."

The Russian waiter approached the table, a sour expression on his thick-jawed face, and set my food down. I took a bite of toast and wiped my mouth with the paper napkin that my silverware had been rolled up in. Michael reached again for his Bloody Mary, and I noticed his hands were shaking. Was he nervous about the meeting?

I tried to remember what it felt like to care about the outcome of a meeting. Everyone at work would be pleased if we established executive relationships at MV1, but I couldn't find any part of me that cared.

I looked down at my breakfast. The toast was sitting in my stomach undigested. I pushed the plate away.

"I was never much of a breakfast person. Our cook made too many cream sauces for the eggs. Those look dry and overcooked." Rose said this as she pointed to my plate with her gloved hand. I just nodded, not replying.

Michael pointed to my abandoned breakfast. "Not as hungry as you thought?" He downed the last of his drink and gave me a mischievous smile. He then motioned to the waiter who was leaning against the faded Formica bar and reading a Russian newspaper.

"Two more of these." He pointed to his empty glass. I started to say no to the drink, but Michael put his index finger to his lip. "It will help. Trust me."

CHAPTER 2

The Bloody Mary had helped. As we walked towards the MV1 offices, I felt almost normal. I had never had a drink in the morning on a workday in my life.

I would have been willing to walk the 15 or so blocks to the MV1 offices, but Michael had hailed a taxi instead. It was 12:30 when the Taxi let us out in front of the MV1 building. Times Square was less crowded than I had ever seen it at this time of day. There was a subdued air amidst the flashing lights of the billboards and marquees. The tourist shops were mostly closed, and the few people walking on the street were professionally dressed and walking with purpose. The taxis were not honking at one another, and this gave the street a surreal quiet.

As we entered the lobby of the MV1 building, we were stopped by a security guard with wavy grey hair and a thick mustache. He was around 50 years old and looked tired. The guard guided us to a makeshift metal detector that had been hastily installed. He pointed to it and motioned for us to put our bags and keys through the machine.

"What is this thing?" Rose looked with a puzzled expression at the X-ray machine.

"They have these at airports, but I've never seen one in an office building," Tess told her, as she too stared at the metal detector with curiosity.

I stood frozen, looking at the guard's blue uniform and badge. Michael watched me from the other end of the checkpoint as I stood there trapped by the blue police uniform. I looked beyond him in terror.

"Ma'am?"

The guard politely urged me to move through the line. I closed my eyes, trying to push away the images that were filling my mind.

Police in blue uniforms running from the dust cloud.

Police pulling bodies into ambulances.

Police telling us to get out of the way.

I could smell the acrid smell of the burning dust. I coughed as if smoke were choking me. I'm not sure how long I stood there, but at some point, I felt a cool, firm hand grasp my elbow. I opened my eyes. Michael was standing next to me, coaxing me to the arch of the metal detector.

"Thank you, sir, for your patience," Michael said as he nodded to the security guard. He let go of my arm and whispered to me, "You can do this." He then gave me an almost imperceptible push towards the archway. I took a tentative step and a deep breath and went through. Michael followed. The guard nodded to Michael with a look of weary understanding.

Rose looked at the metal detector, her eyes haunted, as she whispered,

"I felt like I was standing at a great precipice, with no one to pull me back, no one who cared... or even noticed..."

"I care."

Tess said this as she pushed Rose through the archway.

We walked to the elevators.

"Are you ready to go upstairs?"

Michael's look of concern made me feel self-conscious.

"Yes, of course. Thanks."

The CTO's office was on the 67th floor. Tess gave Michael an approving look as she watched him whisper the elevator pitch that he was going to recite to Dennis when we were introduced. He was tapping his foot, and there were tiny beads of sweat on his upper lip, even though the elevator was air-conditioned. I wanted to feel sympathy for him, but I was just relieved that he didn't ask me any more questions.

When we got out of the elevator, Michael pulled out a container of Tic-Tacs from his pants pocket and popped a few in his mouth. He grabbed my hand and put some into my palm, and I put them in my mouth and followed him to the receptionist's desk, Rose and Tess close behind me.

"We're here to see Dennis Hickman."

Michael gave the young receptionist a warm smile. She was dressed in a garish mini dress with large daisies and an oversized collar and was wearing too much blue eyeshadow. As Michael held the receptionist's gaze, she shifted in her seat and fiddled with her curly red hair, her face flushing. Michael pulled out a business card from a silver engraved case in his jacket pocket. He let his hand linger over the receptionist's hand as he handed her his card. She giggled nervously and then quickly caught herself, pulling her hand away. "I'll let Mr. Hickman know you're here," she said in an overly professional tone.

Tess rolled her eyes. The receptionist rose from her desk and went to an executive office suite behind her receptionist station. As she walked to the suite, she straightened her skirt and turned around to see if Michael was watching. A few moments later, the receptionist returned and smiled warmly at Michael.

"Mr. Hickman will see you now."

She led us to a conference room that was attached to Mr. Hickman's office suite. The conference room had pictures of various MV1 VJs as well as photos of the MV1 Music Awards through the 1980s and 90s. There was a sizeable ceiling-to-floor window in the back of the room that overlooked Times Square.

Michael approached Dennis, shaking his hand. "It's a pleasure to meet you. I'm Michael, and this is my engineer, Stephanie."

Dennis motioned us to take a seat. He was in his late forties, with grey-ing reddish hair. He wore khakis and a navy polo shirt with "MediaCom" embroidered over its left-hand chest pocket. I shook Dennis's hand and then sat down next to Michael. Rose and Tess sat at the other end of the conference table.

I tried to pay attention as Michael talked about how our software company could make things easier for Dennis, but the double-shot Bloody Mary and the stress of getting through the metal detector had taken their toll.

Tess was looking at a bookshelf that ran along one wall. It contained a selection of business and technology books. I noticed that one of the books, *Managing Media in a Digital Revolution*, was written by Dennis.

"I read a lot of things. You never know where a big idea is gonna come from," she said as I stifled a yawn.

Rose was looking around the paneled conference room.

"This room reminds me of the library on the Titanic."

"This place is nothing like a ship. This room is an opportunity in the making. If you impress Mr. Hickman, you can write your own ticket!" Tess looked at Rose with annoyance and then turned to me, her eyes brimming with excitement.

I ignored Tess, putting all my attention into keeping my eyes open and not looking like I was nodding out. I glanced at Michael. He was still giving a sales pitch to Dennis.

"Our response rate is best in class. At Sun Microtek, we excel at stra-tegic partnerships."

Dennis looked bored. He interrupted Michael.

"We're having trouble scaling our web properties and want to add live video events. Have you solved that problem for anyone?"

"I don't know off-hand, but I'll talk with my colleagues and get back to you with an answer."

Michael nervously scribbled in his notebook as he said this. He looked like he was concentrating on every word he was writing. He was about to continue speaking when Dennis held up his hand and turned to me.

"What do you think, Stephanie?"

I was surprised that Dennis remembered my name. Executives usually ignored engineers. I looked over to Michael, who was equally y astonished that Dennis was addressing me.

I wasn't sure what to do. Michael had given me clear orders not to speak in the meeting without his guidance. Account managers owned the relationships with any executives in an account. But to turn to Michael for guidance when asked a direct question would make me look like an idiot.

"Go for it! This is your chance!" Tess pointed to Dennis.

I decided to answer and deal with the repercussions after the meeting. The worst that could happen would be a lecture and hand slap, and frankly, I didn't care. If Michael didn't want to work with me, they could assign me to a different account. One account was as good as the next for me at this point, as long as it was an account that wasn't downtown.

"I think that scaling is a matter of caching as much content as possible along with having burstable bandwidth and standby connected hardware. You should look at video compression as well."

I spoke with confidence. I hoped my voice didn't sound too cocky. Dennis was a CTO and an expert in digitization. I'm sure he knew more than his question suggested. Michael glanced at Dennis nervously. There was a pause.

Dennis turned to me, his eyes lingering on my chest. His nod and knowing smile reminded me of the expressions my professors had always given when I answered a question correctly. He probably knew the answer to his question and was just seeing what Michael and I would say. Dennis spoke directly to me, ignoring Michael.

"Sounds good Stephanie, I'll tell my VP of Media Operations, Rodney Grover, to gather a team to meet with you. We need to solve this problem before the Movie Awards in June and the Music Awards in late August. We plan to have live streaming content for both shows."

Dennis reached out and shook my hand, his eyes holding mine. "Rodney will be in touch." He then turned around and left the conference room.

"Score!" Tess shouted this as she reached over to give me a high five. Rose grabbed Tess's arm, shaking her head. She put her gloved finger to her lips as she whispered to Tess, "Behave yourself."

In the elevator, Michael and I were silent. Michael looked like he was deep in thought. I was wide awake now. When we got outside the building, Michael turned to me and shook my hand, holding my gaze.

"Excellent job Stephanie, you really moved the ball forward in establishing traction in the account. Would you like to go for a drink to celebrate?"

It was 2 pm, and I didn't have any other appointments that afternoon. The thought of going back to the temporary offices depressed me.

"Sure," I said quietly, letting him hold my gaze.

CHAPTER 3

"Hungry like the Wolf' is one of the best videos ever made. It absolutely launched MV1."

I leaned closer to Michael as I said this. I looked at the eight empty shot glasses lined up on the bar. How long had we been here? I squinted as I looked around for Rose and Tess. They were nowhere to be found.

"Bullshit. Duran Duran are a bunch of pussies."

Michael whispered this, leaning in close. I opened my mouth to protest, but he put his finger to his lips and then kissed my nose. Before I could react, Michael had pulled back and motioned to the bartender for another round of drinks.

"No, really! MV1 became a big deal because of artsy videos like 'Hungry like the Wolf.'"

I wanted Michael to see the social significance of what I was saying. If I was going to work on the MV1 account with him, it was important that he understand that I understood that MV1 had been about artsy videos.

"You can't buy me off with drinks! You know I'm right!" I pointed to the empty shot glasses. Michael took hold of my finger, putting my hand on his thigh.

"Duran Duran lack sexual heat. They're neutered, sissy boys."

I was surprised at myself for not pulling my hand away from his thigh. But It felt nice and warm there. Heat.

Michael was right. "Hungry Like the Wolf" had no heat. Like the Towers. They had disappeared so quickly that the fire had not added extra warmth to the air. But the fire from the Towers was a different kind of heat. Wait.

I shook my head, trying to clear it.

The bar was now packed. I squinted and looked at my watch. 6:45. Had I eaten lunch? No, just some peanuts at the bar. I looked at the empty shells scattered amidst a couple of stained cocktail napkins and the empty shot glasses. The bartender hadn't been doing a very good job of cleaning up after us.

My hand was still on Michael's thigh, although his attention was now engaged with trying to catch the bartender's eye. When the bartender looked his way, he ordered another round for us. I wasn't used to drinking like this. I was dizzy. I grabbed the glass of water that was next to my drink and took a gulp. The glass had condensation on it, which made it slippery, and the glass slid from my grasp. I watched it tip over onto the bar, spilling its contents. The water soaked the cocktail napkins and formed a rapidly moving trail towards Michael's arm, which was resting on the bar.

I was glad that he had taken his suit jacket off earlier. I clumsily tried to put the water glass upright, but Michael stopped me and put my hand back on this thigh.

Michael set the glass upright and took his jacket off the stool where he had set it down. He put his suit coat on the bar, and it quickly absorbed the water. I gasped as I watched his expensive designer suit coat take in the water, some stray drops of bourbon, and the lint from the cocktail napkins.

When I gasped, Michael leaned over and kissed me, leaving his suit jacket on the bar to absorb the rest of the liquid.

Michael's kiss felt warm and clean. His tongue lingered lazily in my mouth, casually exploring. My body felt stiff and uncertain. Michael pulled away and grabbed two shot glasses from the bar. He downed his and then put mine to my lips. I drank it. He took the empty shot glasses and put

14

them back on the bar, and continued to kiss me. This time I was more relaxed, although the room was spinning. I clung to him more for support than out of any passion.

Michael pulled away and looked down into my eyes. I grabbed onto the bar to keep from sliding off my stool. I stared at the bar's dark, paneled walls with bar mirrors advertising various brands of beer. I couldn't focus. I squinted and looked over at Michael, who was watching me with amusement. He reached over and ran his hand through my hair, straightening it. He then pointed to my vodka and tonic.

"Take a drink. It'll help settle your stomach."

When had the bartender brought new drinks? I tried to concentrate on the cocktail glass on the counter, but it remained blurry. Michael held the drink to my lips, and I took a small sip. Aside from wearing no jacket, Michael looked like he had just stepped out of a salon. His hair was perfect, his eyes looked clear and sharp, and his clothes still looked pressed. How did he do it? I shook my head.

"What?"

"It's just that you look perfect. How can you look so good after being out drinking all day?"

I put my hand over my mouth. I hadn't intended to say any of that out loud. Michael laughed.

"Practice."

He raised his bourbon to me and took a sip.

We settled in again. The music from the jukebox, the clinking of glasses, and the conversation and laughter of other bar patrons all blurred together and wrapped around me like a colorful blanket. I squinted at the clock on the wall of the bar. 9:30. How had it gotten so late? Michael finally looked drunk.

"Wanna get out of here?"

I nodded, and Michael motioned to the bartender to cash out. Once our tab was settled, Michael grabbed his jacket and helped me up.

We both covered our eyes from the brightness of the lights outside. Michael and I walked towards the cab with his arm around me. He opened the cab door for me, and I climbed in. Before I could give the cab driver my address, Michael gave him his.

"330 West 33rd street."

He looked at me to make sure I was ok with this. I thought hazily of my apartment, with the F-15s flying overhead on security alert and the smell of burning dust.

Michael's apartment was at least in midtown.

I nodded. Michael pulled me closer. I rested my head on his shoulder during the short cab ride and tried not to fall asleep.

When we got to Michael's building, the doorman, a Hispanic man in his thirties, was slouched on a card chair with his red uniform jacket unbuttoned, exposing his frayed greyish-white T-shirt. He looked at us with bleary eyes and nodded to Michael. The building was old, with a faded lobby that looked like it hadn't been renovated since the 1970s.

The elevator could barely hold the two of us. Michael kissed me. I could feel his erection as he pressed against me. The solidity of it made me feel steadier. I pressed back into it and kissed him in return.

When we got to Michael's floor, he slowly pulled away from me and put his arm around my waist, walking me to his apartment. He opened his door and switched on a light. His apartment was small but well-appointed, with mid-century modern furniture and a large flat-screen television. Michael resumed kissing me, taking my purse and putting it on the kitchen counter. He unbuttoned my blouse. I tried to unbutton his shirt, but I was unsteady on my feet, and although I pawed at the buttons, none came undone. Michael pulled back and looked at me, his eyes smoky with passion.

I tried to focus on Michael, but he was blurry. He took my hand and led me to his bedroom, which was filled with a huge king-sized bed on a modern wood platform that took up the entire room.

As Michael came forward, I gave up trying to stand and collapsed on my back and landed on the middle of the bed, my feet dangling off the end of the platform.

Being on my back made it much easier for Michael to take off my clothing. He easily removed my blouse and undid my bra while quickly pulling off his own shirt and undershirt, showing me his pale sculpted chest with just a touch of chest hair. He took off his slacks and underwear, and I could see that he was quite aroused, which was a relief. I wouldn't have to work to get him ready for sex, which was fortunate since the room was spinning again.

Michael kissed my breasts and belly button as he removed the rest of my clothing. I touched his chest and stroked his penis when it was near me, but mostly I let him do all the work.

I watched him hovering over me, thrusting, his pale white skin luminous in the darkroom. His eyes were closed, and he seemed really into his experience. I looked around the room while he pushed hard inside me. There was no art on the walls, and all the lighting in the room was built into the platform bed.

In the dark, I could see three ghosts standing in front of Michael's closet, watching me.

The first ghost was a fireman. His uniform was covered in dust and stained with smoke and blood. He was holding an oxygen mask but wasn't wearing it. His eyes looked sincere and compassionate as he watched me fumble on the bed with Michael. He reached out to offer me his oxygen mask. I shook my head, giving him a polite smile of thanks.

I heard a laugh when I declined the oxygen mask. The ghost of Paul Newman's character Doug Roberts, the architect in the 1974 disaster movie

The Towering Inferno, was grinning. "If you don't need an oxygen mask during sex, then you're not doing it right." He gave me a wink.

Standing next to Doug was Susan, Doug's beautiful fiancée, played by Faye Dunaway in the movie. Susan was wearing her long light brown hair parted naturally. She had on a cream-colored, low-cut Halston silk pantsuit, and her brown eyeshadow and false eyelashes and frosted lipstick made her look the very pinnacle of 1974 glamour.

"We were hoping to borrow Michael's bed to celebrate the putting out of the fire in the building Doug designed. It's the tallest building in the world!"

Susan looked up at Doug proudly as she said this. Doug bent down and kissed her before turning to me. "What are you doing here?" he asked in a teasing tone.

"I don't know."

I'm not sure I said this out loud. The room started spinning again. I closed my eyes to settle my dizziness, and when I opened them, Doug, Susan, and the fireman were gone. I had missed my chance to tell Susan that Doug's building was no longer the tallest building in the world. Willis Tower in Chicago now held that honor.

The Twin Towers had been second and third tallest.

With the ghosts gone, there was nothing for my eyes to focus on except Michael. His body was lean and toned, and he had a tattoo on his right arm that looked like it was some abstract Celtic symbol. I moved my hips to make the sex easier for him. His thrusts were faster now, and I tried to keep up, but the movement made me dizzy, and I felt bile rise in my throat.

I didn't want to throw up during sex.

I swallowed hard. Michael took my legs and put them on his shoulders, and thrust fast and deep. I held onto the sheet for traction, waves of nausea making my body shudder. Michael interpreted this as me having an orgasm and thrust a few more times, his face contorted with his own climax.

He was quick and neat. I moaned one more time for good measure, and then he collapsed beside me on the bed. His pale body was now glistening with sweat. He brushed the hair out of my eyes and kissed my nose sleepily.

"That was great."

"Yes, great."

I managed a small kiss back.

"Where's your bathroom?"

Once in Michael's bathroom, I vomited as quietly as possible.

I didn't want him to hear me, so I turned on the sink full blast. The bathroom floor felt cool, and I wished I could just sleep there, next to the toilet. I started to drift off, but someone cleared her throat, and I looked up.

Standing near the shower, in a blue velvet floor-length party dress, was Rose. She gave me a sympathetic look as she said,

"A woman's heart is a deep ocean of secrets."

"You said that as an old woman in the movie, but you're young now," I mumbled as I tried to focus.

Rose smiled and shrugged.

I stood up slowly and grimaced as I held on to the towel rack for support. Once upright, I took some toilet paper and made sure I wiped up any stray vomit. I splashed my face with the running water. Rose kept her position near the shower, her hands clasped demurely, her eyes taking in my sloppy cleanup routine.

I turned off the faucet and looked at my reflection in the mirror over the sink.

I looked like someone who had just thrown up.

I didn't turn back to face Rose as I opened the door to leave the bathroom. But she called out to me anyway. I sighed and turned around. Her eyes were bright and earnest.

"My first love Jack said this to me before he died, and I'm going to pass it on to you in hopes that it will help you: 'Promise me you'll survive. That you won't give up, no matter what happens. No matter how hopeless.' I made Jack that promise. Can you do the same for me?"

Who was Rose to tell me not to give up?

I had survived. That was the problem.

I half-heartedly gave Rose my middle finger in reply as I left the bathroom.

Michael was already asleep on the left side of the bed; his back turned to the wall. I climbed into the bed, my back to him. Within what seemed like a few minutes, I fell asleep.

When I woke up, I felt the weight of my watch on my wrist. Michael hadn't taken it off when he undressed me. 6:00. If I left now, I could go home, shower, take a quick nap, and be awake for my 10 am team conference call. I looked around for my clothing and quietly got out of the bed. Michael was sleeping face down in his pillow, snoring.

I grabbed my purse and opened the door, cringing when it made a squeaking noise. As I walked through the lobby of the building, I recognized the doorman from last night. His uniform was now buttoned. The doorman nodded but didn't look up from his *Daily News* as I left the building.

I kept my eyes closed for the twenty minutes it took to get to Brooklyn. Once home, I gave the cab driver a decent tip and went up to my apartment. Everything was just as I had left it. There was a bowl full of uneaten cereal in the sink. The blinds were drawn. There was a faint smell of dust.

I pulled my clothes off and collapsed into my bed. As I felt the familiarity of my sheets and comforter, I soon fell back asleep.

CHAPTER 4

My cell phone was ringing. I grabbed it, trying not to sound like I was still in bed. I looked at my clock radio. 2:00.

"Stephanie, this is Chris. You missed the team call."

Chris sounded displeased. Tess was watching me from the doorway to my bedroom. She tapped her watch.

"You should never keep your boss waiting. He could blow this deal for you."

I put my finger up to my mouth to quiet Tess and answered Chris.

"I tried to call into the meeting, but cell service is still spotty here. I don't have a replacement laptop yet, so I couldn't email."

"I'll expedite getting you a new laptop. But since the team is spread out right now, it's important to make the team call. We went over accounts. How did the MV1 meeting go?"

"The CTO needs help with video streaming and wants me to meet with his team."

"How's the new account manager? I haven't met him yet. We just hired him from HP."

I thought of Michael lying naked and prone in his bed where I had left him.

"He was nervous with the CTO, but he's very dedicated."

Tess was leaning over me, listening to my conversation with Chris. She rolled her eyes at the mention of Michael. Chris seemed appeased that the meeting had gone well. I was relieved when I heard the click of him hanging up.

"You need to be careful with Chris. Katherine, my boss, once said to me that you should never burn bridges. Chris could be a senior partner someday." Tess said this to me as if she were an "Intro to Business 101" professor at Staten Island Community College, giving me an important piece of information that would be on the midterm exam.

"I thought you hated Katherine?" I said this offhandedly as I looked around my small bedroom. I needed a walk to clear my head.

After I showered, I listened to my voicemail. There were three messages from Michael. I didn't remember giving him my number. I didn't call him back. I would talk to him tomorrow. We had to debrief on the next steps for MV1.

Twenty minutes later, I went downstairs for my walk. It was sunny and cool outside. The air still had an acidic pinch of leftover smoke. In front of my building, a toddler in cornrows and a bright yellow velour jogging suit tugged at her mother's coat. She cried as she pointed to her red Tootsie Roll Pop that she had just dropped in the wet paper-clogged gutter. Her mother didn't turn around but instead dragged the child along as she doggedly made her way to the Rite Aid across the street. There was no music on the street and no horns blaring. The few people that were walking were looking down at their feet, with their shoulders hunched inward. I headed towards the Starbucks on my corner.

I was surprised by how crowded the Starbucks was. Every seat was taken, and there was a long line at the counter. There was subdued chatter at the tables, and slow jazz music was playing on the stereo system.

As I took my place in the slowly moving line, my eyes immediately went to the young fireman waiting for his drink to be prepared. He was dressed in full fireman regalia: hat, boots, coat, tools, the works. He looked so young, and there was a sincere, hopeful energy exuding from him. He was engaged in conversation with the person making his drink.

I couldn't avert my gaze. His whole presence was a magnet pulling at me. When his drink was done and he was headed to the door to leave, I found myself speaking to him.

"Thank you so much for everything you are doing." I wanted to touch his arm, to show my appreciation in some way, but I maintained a respectful distance. The young fireman nodded in acceptance of my thanks. He started talking to me, but his eyes were looking beyond me to a horizon of his own.

"My dad and my two brothers were all firemen, and they were down there. They ended up being on the list of missing. I'm going back as soon as I can. We all went down there that morning together. We probably won't find any more survivors, but we have to at least help the families find the bodies."

The young fireman's eyes were a mixture of shock, exhaustion, hope, and conviction as he said this. His fervent tone suggested that he held a strong belief in what was right and had faith that justice would prevail. If I had seen such a character in a movie, I would have thought the part was overplayed, and a cliché, but the man standing in front of me was real.

I nodded in acknowledgment of the fireman's speech. He gave me one last exhausted wave and turned to leave Starbucks, saying nothing more. I quickly bought my coffee and left.

As I walked from Pacific street towards the Brooklyn Heights Promenade, I passed several homemade altars. I paused in front of one. It was a collection of Xeroxed pictures, notes, flags, cards, and flowers. Three prayer candles with colorful images of the Virgin Mary were still burning. At the front of the altar was a frayed, stuffed pink bunny with one plastic eye missing. The doll had around its neck a Polaroid picture of a young man holding a grinning toddler boy in a Yankees baseball cap. My eyes locked with the stuffed bunny. I stood silent for a moment giving the bunny a visual salute. I then continued walking towards the East River.

I took a seat on a bench facing the river. Tess sat down next to me. We sat in silence and stared at the wounded skyline with its gaping hole. A thick cloud of greenish dust and smoke hung over the wounded skyline like something The Joker might have put into the sky in an old Batman movie.

"I know I could do a job like the people in those buildings," Tess said with longing, pointing to the skyline. Her eyes were hungry, just like they had been as she tried to climb out of the rut of being a secretary in *Working Girl.*

"Why are you always so obsessed with working?" Rose interjected. She approached the bench and sat down. Not waiting for Tess to answer, she turned to me instead.

"Feeling better?"

"Some of us weren't born with a silver spoon in our mouths."

Tess said this to Rose, a condescending look on her face. I didn't reply. Rose placed her gloved hand on my arm. Her eyes were as earnest as they had been last night.

"You have to go on, Stephanie."

"She's doing what she needs to get ahead."

Tess looked wistfully at the Manhattan skyline as she murmured this more to herself than to Rose or me. I ignored both ghosts and shivered as a waft of cool air tickled my face.

Today seemed so far away from five years ago when, at twenty-eight, I had arrived from Ann Arbor, Michigan, enthused and eager to begin my life as a New Yorker. My head had been filled back then with the success stories of every movie, TV show, and novel about NYC that I had ever watched or read. I had been certain that a career in New York was worth sacrificing everything for.

But now, I wasn't sure of anything.

I didn't look back at the skyline as I rose from the bench and continued my walk home alone.

CHAPTER 5

"Are you coming to mandatory crisis therapy?"

My co-worker Ralph was standing by my desk. He pointed to a room down the hall. Usually, when I saw Ralph, he complained about his teenage daughters or joked about something silly that an account executive had said, but today he was quiet. Ralph lived deep in Jersey somewhere and hadn't been downtown on 9/11. I guessed that this was his first time in the new office. He kept looking around like he had just been hired.

"I guess so; I didn't get the invite." I gave Ralph a weary smile, my eyes acknowledging the kindness in his.

"I'll forward you the memo later. Let's go get a seat."

I followed Ralph to the makeshift conference room, which looked like it used to be a filing storeroom. It was lined with black file cabinets with drop cloths on top of them, and in its center were about thirty card chairs set up in a circle.

I was settling into mine when Michael walked in. Knowing how he spent his nights, I was amazed at how good he looked. He had on black sunglasses, and a grey fashionably cut suit with a dark purple shirt. He took off his glasses when he saw me and gave me a sheepish grin.

Michael motioned to the seat next to me, and I nodded. Although we had exchanged emails and had talked briefly on the phone about Dennis's video streaming questions, Michael and I hadn't seen each other in person since our drunken hookup after the MV1 meeting the previous week.

I had worked from home and stayed in my apartment most of the week, taking conference calls and curling up on my sofa watching movies from my VHS collection. The movies reminded me of my dad. I wondered whether my mother had told him I had been in one of the Towers.

My thoughts were interrupted by one of the psychologists, who cleared his throat nervously. He was in his late thirties or so and had curly black hair and a trimmed beard. All of the chairs were now filled, and six facilitators were walking around the circle handing out Xeroxed meditation instructions.

"Can I get everyone's attention, please? I'm Dr. Thompson, and I'll be leading today's discussion. We have facilitators present who are here to help. Just raise your hand if you want to speak. Many of us flew out here from all over to aid in helping all of you heal."

As I listened skeptically to Dr. Thompson, I heard a snort. I turned to Michael thinking it was him, but it was one of my ghosts instead. Angelina Jolie's character Lisa from the movie *Girl, Interrupted* was sitting across the circle from me. She was dressed in the same faded T-shirt and hip-hugger jeans that I remembered her wearing in McLean mental hospital in the movie when I watched it the other night. I had seen the film numerous times since it had come out a couple of years ago. I loved Lisa's no-holds-barred insanity in *Girl, Interrupted*. It was a guilty pleasure of mine to witness her destruction as she annihilated herself and everything around her in a storm of passion and fury.

I watched Lisa now, secretly hoping she might somehow disrupt this painful healing circle like she had upended so many meetings and gatherings in the movie.

Lisa had her copy of the meditation instructions in her hand and was folding them into a paper airplane. I stared at her for a minute, waiting for her to act. When nothing happened, I turned back to Dr. Thompson, who was addressing the group.

"Our process is to have everyone share how they feel about what happened on 9/11. There is no inappropriate thing to say, and the goal is to bring the feelings up for healing."

As Dr. Thompson looked around the circle, Lisa finished the final creases of her paper airplane. She pointed it at Dr. Thomson, as she proclaimed,

"You lie down, you confess your secrets, and you're saved. Ca-ching! The more you confess, the more they think about settin' you free."

Before I could react to Lisa, Michael whispered in my ear,

"Let me lay my hands on you and heal you."

I grinned in spite of myself, covering my mouth so that the hovering therapists wouldn't see.

"If there aren't any questions, let's get started. Who'd like to go first?"

There was a long awkward silence. Finally, a woman I didn't know raised her hand. She was in her mid-thirties and had straight blond hair with highlights in it. She was dressed in a tailored beige wool suit and had a pad in her lap to take notes.

"Hi, I'm Stacy..."

Stacy's eyes were welling with tears.

"I just can't get the images of that day out of my mind. All those people jumping. I'm not sleeping."

Stacy started crying. Immediately four facilitators were hovering over her. Each handed her a tissue. She took one of them and blew her nose.

Lisa watched Stacy cry. She crossed her arms and scowled as she muttered,

"Good luck, crazy bitch."

I glanced over at Lisa in disappointment. Where was all her fury now?

As Stacy continued sobbing, several others in the circle started sniffling as well. Most of us just sat uncomfortably, waiting for the tears to stop.

As I listened to Stacy, I waited to feel grief for the innocent 9/11 victims. But I only felt tired.

Tired of getting up in the morning.

Tired of my frequent flashbacks.

Tired of the grey dust that covered me, that couldn't be washed away.

"Who'd like to speak next?"

Dr. Thompson looked around the room as he asked this.

Michael leaned in and whispered in my ear.

"Want to get out of here and get a drink?"

I scanned the circle of coworkers in various stages of discomfort and nodded.

CHAPTER 6

The early November air had a bite to it. After our meeting with Dennis, Michael and I walked ten blocks or so to a dive bar in the lobby of a faded Theatre District hotel on 47th Street, called the Hotel Edison. Pictures of Broadway plays from the 1950s through the 1980s lined the walls. We had come here several times since the group therapy session a month ago.

The bar was dimly lit. The bartender had a goatee and a shaved head with a tattoo of a dragon on his scalp. He was filling a container with lime slices. Michael ordered for us. When our drinks arrived, Michael took a sip of his bourbon, and I took a sip of my beer.

"What was your childhood like in Birmingham?"

I leaned in closer to Michael as I asked this, my hand on his arm. Michael and I had been seeing each other for over a month now, and I was determined to stay sober enough to get to know him more. I wasn't that familiar with Birmingham other than it was an industrial city in England. Michael gazed off into the distance as he answered my question.

"I don't know who my father was. My mother really didn't work. She was part of Black Sabbath's entourage and hung out with the band and the roadies. When she wasn't partying, she raised my sister and me."

Michael's facial expression was a mixture of longing and anger as he said this.

I thought of how distant my mom had been when I was a girl. Our relationship was still superficial. Yet she had sat at work with her entire office on 9/11 waiting to hear if I was alive, and she had been the first person I had called when my phone finally worked again late that evening.

"I grew up in an average family. My mom was depressed a lot when I was a kid." I said this matter-of-factly and took a gulp of my beer.

Michael replied quietly, "I came to New York with nothing. I never finished secondary school." Michael looked at me as if to dare me to make fun of him after he said this.

"You never finished high school? How did you become an account executive?"

I regretted asking the question. But account executives usually had MBAs or at least Bachelor's degrees. Michael must have had to work hard to get where he was now in his career. This actually made him more interesting to me.

Tess had joined us. She downed a shot of tequila and then turned to me.

"There's nothing wrong with being self-made," she said. "I'm thirty years old. Took me five years of night school, but I got my degree, and I got it with honors."

I nodded absently to Tess in reply. Michael continued.

"I worked at terrible companies at first, doing anything I needed to survive. I worked my way up to a job with a local subsidiary of Hewlett Packard downtown that sold ink cartridges. The company was a poor stepchild to HP, but it was still better than any other job I had ever had. I watched how the account executives acted there, how they dressed, and what they said. I learned a lot. There was a successful account manager who took me under her wing and mentored me."

Michael said this with his arms crossed over his chest.

"That's great, Michael."

I had a sinking feeling that Michael was still being mentored all over town. There had been many times in the last month when he didn't return my call, even though my messages had been about preparing for our next meeting with Dennis. I had assumed he was out drinking somewhere. It was none of my business, really.

"I started out getting my Ph.D. in German Literature at Yale, but I hated academia, so I went back to school at the University of Michigan and got a second degree in Computer Science."

I sounded like a pompous asshole. I had never cared about my over-education. Why was I reciting my resume to Michael?

Rose had joined us. She sat down next to Tess. I gave her a nod and turned back to Michael, who leaned in towards me and said,

"Yale, impressive."

Michael said this with genuine admiration. His lips brushed my ear as he said, "I'm dating a brainiac. Sexy."

Michael nibbled my ear and whispered, "Want to go to your place?"

Even though Michael and I had been dating five weeks or so, he had never been to my apartment. Somehow it had always been easier to go back to his place in Midtown.

"It's in Cobble Hill. Have you spent much time in Brooklyn?"

"My best friend Peter works as a doorman in a building on Broome Street. He lives in Bushwick. I've known him since I first came to New York eight years ago. Every couple of weeks, we get together, usually in his neighborhood. We met at the Coney Island Mermaid Parade. I had just been kicked out of the house I was staying at, and he took me in when I had nothing. We were roommates until I bought my place two years ago."

"Does Peter like being a doorman?"

I winced at my question. Rose gave me a disapproving look and whispered,

"Even people traveling in the lower decks have dreams."

"Damn straight!" Tess pounded on the table for emphasis as she said this.

Michael gave me a reproachful look. There was something more in his expression that I couldn't quite put my finger on, a protective challenge to me. Michael defended Peter in his reply to me.

"It's a job. He's a poet and was never ambitious like me. He managed our band for a summer, though, and did a pretty good job of it."

"You were in a band?"

My tone showed surprise. I didn't try to hide it.

"I was the bass player in a band called Sons of Discontent. We toured and had a decent following. We played for five years and even cut a couple of demo tapes but broke up a couple of years ago."

"Why did you stop playing?"

"There was infighting in the band, some drama around the lead singer's girlfriend."

"Is that the only reason you guys broke up?"

"No, my career was starting to take off, and I couldn't afford to take time off to travel anymore," Michael said this frankly, but there was a trace of wistfulness in his eyes. He downed the rest of his bourbon.

Michael turned his gaze away from me and signaled the bartender for another round. I watched him as his eyes lingered on the bartender's muscular tattooed chest that was peeking out of his half-buttoned black shirt. The bartender gave Michael a leisurely review that traveled from Michael's face to his crotch and back. I felt alone in the bar for a moment, as if Michael had suddenly disappeared. Michael had a past that I knew nothing about.

I tapped my fingers on the bar absently as I watched Michael staring at the bartender. Lisa approached the bar. She pointed to Michael as she said, "Don't get too hung up on him. He's just a man."

She took a drag of her cigarette and stubbed it out on the table, continuing to hold my gaze as she said,

"A man is a dick is a man is a dick is a chicken...is a dad...a Valium, a speculum, whatever, whatever."

I nodded in reply. Although it was odd that I would agree with a diagnosed sociopath, Lisa was right about Michael.

Lisa pointed to Michael and grinned, sticking her tongue out at him as he stared at the bartender. Michael downed his bourbon shot. He then finally turned to me, giving me an inviting smile as he leaned in towards me. He put his hand on my thigh. He always did this when he wanted to change the subject to one he was more comfortable with, which was usually sex. Michael squeezed my thigh and leaned in closer.

"Let's go visit my friend Peter tomorrow. It's his day off."

I was curious to meet Michael's best friend. I took a sip of my beer and nodded.

CHAPTER 1

According to Michael, Peter's Bushwick neighborhood was quite rough. No subway went there, so we decided at Michael's suggestion to take the bus. I was surprised he didn't want to take a cab to Peter's apartment. The cab ride would have been $25-30 from my apartment, assuming a driver was willing to go into Peter's dicey neighborhood. That was pocket change for Michael, who probably made over $400,000 a year. But I didn't question his decision to take the bus. It made no difference to me either way.

Rose had joined us on the bus ride. She looked out the window for most of the trip. When the bus stopped near Peter's house, Rose pulled her hands away from the window. Soot had left dusty grey streaks on her white gloves. She looked down at her hands and shrugged, giving me a rebellious grin.

"Mama would be horrified. She always said that you can tell a lady by her gloves."

Michael had told me that Peter dabbled in art in his spare time but hadn't said much else about him, other than he was a doorman. I had brought a good bottle of wine that I had been given as a Christmas gift from Chris last year. Michael had told me that Peter loved wine, and I thought it would be a nice gesture to share a bottle with him.

The bus ride took about forty minutes. I looked at my watch. It was 3:00 when we started the short walk from the bus stop to Peter's place.

Peter's row house was badly in need of a paint job and had a top floor that was boarded up. The porch was caving in, and there was cracked glass in the front window that was covered up with duct tape. I was surprised when Michael pulled out his keys and opened the front door for me. He must visit Peter often if he still had a set of keys despite moving out two years ago.

I stepped into the small foyer, which had peeling paint and water spots on the ceiling, and the floor looked like it hadn't been washed in decades.

"Peter! We're here."

Michael used another key and entered Peter's living room as he shouted this. As I stumbled behind Michael into Peter's front room, I nearly tripped over a pile of empty pizza boxes sitting on top of a rusty overturned patio chair. Rose followed us inside. As she entered the living room, she wrinkled her nose and put her hand over her mouth.

There was trash everywhere. Clothing, empty liquor bottles and beer cans, wadded-up paper, half-empty cans of food, and dirty plates covered every surface of the floor, tables, and counter space. There was a rough mural of a face painted on the back wall of the living room. I couldn't tell if the face was male or female. The mural looked half complete.

"Peter painted that. Like it?"

Michael pointed to the face on the wall. Although I wasn't going to judge his friend's talent from an unfinished wall painting, I wasn't impressed. The mural looked like an adolescent copy of Matisse.

"Is it finished?"

I looked at Michael innocently as I asked this, giving him as warm a smile as I could muster while standing in a pile of trash.

"Yes. Well. Nothing is ever finished, but Peter says that he's moved on to other projects."

"I have many new projects. Better projects."

Peter approached me unsteadily as he said this. He was a slight man with pale skin and short black hair. He had on dark sunglasses even though the curtains and shades were drawn. Peter was wearing a wrinkled navy-blue button-down shirt and jeans that were so big on him they looked like they were about to fall off. He also had on a purple tie, which was loosely fastened and hanging to the side of his neck and shirt, giving the impression of a noose.

"Peter, I'd like you to meet my friend, Stephanie. Stephanie, this is my best friend, Peter."

Michael pointed to me as he made introductions. Peter hugged me, and he felt so fragile I thought my gentle reciprocation might crack his ribs.

"Peter put a tie on just for you."

Michael smiled at Peter with affection as he said this. They held each other's gaze for just a moment longer than I expected them to. I took the bottle of wine out of my bag while Peter walked to the torn rust-colored velour sofa and sat down on the floor cross-legged in front of it. He took off his dark glasses and squinted at me.

"It's a pleasure to meet you, Stephanie. What kind of wine did you bring?"

"It's a French Burgundy."

I handed the bottle to Peter to show him the label.

"Do you have a wine bottle opener? I usually don't drink wine that has corks."

"We can use this."

I pulled the combination swiss-army-knife-flashlight-keychain out of my purse that my brother Steven had bought for me two years ago as a Christmas gift. It had a tiny corkscrew as one of the attachments. I took the wine bottle from Peter to open it and sat down on the faded blue armchair next to the sofa. Rose walked gingerly around the garbage on Peter's floor and sat down stiffly on one end of the couch, holding her hands in her lap.

"I always hated wearing gloves, but today I'm glad I have them," she said as she looked around the filthy living room.

Lisa had joined us. She was wearing hip hugger bell-bottom jeans, a large white leather belt with a double row of hooks going all around the belt, and a faded T-shirt with the Harley Stevenson logo on it. She fit right in with the bohemian squalor of Peter's apartment. Lisa pulled a pint of whiskey out of her denim jacket and took a swig as she stood in the entryway. She walked around the trash and sat down on the sofa next to Rose.

Michael reached into a sooty ashtray sitting on the coffee table, retrieved a half-smoked joint, and lit it. He took a long drag and offered it to me. I was struggling with opening the wine bottle, so I shook my head.

Michael blew smoke out his nostrils, passing the joint to Peter, his fingertips lingering for a moment. Peter took a long drag of the joint. At the end of the toke, he seemed to be nodding off, and the joint almost fell from his loosening grip.

"Peter, watch it. You're going to set yourself on fire again."

Michael said this tenderly and took the joint out of Peter's slack fingers. I wasn't surprised to hear Michael say this. Peter looked right now like he was on several different drugs, all in lethal doses. But I was taken back by Michael's tone. In the five weeks, we had been dating, I didn't recall Michael ever speaking to me with the warmth he was showing Peter.

Lisa looked pointedly at Peter and Michael as their fingers touched again. She gave Michael a wink as she said,

"Your boyfriend has a substance abuse problem."

She addressed her comment to Michael, not me. Of course, he didn't hear her.

Michael and Peter continued to pass the joint back and forth between themselves as if they were alone. They remained silent, occasionally glancing at each other with deepening intimacy, as they sat back and let the pot kick in.

I didn't have time to fully process the vibe between Michael and Peter. The task of opening the bottle of wine required my full attention.

The bottle had a dried crumbly cork, and it took me a few more minutes to open it. When Peter heard the cork come out of the wine bottle, he sat up and opened his eyes.

"Wine is just what I need right now. Michael, honey, can you get some glasses?"

Peter said this is such a campy way that I laughed. He turned to me and smiled, and I got the impression from the way his eyes focused on me that he was just seeing me clearly for the first time since I had come in.

Michael pulled three large red plastic tumblers from a bag on the floor. He handed Peter one. Peter reached for the wine, taking the $200 bottle and filling his tumbler to the top. He took a gulp.

"Nice."

"Peter, don't hog all the wine. Stephanie didn't get any yet."

Michael filled a tumbler up about halfway full and handed it to me. He then picked up a whiskey bottle sitting atop a pile of yellowing news-papers and took a large gulp from it. Lisa took a swig from her own pint of whiskey. She offered the bottle to Rose, who wiped the rim before she took a tiny sip.

"I don't have cooties, babe."

Lisa whispered this in Rose's ear as she reached over to grab the bot-tle back.

Peter finished his wine in several gulps and poured what remained in the bottle into his tumbler. Michael turned to me.

"Sorry. Peter has a drinking problem."

"No Bitch you did not just say that!"

Peter leaned over, spilling his last few drops of wine down his front. I watched as they formed purple splattered polka dots against his faded navy-blue shirt. Michael grabbed the cup from Peter, who was still on the floor. The two of them became entangled in a wrestling grapple, laughing, and seemed to have forgotten again that I was still there.

I set my untouched wine on the coffee table and looked around the filthy room. Peter had a broken laptop on the coffee table, and there was an old battered television sitting in a cheap plywood entertainment system against the back wall. There was a large bookcase filled with paperbacks next to the television. Otherwise, everything else in the room seemed to be trash.

"Don't you like the wine? I'll go to the corner and get some stronger spirits."

Michael sat up from his tangle with Peter on the floor and looked over at me as he said this. I didn't reply. Michael didn't seem to notice. He walked towards the door, leaving without saying anything further to Peter or me.

With Michael gone, I had the challenge of talking to Peter. I took a sip of my wine. Peter lit the joint, took a drag, and exhaled. He reached over and handed it to me.

I accepted the joint and took a hit. There was no reason to stay sober at this point.

Peter and I passed the joint back and forth between us, not talking. I was starting to get buzzed. Peter had The Cure playing. I closed my eyes and settled into a quiet cloud of smoke and music. I heard a thud, and my eyes jerked open. Peter was lying on the floor. He had a thin paperback book in his hand.

"Found it."

"Found what?"

"My poetry. This is the first volume, but I'm working on a second volume. Can you pass me the joint?"

Peter mumbled this from the floor, and I had to strain to understand him. I reached over and handed the joint to Peter's outstretched hand. He threw the book on the floor and pushed himself up with his free arm, turning on his side. He took a hit of the joint and handed it back to me as he finished sitting upright. I took one last drag and pinched the roach to snuff it out.

"I have more pot."

Peter said this slowly as if he were concentrating on each word. He then reached for the book he had thrown and opened it to a random page.

Your cock could have been bigger

My mouth only half full

Toilet flushes

Will your cum taste salty?

Or will it run

down my chin

Eternal

Forgotten

Next cock down the line

Assembled

Poised for jagged release.

Peter's words were remarkably clear for someone who was so wasted.

I was pretty high, but I was able to get the gist of what he was saying, not that it was rocket science.

"Peter, are you reciting that thing out loud again? Read something else for a change."

Peter, Lisa, Rose, and I all looked towards the door.

Michael had returned. He pulled two large bottles of whiskey and a bottle of vodka out of a paper bag and set them all on the coffee table. He also pulled out a frozen pizza and some Cheetos.

"I bought your favorites."

Michael opened the bottle of whiskey for Peter, kissed him on the lips, and poured him a generous amount.

"Here, Doll. Pace yourself."

"Thanks, Precious."

Lisa grinned as she watched Michael kiss Peter. She pointed to him and gave me a wink, and blew me a kiss. I glared at her.

Peter squeezed Michael's hand as he took the cup from him. He then took a large gulp of whiskey, shivering as it went down. "My pot's in the kitchen in the freezer."

Michael nodded. "I'll get it. And I'll heat the pizza. You probably need to eat something."

Peter shrugged and took another drink of the whiskey. I could hear Michael banging around in Peter's kitchen. He seemed so comfortable in Peter's shithole of an apartment.

Michael had told me that he had lived with Peter, but he had never hinted that their relationship was sexual. I couldn't imagine Michael, who was so persnickety about his appearance, living in a house like this, or with a mediocre artist like Peter. When I saw how at home he was in the squalor of Peter's place, I realized I didn't really know him at all.

Two longish Depeche Mode songs and a Pet Shop Boys track played before Michael re-entered the living room carrying three plates of baked frozen pizza lined up along his arm. In his other hand, he had a Ziploc bag of weed that had a few ice crystals near its top from being in the freezer.

Michael handed me a plate with one third of the pizza on it. He put the other two plates down on the coffee table.

"Peter, wake up! The pizza's ready."

Michael gave Peter a nudge with his toe. Peter got on all fours and slowly turned around to face Michael.

"Sit up and eat some pizza."

Michael said this as a parent might order their child to eat their vegetables. He reached for the bag of weed and picked up some rolling papers sitting on the coffee table near the ashtray. Michael sprinkled some of the pot from the bag onto a paper. He then rolled the paper tightly and licked the end to seal it.

I set my plate in my lap. I took a bite of the hot greasy pizza, and it tasted surprisingly good. I licked the salty sauce off my lips.

"How's the pizza, babe?"

I was about to answer Michael when I saw that he was talking to Peter, not me. Peter was holding his slice of pizza with both hands and had taken a bite. Tomato sauce was dribbling down his chin. Michael reached over and wiped it off with his fingers, and then to my surprise, licked the sauce off them. The gesture was suggestive and sexual.

Lisa was watching Michael and Peter with amusement. Rose was looking at them in curiosity. Michael lit the joint he had just rolled and took a drag. He reached over and handed it to me next, which surprised me. I had almost forgotten I was in the room with him.

"Why don't you take your tie off before you ruin it."

Michael said this to Peter as he hugged him from behind, gently easing the tie over Peter's head.

"They make a cute couple," Lisa said, staring at Peter and Michael.

"What do you mean by that exactly?"

Rose turned to Lisa as she asked this. She looked genuinely confused. Lisa ignored Rose and got up from the sofa. She turned to me and pointed to Michael and Peter.

"I'm going to let the lovebirds nest. I'm out of here. Are you coming?"

I shook my head.

Lisa shrugged, "Suit yourself."

Lisa then left. Rose followed her out. I could hear her asking Lisa another question about Peter as the door shut behind them.

I turned back to Peter and Michael. Michael was laughing as he said,

"You're such a beautiful disaster, Peter."

"You wouldn't have me any other way, baby."

Peter stuck his tongue out, wiggling it. Neither of them looked in my direction, which made sense because I wasn't there. Not really. I was invisible.

I looked at the remains of my greasy pizza, now getting cold. It was time for me to go. I set the plate down and got up without saying anything.

Michael turned to me as I stood up and said, "If you need to go to the bathroom, I'm going to have to go there with you. Peter's toilet is broken, and I'm the only one who can get it to flush."

I did have to pee, and it was easier to do it here.

Michael followed me to a dark room next to the kitchen. He turned on the bare exposed light bulb that lit the bathroom, and I put my hand over my nose and mouth to mask the smell of raw sewage coming from the room.

There was toilet paper floating in the toilet in murky brown water. The top of the toilet was off. Next to the toilet was a rusted shower that had undefined grime all over it. Mold was growing on most of the tiles of the shower. Dirty towels were scattered on the floor, and the mirror over the sink had large water spots, and toothpaste, on it. I walked gingerly towards the toilet, stepping over a few pairs of Peter's scattered dirty underwear.

"Let me get something to hold the stopper."

Michael grabbed a half broom that was near the toilet and put the handle in the toilet tank. He then stepped back into the kitchen to give me privacy. I closed my eyes, pulled down my pants, and aimed for the bowl, hoping for the best.

I tried not to breathe while I emptied my bladder and pulled up my pants. Michael reentered the bathroom to do whatever he was going to do with the broom handle. As I heard the toilet flush, I made the mistake of breathing in the sewage smell. I gagged. I was going to throw up, and there was nowhere to do it that wouldn't make me even sicker. I rushed out of the bathroom. The kitchen smelled smokey from baked pizza.

Smoke.

I felt the tingle in the back of my head that usually signaled the onset of a flashback. I used all my remaining energy to stay focused on the here and now, which, unfortunately for me at the moment, was vomit.

I leaned over the kitchen sink. The pizza came up in chunks that looked like they hadn't even been chewed. Clear bile then followed. My puking was over quickly. I wiped my mouth on my shirt, not wanting to touch anything in Peter's kitchen. I turned on the faucet and put dish soap on my hands.

I scrubbed my hands.

Michael watched me as I cleaned my hands roughly, washing each finger over and over. I didn't look at him, and I didn't stop washing my hands. I soaped my palms, the top of my hands, and each finger. I scrubbed the wine away. I scrubbed away the pot, the pizza grease, the pee, the mold, the sewage, the dirt, the dust, the fire, and the smoke. My hands were now red and chapped. I didn't care. I poured more dish soap on them and continued to scrub them.

"I think your hands are clean now."

Michael came over to the sink and turned the water off. He took my chapped hand, bringing it up to his lips and kissing it.

"What's wrong?"

Michael looked into my eyes. His pupils were dilated, and he was slurring, but the tenderness in his eyes was real. It was the first real moment of connection I had felt with him during this entire visit.

"I want to go home."

Michael squeezed my hand and went into the living room. Peter was staring at the television, which he had turned on without sound. His stereo was still playing. Echo and the Bunnymen were now on. I liked Peter's taste in music. I was glad that I had something nice to say if I were later pressed by Michael to come up with a compliment.

Peter kept clicking the TV remote, but the channels weren't changing.

"I can't find *Ab Fab*. Michael Hon, can you help me?"

"You have the wrong remote. That's for the VCR player. Here."

Michael handed Peter a different remote. He then poured some whiskey into Peter's tumbler before capping the whiskey bottle and putting it on the table. He turned the stereo off and adjusted the volume to the television, and the laugh track and British accents of *Absolutely Fabulous* filled the room.

"I'll give you a call or swing by tomorrow to see how you're doing."

Michael bent over and kissed Peter's lips after he said this.

I pretended I didn't notice the kiss and headed for the front door. I didn't want to delve into Michael's sexuality or relationship with Peter right now. I just wanted to get out of this shit hole. Michael took one last look at Peter as he followed me out of the apartment, shutting the door behind us.

CHAPTER 8

Michael and I didn't talk as we walked to the bus stop. The silence between us wasn't a comfortable one. I would have preferred to take a cab, but there was no way we would get one in Peter's neighborhood even though it was only 9 pm.

Michael pulled a pack of Marlboro cigarettes out of his jeans pocket. He lit one. An Asian-looking middle-aged man was riding a sizeable three-wheeled bike in the middle of the road. The bike had several milk crates strapped to the back of it, which were filled with what looked like carry-out Chinese orders in white plastic bags. I watched the man slowly pass us by us, his face straining as he pushed the tricycle of takeout up the hilly street.

Michael exhaled cigarette smoke, which hung in the air between us.

"You didn't like Peter much, did you?"

"He's quite a character."

"Peter's a creative type, an artist. He suffers every day in a job that doesn't stimulate him. You can't hold that against him."

Michael took a long drag of his cigarette after he said this. He was looking out towards the blue graffiti-covered door of a warehouse across the street, a melancholy expression on his face. His voice sounded more reflective than angry.

"I just said he's a character," I replied, in a tone more apologetic than I wanted it to be.

"Peter's always been there for me."

Michael was pacing between the outside of the bus shelter and the bench. I sighed. I hadn't slept much last night, and I was exhausted. Michael's relationship with Peter was a topic for another day. I apologized. Again.

"I'm sorry, Michael. I know you and Peter are close. I'm just tired."

I put a contrite look on my face and made my voice sound regretful. I sounded more sad than sorry this time, though, which made sense. I was sad. But not for offending Michael. I was sad because getting to know Michael was beginning to be too much work.

Michael held his cigarette up to my mouth to take a drag, to show me he was accepting my apology. I took a puff.

"Peter wasn't at this best today. He'll be better next time."

I shivered and nodded, saying nothing. The bus showed up a minute or so later. I took a seat next to Michael and closed my eyes. After what seemed like a few minutes, Michael nudged me and whispered in my ear.

"This is our stop."

I rubbed my eyes and followed Michael to the back door of the bus. We were at the Port Authority Bus Terminal. Michael hailed one of the few taxis that had their light on, and we climbed in. It would have made more sense to walk the ten blocks to Michael's apartment, but I was grateful to slump in the backseat of the cab.

Michael gave the taxi driver his address, and we both settled in for the short ride to Michael's apartment on West 33rd Street. When we got to his building, the same Hispanic doorman that always seemed to witness my visits to Michael's apartment gave us a nod. He was eating a steak hoagie, and the cheese and mayo were dripping out the side of the long bun, landing on his fingers and the tinfoil wrapper that was on his lap.

Michael put his arm around me in the elevator. His arm felt like a weight on my shoulders, but I didn't remove it. Once inside Michael's apartment, I put my messenger bag down on the now familiar, orange mid-century modern sofa. Michael led the way to the bedroom. The bed was unmade, and a grey sateen comforter was sitting in a tangled lump in the middle of the bed.

"I'm going to make a drink. Want one?"

Michael didn't wait for me to answer and headed into the kitchen. As I sat on his bed, I took a look around the room. I couldn't reconcile the enormous, expensive platform bed, bare white walls, and closet full of designer suits with the squalor I had just experienced at Peter's place.

I let my guard down a sliver and reflected for the first time that day on the intimacy between Michael and Peter that I had witnessed earlier. Michael had never hinted to me that he was bisexual. But I had never asked either. Had there been signs that I had missed in the past five weeks? I had studiously avoided thinking much about Michael's sex life. I never asked him who else he was seeing. I had barely begun to delve into his present, let alone his past.

A chaotic mix of emotions swirled within me as I sat on Michael's bed. Anger, embarrassment, curiosity, exhaustion, and a thin, knotted strain of hopelessness, threatened to disturb my surface calm. I pushed the emotions down, the best I could, into the recesses of my stomach. As I pondered Michael's life outside the narrow window of his interactions with me, I heard a long whistle. Lisa was looking through Michael's clothes.

"This would look great on me," she said, eying a black leather jacket in Michael's closet.

Michael entered the bedroom and handed me a vodka on the rocks. He gulped his drink and sighed in pleasure. He turned to me.

"What were you looking at when I was in the kitchen?"

"Do you like Hunter S. Thompson?" I pointed to a paperback novel that was on the floor.

Michael pulled a crumpled pack of cigarettes out of his pocket and lit one of its contents, avoiding my gaze.

"Someone recommended it to me and bought me a copy."

Some woman that he was sleeping with must have given him that book. Or man. It was the only book that I could see in his apartment.

I looked back down at the book as I said,

"Fear and Loathing in Las Vegas is a great book. When I was an undergrad, I gave a thought for a few minutes to being a gonzo journalist. I enjoyed the movie too. I like anything Johnny Depp is in."

"I know the type of men you like."

Michael took a sloppy gulp of his drink after he said this. He expelled a burp and didn't say, "excuse me."

Michael had no idea what men I liked.

But I guess that made us equal because I had no idea what men he liked either.

As I watched him, I just wanted to go to bed. My bed.

Michael looked into my tired eyes. He took my face in his hands and kissed me. I could feel his breath inside me as I passively let his lips probe mine. Michael pulled away from the kiss. He took a sip of his drink and set the glass down on the side table built into the bed. He pulled me closer and murmured in my ear, his words slurred.

"Are you my girl?"

It was a strange question to ask me after spending the day being so intimate with Peter. Before I could reply, Michael started to undress, struggling to get his t-shirt off. With an impatient yank, he flung it across the room and again picked up his drink from the side table, taking a gulp, rewarding himself for his effort. He swayed in his position on the bed, and I thought he was going to pass out.

"He's not going to be much of a fuck tonight."

Lisa grinned and pointed to Michael. Rose had entered the bedroom. She looked at me with concern.

"Are you going to be alright?"

I shrugged. The truth was, I had no idea what being "alright" was anymore.

Michael had taken his jeans off and was now sitting on his pillow, his back against the wall. He was pulling off his blue cotton bikini briefs. I dragged the comforter out of the tangle it was in and spread it clumsily over the mattress. Michael's eyes were closed, and he looked like he was nodding off.

"Let's go to sleep Michael."

I unzipped my jeans partly so that they wouldn't dig into me when I slept.

"No! I want to fuck."

Lisa, Rose, and I looked skeptically at Michael's flaccid penis.

Michael reached over and finished unzipping my jeans with a clumsy tug at the zipper. I toppled over easily from the force of his sudden movement. As I landed on my back in the middle of the mattress, Michael bent down and tugged at my jeans, yanking them off in two strong pulls. He removed my panties and climbed on top of me, spreading my legs with his right hand.

I looked at Michael's limp penis bobbing up and down as his fingers entered me. His eyes were closed, and he had a drunken smile of enjoyment on his face.

Both Lisa and Rose were watching Michael. Rose had an uneasy look on her face. Lisa looked amused.

"Do you want me to call for help?" Rose's eyes were filled with compassion as she asked this quietly.

Lisa laughed and said, "If help was called for every time a woman had bad sex, the police would be busy 24/7 and have no time for crimes."

"How can you be so callous?" Rose pointed her finger accusingly at Lisa. The latter leaned in aggressively, her lips close enough to touch Rose's.

Lisa's eyes were filled with rage, and at this moment, she truly looked like the sociopathic mental patient she was. She hissed one of her lines from *Girl, Interrupted.*

"Some advice, okay? Just don't point your fuckin' finger at crazy people!"

Rose gasped and was about to continue when I interrupted them with a stare.

There was no room in my life at the moment for ghost infighting.

As Michael continued to nudge his fingers in and out of me, I turned away from both my ghosts and focused on the ceiling instead. It was cool, blank, clean, and white.

My fireman ghost entered the room and positioned himself at the side of the bed. He offered me a blanket and some water. I shook my head.

I had had a long day, and I wanted Michael off of me. I decided to fake an orgasm, like I had many times in the last month, hoping that that would hurry him up. I instructed my mouth to groan, and I built to a moan of fake pleasure as my body thrust its hips up to meet Michael's clumsily jabbing fingers.

Hearing my moan must have convinced Michael to release me. He finally pulled his fingers out of me. The sudden movement toppled him over on his side.

Lisa started clapping.

"Great fuck lover boy!"

I ignored Lisa and turned to the fireman, my eyes begging him to help me clear the room of ghosts. It always took a lot of energy out of me to pretend to enjoy the sex with Michael. I needed a few minutes to myself.

My fireman ghost nodded in understanding at my silent plea. He turned to both Lisa and Rose and picked them both up, carrying them out of the room as if he were carrying them out of a burning building.

Neither ghost fought him. I watched them go. I then tentatively stood up and headed to the bathroom. Michael was on his back, his eyes closed.

I shut the door to the bathroom and locked it. I then splashed cold water on my face. I didn't look my reflection in the eyes.

I closed the lid to the toilet and sat down, glancing around the small bathroom. There were towels strewn over the shower door and on the floor. The trash can next to the toilet was full of Kleenex, cigarette butts, and beer cans. A thin pink plastic tube stood out amongst the Kleenex and cigarette butts. It was a tampon applicator.

There was a fungal smell coming from the floor by the toilet paper holder. I looked down, trying to determine where it was coming from. At the edge of the toilet, about an inch from my feet was a used tampon. The blood on the tampon was brownish-red. The tampon looked fuzzy and dried out like it had been on the floor for a while.

The bloody tampon was one too many pieces of garbage for me on a long day filled with trash. I got up from the toilet and didn't look at the tampon again, but instead took a towel that was hanging precariously from the towel rack and dropped it angrily on top of it.

I returned to the bedroom. Michael wasn't in bed. I quickly dressed and walked towards the kitchenette. The light was on, and the refrigerator door was open. A bottle of vodka was on the counter. I looked in the refrigerator. It was almost empty. There was a bottle of HP sauce, some Chinese carry out that looked like it had been sitting there a while, and a few cans of PBR.

Michael wasn't in the living room either. I heard a soft snoring sound coming from the front hallway and walked hesitatingly over towards the sound. The hallway was dark, but with the light of the kitchen, I was able to see the outline of Michael, passed out face-down on the floor. I walked over to him and nudged his leg with my toe.

"Michael?"

He didn't respond. But his snoring let me know he was breathing at least. I stepped over him, went back into the living room, and put my shoes on.

I took a last look at Michael passed out on the floor. There was a train of milky orange vomit hanging out one side of his mouth, leading to a small puddle of puke that the left side of his face was resting in. Either this had happened in the short time it took to tie my shoes, or I hadn't noticed it earlier.

Either way, I didn't care.

Fuck him.

I kicked Michael as I stepped over him and made my way to the door. I exited the apartment and slammed it behind me, not caring if the noise woke him.

Once outside, a lone taxi drove slowly towards me on the empty street, and I hailed it. I kept my eyes closed for the entire twenty-minute ride to Brooklyn. When I got to my building, I took the tiny elevator upstairs to my floor, relieved that it was one of the few times it wasn't out of order.

I let myself into my apartment, pausing for a moment to take in the clean and quiet serenity of my small living room. I went into the bedroom. My clothes came off quickly. I took the panties that Michael had pulled off of me, threw them into the wastebasket, and climbed into bed.

I pulled the covers over my exhausted body. I felt the hot sting of tears. For the first time in six weeks, I let myself cry.

I cried for the emptiness of Michael's apartment.

I cried for Michael's fingers inside me.

I cried for bad gay poetry and half-done murals.

I cried for the drinks, joints, and bloody tampons.

When I couldn't cry anymore, I reached for a tissue from the box I kept on my bedside table and blew my nose. I threw the used tissue in the wastebasket, letting it land on top of my discarded panties.

I was sick of having a life that made me cry.

I needed to take better care of myself somehow. Maybe tomorrow I would call a therapist. Not group or corporate crisis counseling, but someone I could talk to one on one.

I let go of my tears and floated into blackness. The last image I had as I lost consciousness was of my fireman ghost. He had returned. He lifted me from my bed and carried me in his arms, and laid me down on a soft feather bed in a sunny, clean grassy field of daisies, with the sunlight gently caressing my face. He handed me an oxygen mask, and I took several deep breaths before returning it to him. I gave him a grateful smile. He nodded and waved as he turned to go, walking away from the field onto the horizon, where there were thousands of smudged smokey faces waiting for his help.

CHAPTER 9

I heard the shrill buzz of my cell phone and opened my eyes. I snuck a look at the alarm clock at my bedside table. 4:00. I had slept through most of Sunday. The long, strange interlude yesterday with Peter and Michael came back to me, and I winced. I picked up the phone without thinking, just to stop the noise of the ringing. It was Michael, who was in a bar somewhere. I could hear the background noise.

"I'm grabbing a beer. Want to join me?"

I certainly didn't want to join him. I needed to end things. But I wasn't sure how to handle the conversation over the phone.

I still had to work with Michael. If the breakup didn't go well, my job could end up being miserable. I was trying to come up with what I was going to say when someone cleared his throat and started speaking.

"Living the same day over and over again is such a drag."

The ghost of Phil Connors, played by Bill Murray in the movie *Groundhog Day*, was standing over my bed. Phil gave me a wink and continued,

"I was in the Virgin Islands once. I met a girl. We ate lobster, drank piña coladas. At sunset, we made love like sea otters. That was a pretty good day. Why couldn't I get that day over and over and over?"

I looked up at Phil and nodded. I couldn't agree with him more. It was time to say goodbye to Michael. The time I spent with him felt like the same drunken interlude played out over and over. I didn't want that to continue. I took a deep breath, ready to say the breakup words to Michael, but he spoke first.

"Stephanie, are you still there?" Michael's voice sounded like he was shouting to be heard over the noise in the bar.

I stared at the phone, my mouth was open, but no sound was coming out. The long uncomfortable pause was punctuated by the shrill laughter and clinking of drinks in the background on Michael's end of the phone. Michael broke the silence.

"You know I love you, don't you?"

I was shocked that he was saying this. Granted, he was probably drunk, but we barely knew each other.

I could hear a faint crackling of static on the line. Why was it such an ordeal for me to break things off? He would have me replaced within the hour. I turned to Phil for guidance. Phil pointed to the phone and said, "Make it the end of a very long day."

I took a deep breath. My voice sounded both nervous and formal as I said, "Michael, I have something to tell you. I just don't think that I can date anyone right now. I think I'm going to take some time to be alone."

I should have hung up right after I said my piece, but I waited for Michael to reply. I had no idea how much time was passing. My nervousness was making time stand still. Finally, Michael answered in an icy tone.

"Whatever. You don't have to announce your plans to me. We aren't a couple or anything."

"I'm sorry, Michael."

To my surprise, Michael started laughing.

"Don't take things too seriously. It's no big deal."

Of all the responses, laughter was the one that I had least expected.

"Goodbye, Michael."

I hung up quickly after I said this. I couldn't take any more of the uncomfortable pauses laced with background bar noise. I turned my phone off so that I wouldn't see or hear if Michael called me back. For me, the conversation was over.

My hands were shaking. I clasped them together until they stopped. I then used my blanket to wipe the sweat off my forehead as I looked around the bedroom. Phil was gone. I got up and quickly showered and dressed and made myself some coffee, and ordered Chinese carryout.

As I ate my Kung Pao Chicken, I opened my laptop and sifted through my work emails and notes on the MV1 project. What would working with Michael be like now that we had broken up?

That night when I went to bed, I fell right asleep, but my dreams were disturbing and took me back to 9/11. There was an enormous dust cloud pushing its way through the street. The cloud looked like something out of an old Japanese horror movie you would watch on late-night television. The crowds around me started screaming and running in terror. Instead of calming the crowd, the police were infecting it with their panic.

But I stood still. I was sick of running.

"Help, stop. Please!"

A woman in her late twenties, with curly brown hair, wearing a blue cotton floral dress, cried out from the street. She had fallen after being kicked and trampled by the running cops. She was pregnant. Her skirt was caught under a large crate that somebody must have left behind to make their fleeing easier. I lifted the crate and helped her up.

"Thank you."

The woman tried to say this through her intense coughing. I needed to get her somewhere safer, but there wasn't anywhere safe. I saw an ATM booth across the street.

I didn't try to talk to her but instead pulled her arm, leading her to the booth. Its windows were scratched and had graffiti on them. There were discarded ATM receipts on the cement floor. I shoved the woman inside.

There wasn't room in the atm booth for both of us, so I crawled under a truck that was parked on the street. I gasped for air, coughing and wheezing. By flattening myself under the truck, stomach to the ground, I was able to take in some air.

After an indeterminate amount of time, I climbed out from under the truck. Every surface was covered with six or more inches of whitish-grey dust. It was everywhere. I waded through it, keeping my shirt over my mouth. I wanted to make sure the pregnant woman was ok, but when I finally got to the atm booth and looked inside, It was empty. I covered my eyes the best I could and blindly walked towards Church Street and the Manhattan Bridge.

CHAPTER 10

I woke up from my dream drenched in sweat and gasping for air. The room was pitch dark, and my blanket was in a pile at the foot of the bed. I looked at my alarm clock. 7 a.m. What day was it? Tuesday. I had my biweekly meeting with Chris today. I quickly showered and dressed and walked to the subway.

The 4 / 5 train was crowded, and I couldn't get a seat. My head was right up to the armpit of a tall, middle-aged man with horn-rimmed glasses and a stained oxford shirt. The man had a scraggly beard and was balding. He kept folding the New York Times into tiny sections so that he could read it on the crowded train. He reminded me of Arthur, my string theorist ex-boyfriend from Ann Arbor. I hadn't talked to Arthur recently and wondered how he was doing. I missed him.

I got off the subway at Grand Central Terminal and walked to 51st Street and the office. I checked my watch. It was 7:59 am, and I was just on time. Chris was at his desk sipping a cup of street vendor coffee when I arrived for our meeting.

"Good morning Stephanie. Have a seat."

Chris motioned to a chair without looking up from his laptop. His voice was polite but formal. He was dressed in a tailored grey suit and a navy tie. This was exactly the same outfit I saw on just about every account manager or executive I came across, except Michael, who, for all his flaws, at least had some flair.

"Ugh!"

Chris mumbled this as he jumped back in reaction to the coffee that splattered on his arm as his cup tipped over. He ran his hand distractedly through his curly light brown hair as he reached for the thin napkin that had come with the coffee.

I removed Chris's leather laptop bag from the one guest chair and sat down. Chris continued to wipe up the coffee with the napkin, and when that was soaked through, he took an office memo and placed that over the coffee to finish sopping up the liquid.

"How was your commute?"

I asked this politely to try to expel the awkward silence in the room. I was used to such silences with Chris. He had been my manager for about three years, and we had never been particularly close.

But our relationship had deteriorated further when I had asked to be removed from financial accounts after 9/11. Chris hadn't wanted to upset any of the financial sales managers by introducing a new engineer into their accounts. He had strongly encouraged me to stick with the financial vertical so that I didn't offend the clients or the account executives. Frustrated with Chris and desperate not to work downtown near Ground Zero, I had called Chris's manager, Brett, and had pleaded my case to him. Breaking from my usual cadence of uncontroversial small talk, I had described to him in a monotone what it was like to flee the building that day.

Brett had been uncomfortable listening to my detailed, matter-of-fact description of how I survived the collapsing Towers. He had quickly ended the conversation with a promise to put me on the MediaCom account.

Although it was mid-November and had been over two months now since I switched to the MV1 account, Chris resented that I had gone over his head to achieve my transfer, and we hadn't quite gotten back to an equilibrium.

Chris didn't look up from mopping up the coffee as he replied to my question.

"Holland Tunnel was down to one lane. Took forever. I should have taken the train, but I'm having dinner with Vince, the VP of Media Accounts, and Brett tonight. I want to brief them on MV1."

I was surprised that Chris was sharing so much detail with me. Usually, we kept our discussions to the weather. I was the only woman on his team, and he always seemed flustered that he couldn't talk about professional sports, his golf handicap, or the other small-talk topics he usually engaged in with the men on the team.

Chris threw the wet napkin and memo in the trash at the side of his desk. He finally looked up,

"How's MV1 going? Is the deal going to close this quarter?"

I didn't have an answer for him. Contracts were Michael's job.

"Tell him it will close. You need to project an air of confidence."

Tess was standing next to Chris, looking over his shoulder as she said this. Chris continued.

"Michael hasn't updated his account forecast, and I'd like to get an idea if the streaming deal will close this quarter."

Chris scanned my face, his eyes stopping just short of meeting mine directly as he waited for my answer. His mouth was pursed in a much-practiced half-smile that neither gave offense nor encouraged.

I was sick of covering for Michael. Since I had broken up with him three weeks ago, our working relationship could best be described as a failed detente. As I took on more and more of his duties in the MV1 account, Michael was acting out more. When I called him for our weekly briefings, he was often drunk, even if it was a morning midweek call.

Michael was mocking and hostile when we briefed on the account together. Michael showed up unprepared when we met with Dennis, stringing a non-stop series of marketing and technical buzzwords and cliches. The first time this had happened, Dennis had cut the meeting short and had turned to me for status on the progress we were making with his team. Now Dennis simply refused to meet with Michael and met with me instead.

Chris didn't know that Michael was persona non grata in the MV1 account. For the last three weeks, I had been meeting with Dennis alone several times a week and covering for Michael with Chris. That was more because I didn't want anyone thinking that the account was in a bad place than for any loyalty I had to Michael.

"If you tell Chris the deal will close, you can take charge of the MV1 account. Then you can go close the deal yourself and really kickstart your career!"

Tess walked around Chris's desk after she said this and peered wistfully out the small window. She continued,

"It took me everything I had to move up from being an administrative assistant. Don't mess up your big chance Stephanie."

I resisted the urge to roll my eyes and didn't reply to Tess.

"Brett is on my back for forecast numbers. I need to have something to tell him tonight, Stephanie. Brett wants to give Vince an idea of where we're at."

Chris's tone was skirting the thin line between a whine and an order to produce numbers out of thin air.

"You've got your boss where you want him. Make up some numbers, and then go make it happen!" Tess looked at me, her eyes earnest.

I resisted the urge to roll my eyes. I wasn't going to cover for Michael, not this time, and I wasn't going to lie to Chris either. I turned to Chris and spoke in a calm but firm tone.

"I understand, Chris. But contracts and forecasting are Michael's job."

There was an uncomfortable pause. I held Chris's gaze. It was he who looked away first.

"You're blowing it, Stephanie." Tess gave me a look of disappointment, shaking her head in disgust as she left Chris's small office.

I looked at Chris's tense face. I didn't have the numbers he was asking for. And even if I did, I wasn't sure that I wanted to own the responsibility for forecasting in the MV1 account. Even though closing the deal wasn't my job, I didn't want to blow Chris off completely. He wasn't a horrible manager; he was simply a mediocre one.

Like many men I worked with, he was a family guy from Jersey, living a life dedicated to offending no one. I didn't want to exacerbate the stress ween us, so I lightened my tone and gave him a deferential look.

"Why don't I set up a meet and greet dinner with you and Dennis? I think it would be great to get your read on him. You'll be able to ask him about the contracts then."

Chris's face visibly relaxed when I offered dinner.

"That's a great idea, Stephanie. Hearing Dennis's needs in person will help me align to his strategic plan."

"I'll set it up." I gave Chris a perfunctory smile and made my exit soon afterward.

Back at my cubicle, I contacted Le Bernardin and managed to get reservations for Friday night. When I called Dennis, he accepted the dinner invitation immediately.

"Sounds great, Stephanie. I have some exciting news for you. We can discuss it Friday."

Maybe Dennis was ready to tell me the contracts could be signed. By meeting with Dennis several times a week, I had gained influence in the account. I was the one that Dennis would tell if he was ready to close the deal.

Michael had been angry and resistant to me meeting with Dennis by myself, but he didn't want to lose the MV1 deal. Figuring out how to handle my awkward and uncomfortable work situation with Michael was still on my "To Do" list, along with scheduling a meeting with a therapist. I kept putting both tasks off. The truth was, I was avoiding people these days. I preferred being alone with my ghosts.

I spent my nights, and even some of my days, curled up in front of my television with them, watching old movies. I often thought of my father when I watched the classic musicals and film noirs in my VCR collection. My father had taught me so much about movies when I was growing up. We hadn't seen each other in over a decade, however, and our movie-watching days together were long over. Still, I could feel his presence sometimes when I watched certain musicals or Hollywood classics.

I worked on the streaming architecture for the rest of the day and left the office at 3 pm to avoid the rush hour crowds on the 6 train and 4/5 train. Once home, I poured myself a glass of wine and was about to sit down and put a movie on when the buzz of my cell phone drilled through the air. I flipped the phone open.

"Stephanie? It's Mom. Can you hear me?"

"Hi, Mom. What's up?"

"I'm just checking to see how you're doing."

"I'm fine."

"What does that mean, 'fine' Stephanie? Are you coming home for Thanksgiving? We're all worried about you."

"I've been busy."

"You always come home for Thanksgiving. What's so important there? Isn't everything going to be closed at work anyway?"

"New York doesn't shut down just because it's Thanksgiving, Mom."

"If you have to stay in the city, maybe I should fly out there for a couple of days."

I could hear in my mother's voice that she was starting to perk up at the idea of a holiday trip to the Big City. I needed to stop that idea before it took root.

"It's generous of you to offer to spend some time here, but I'll be busy with work. I'll come home soon, I promise. Maybe even for Thanksgiving. I just need more time to figure it all out. How's Dan? Has it snowed there yet?"

My mother responded enthusiastically to my polite questions, and I settled into half listening to her describe the goings-on of my stepfather Dan, my brother Steven, and various friends and coworkers of hers. After about fifteen minutes, my mother had caught me up on everything going on in her world, and the conversation wound to a close.

"You know you don't have to wait for me to call you; you can call me too."

"I know. I'll let you know if I am coming home for Thanksgiving by the end of the week."

I hung up with relief. My Mother and I always seemed to be having the same phone conversation. When I talked with my mother on the phone or spent time with her in person, her choices just made me want to flee back to the safety of my own life.

This was especially true during my visits to Michigan. When I went home, I always had to deal with my stepfather Dan. He was nothing like my father. Dan was prone to get-rich-quick schemes and loved to gamble. This wouldn't cause alarm if he had some sort of self-control, but unfortunately, Dan was a particularly bad gambler, which had caused my mother to be in a perpetual state of burdensome debt.

Dan also was drawn to political conspiracy theories, which had caused many a family fight at the dinners I had to suffer through with him when I came home for the holidays. He didn't seem to like movies at all. He watched wrestling on TV. If he hadn't been my stepfather, I would have thought he was a character from a poorly written situation comedy.

I had no idea really why my mother had ended up marrying Dan. But they seemed to keep each other company. Anyway, it was none of my business really at this point in my life.

My mother had her life, and I had mine.

It was ironic that my Mother was asking me to call her more often. When I was in middle school and high school, I thought of trying to get her to go to one of my school events or spend some time with me discussing what was going on in my world. Busy with her job working for my grandfather and her nights out with her friends, she always had some excuse for why she didn't have the time to spend with me.

Later, when I was a young woman in college and graduate school, I would leave voice messages on her answering machine that rarely were returned. I would try to schedule a time to hang out with her, but if she wasn't busy losing money at some casino junket, she was joining Dan on another sales road trip. We rarely talked. When I first moved to New York, I didn't hear from her for many weeks at a time. But now, I was hearing from her several times a week.

I guess terrorism was a family bonding event.

But my mother was right. It was time to get my first post 9/11 visit home over with. It was as good a time as any to go home. I walked over to my desktop computer and brought up Expedia, searching for Thanksgiving flights. Thanksgiving was the following week, and most were sold out, but I found an early morning one that still had seats and bought my ticket.

CHAPTER 11

I woke up with a start and glazed at my bedside clock. 5 am. Tonight was the Le Bernardin dinner. I had tossed and turned all night. There was no point in trying to grab another hour of sleep. Besides, if I left the house early, I would probably get a seat and some elbow room on the subway.

I showered and pulled out a pair of black leggings and a low-cut black tunic sweater. The tunic was body-hugging, and I usually felt self-conscious wearing it since I thought my breasts were too large, but today I was going to go for broke.

As I was drying my hair, I looked at my reflection in the mirror. I looked pale and tired. I reached for my makeup bag, which was on the counter near the sink, applied my makeup, and put on a simple gold chain, dangle earrings that had a Mediterranean look to them, and a thin link belt made of interlocking squares.

When I left the apartment, it was 6 am, and Court Street was just beginning to fill with morning commuters. As I walked to the Borough Hall subway station, I looked at the steam coming out of the manhole covers on the pavement. The sounds of early morning surrounded me. There was a big green garbage truck barreling down Court Street, with two men in reflector vests and hard hats hanging to the side; the newsstand next to the subway entrance was just opening. An older, frail, Indian man was hovering over a pile of *Daily News,* neatly stacking them. I entered the subway station, scanned my MTA card, and walked down to catch a train.

When the train arrived, I sat down next to a professionally dressed black woman in a bright fuchsia suit, with nails to match, her hair in a perfect updo with no hair out of place. The woman and I nodded to each other in the half-full car. I closed my eyes for the twenty-minute ride into midtown, my mind wandering to thoughts about the MV1 account. Chris's manager Brett was encouraging me to take more active control of the account, and that could only mean that he was concerned with Michael's handling of it.

I departed the train at Grand Central Terminal. As I walked to the exit, I was surrounded by the "Missing" signs for those lost in the Towers. Although the hundreds of such signs had recently been cleared from the walls of Grand Central Station, there were still quite a few mimeographed entreaties taped to the many poles, trashcans, and notice boards around the station. As was my habit these days, I tried to ignore the innocent Xeroxed faces as I made my way out of the station.

Lexington Avenue was crowded with commuters. Honking horns and the loud rumbling motors of buses filled the air with chaotic noise. I headed for the Korean deli that was two doors down from the office. When I entered, the line at the grill was long but manageable.

I bought a coffee with cream and sugar in its familiar blue and white cup and an egg and cheese sandwich on a roll. I watched with sleepy antic-ipation as the Mexican man at the grill nodded to me, remembering my regular order. He quickly made my egg and cheese sandwich without me having to say a word. Breakfast in hand, I continued to the office, where I entered the building, putting my laptop and purse through the security checkpoint without even thinking. Every building I entered these days had beefed up its security since 9/11, and I was now used to guards and metal detectors and didn't get triggered by them anymore.

As I rode the elevator to my floor, my thoughts wandered to the Le Bernardin dinner. Before 9/11, it would have been impossible to get a table for dinner there on such short notice. It was still surprising how easy it was since September to get into plays and five-star restaurants. But I rarely felt like going to expensive or trendy places these days. There was too much pressure in those places to enjoy myself.

I headed for a cube at the back of the office. The floor was still relatively empty, and I had my pick of cubes. I chose one against the wall with a window and sat down, gulping my coffee as I turned my laptop on and opened my email. As I read through my messages, I devoured my egg sandwich, letting the warm creamy American cheese ooze out, catching it with my finger, and then licking my finger. The salty eggs in the sandwich seemed to go down my throat almost without me chewing them.

When I finished my breakfast sandwich, I got up to throw out my empty coffee cup and the foil that the sandwich had been wrapped in. As I walked to the nearest trash can, I took a look around the office. All the cubes were now filled, and people were talking on conference calls or working at their desks, the clicking of their keyboards filling the air. Even though it was late 2001, the office activity I was witnessing could have been from any era in the last 50 years. The fashions had changed, and there were not as many secretaries, but otherwise, the conference calls, memo typing, and polite office conversation could have been from any time.

"When you finish the slush files, then you may go. But I want my comments on each."

I turned around to see who was talking. The ghost of Amanda Farrow, as played by Joan Crawford in the 1950's movie *The Best of Everything*, was giving me a disapproving look. *The Best of Everything* was a 1950's office drama. I had watched the movie the previous night, enjoying the escape into work life in the 1950s. Everything was so much simpler then. Roles and rules were rigid and understood by everyone. Looking at the limited opportunities of the women in those movies always made me feel like somehow I had made progress.

Amanda pointed to a cubicle.

"Am I not being clear, Miss Willis?"

Amanda's question was straight from the movie. I thought I would be more surprised that Amanda was here with me, but it felt oddly natural to run into her this way. Amanda's character in the movie had sacrificed love and marriage to have a career. *The Best of Everything*, much like every other film from the 1950s, portrayed a woman's career choices as binary. Amanda could have love or a career, but not both. In the movie, she took out her frustrations on the beleaguered steno pool, who typed her endless memos and stayed late to process her editorial dictation.

Of course, things had changed since the 1950s for women. It was now socially acceptable to be a married working mother. At the beginning of my career, I had bought into the notion that professional success was worth enduring hardship for. I had left my ex-boyfriend Arthur and Ann Arbor to take this job. But now, five years later, I wasn't sure if I wanted to sacrifice anything for my so-called career.

My dilemma was different from Amanda's.

As if hearing my thoughts, Amanda sighed and continued, "You young girls these days think it's so easy to get to the top. You know nothing."

Amanda pointed to the cubicle again.

"Today, Miss Willis. I want my comments typed today."

Amanda then turned around and left. I thought about Amanda's comment. I didn't think it was "so easy" to get to the top. Women usually were not promoted in technical sales organizations or engineering. I was the only woman engineer on the team, and there were no female sales executives either.

I wasn't even sure I wanted to get to "the top." I didn't want to be like Chris or Brett, only thinking about money and closing deals. And I certainly didn't want to be like Michael, although he was in a downward spiral and wouldn't be promoted any time soon.

In *The Best of Everything*, the main character Caroline worked her way up from the typing pool to an editor at rapid speed. By the end of the movie, Caroline had given up caring about her career and instead turned towards the promise of love with one of her older male coworkers.

Had leaving her career behind made Carolyn happy? I looked around at everyone being productive and focused. An intense wave of sadness washed over me. I wanted to go home. But I wasn't sure where my home was. Before I could get too melancholy, my cell phone rang.

"Hey Doll, it's Dennis. Got a sec?"

I ignored Dennis's familiarity. He had been calling me "Doll" for some time now. Dennis was in his late forties, and the fifteen-plus-year age difference between us probably explained the endearment. I wondered if he called his wife "doll" too.

"Hey, Dennis. What's up?"

"There are some people I'd like to come to dinner tonight if possible. The President of the Content division and his team are in from LA, and they expressed interest in discussing your ideas. Eight people total."

"That's great, Dennis. Thanks so much for arranging this!"

I made sure I made my voice sound properly thankful and excited as I hung up. It was a great reflection on me that the West Coast executives wanted to spend time with me at dinner. In media accounts, West Coast content executives were considered higher in the pecking order than IT executives like Dennis. They controlled more money.

This was a career high point. I sat for a moment and tried to feel happy. I thought about the scene in *Best of Everything* where Caroline ran around the office in excitement when she got promoted out of the typing pool and became a manuscript reader. Hosting such a critical dinner was a step up for me. I wanted to feel excited like Caroline.

Yet, I just felt exhausted.

I called Chris to let him know the good news. I looked at my watch. It was only 10 o'clock. I had quite a few hours before dinner and nothing much to do before I met Dennis. Coming into the office so early didn't feel like such a brilliant idea anymore. I decided to take a walk. The cool fall air would clear my head.

I headed towards Times Square. As I walked near the 42nd street subway station, a busker playing drums made out of large white plastic pails turned upside down. I reached into my small wallet and threw a couple of dollars into the hat by his feet.

I didn't have anywhere to go and wasn't sure where I was walking to. Even though it was still morning, a cold beer and a dark corner were exactly what I wanted. I walked to one of the bars Michael had introduced me to. It was on 43rd and 8th, just a block from the Port Authority bus terminal, where some of the classic pre-Giuliani Times Square culture remained. There were still porn shops, dive bars, and questionable electronic retailers on the block, and I loved the seedy feel of the street.

I walked past a pink neon sign of a naked woman with her back arched and smiled to myself when I saw the red "BAR" sign of Smith's next door, flashing much the way it probably had for fifty years. This is the New York that I needed right now.

I opened the door and was greeted by the bartender Joe, who knew me from my visits with Michael. Joe was watering down a bottle of Ketel One vodka with a gallon-sized bottle of cheap vodka. He grinned when he saw what I was looking at, but he didn't stop what he was doing. His sleeves were rolled up, revealing muscular arms that were covered with faded tattoos. His straight brown hair was tied back in a neat ponytail.

"Morning. Is Michael with you?"

It was hard to believe that my life was such that I could walk into a bar like Smith's in Midtown and the bartender knew me. This wasn't the New York experience that I had imagined in my fantasies when I had moved here. But I liked the comfort of the dusty old bar, and I enjoyed being recognized by Joe. It was a relief to be seen, even if it was just for a moment, and even if it was just by a bartender.

I shook my head and gave Joe an amused smile in reply as I looked pointedly at his watering-down procedure. I took a seat. The bar was empty. There was one table taken with two middle-aged guys in construction gear, drinking a beer with a shot and reading the sports section of the *Daily News*. Joe brought me over a PBR and a shot of Jack Daniels. I quickly downed the shot. Joe winked and poured me another one.

I wasn't alone for long. I was soon joined by the ghost of James Dan's character, Jett Rink, from the movie *Giant*. *Giant* was an epic tale of a Texas ranching family. Although I hadn't seen *Giant* in a while, I had watched it quite a few times over the years. I was a fan of the tragic disillusionment and alienation of James Dean.

In *Giant*, Jett starts as a low-paid worker on the Bennett family's Texas ranch. He becomes an oil baron by the movie's end, but his riches don't provide him love or fulfillment. In the three-and-a-half-hour film, Jett spends the entire time chasing after a vision of success that he can't even define clearly.

I glanced over at Jett, who was dressed in jeans, a denim jacket, and a work shirt. His jeans were stained with mud and oil. Jett's hair was in a classic James Dean pompadour. He walked over to the other end of the bar and leaned against it, watching me down my shot. Jett pulled a whisky bottle out of his denim jacket and gave me a maudlin look filled with both desire and self-pity. The line had been originally aimed at his boss and romantic crush in the movie, Leslie Bennett, as played by Elizabeth Taylor:

"You are the boss, and you know it too, don't ya."

I looked at Jett with distaste. He reminded me of Michael. In fact, this bar reminded me of Michael. Why had I come here? I sighed.

"I'm not the boss."

I thought this to myself without meeting Jett's eyes. Jett grinned, hearing my thoughts. He took another swig from his whiskey bottle and looked around the bar, much like Michael might have. He sounded very drunk as he slurred another line from *Giant*.

"Imma rich boy. And Imma make more money than you ever thought you could have—you and all the rest of you stinkin son of a Benedicts."

Jett then approached me, stumbling. I held my hand up to ward him off. I just wanted Jett to leave. I still had to deal with Michael since we shared the MV1 account, but I was under no obligation to entertain Jett. I gestured to the exit.

Jett gave me a lopsided grin. He then turned from me and stumbled back to the bar. He sat down unsteadily on a barstool and took another swig from his whiskey bottle. He closed his eyes, and his head dropped as if he had passed out. I had seen Michael in this exact pose many times.

I turned away from Jett. I didn't want to deal with any drunken, tortured men right now. Even if they were ghosts. I closed my eyes, willing Jett away. I didn't expect my gesture to have any power, but when I opened my eyes, to my surprise, he was gone. I motioned to Joe.

"Can I have a cup of coffee?"

"I'll make a fresh pot."

Joe brought a spoon wrapped in a napkin over to my table. I pulled out my memo pad and looked over my notes on MV1. The construction guys were gone, leaving me in the bar by myself. As Joe filled my coffee, my cell phone rang. I flipped it open. It was a number that I didn't recognize.

"Stephanie, is that you?"

The voice at the other end of the phone sounded frail and confused.

"Who is this?"

"It's your father. Your mother gave me your number."

My father hadn't seen me or called me for over a decade. We had had a big fight when I moved to Yale for graduate school, which had never quite healed itself. Our only communication for years had consisted of the card I sent him each Christmas and birthday that accompanied a gift pack of gourmet brownies and his return thank you note. It was unsettling to hear his voice on the line.

"I've been trying to reach you. I'm at University of Michigan hospital. My defibrillator keeps shocking me, and I have a very irregular heartbeat. The doctor is going to try to turn it off."

I could hear my father take a gasp of air after his lengthy explanation.

"When's the surgery?"

"Tomorrow. I just wanted you to know, in case anything goes wrong."

I listened to my father's jagged breathing on the line. He sounded scared. But I couldn't just drop everything and fly to Ann Arbor tonight.

"I'm coming home for Thanksgiving, Dad. I'll come see you then. I promise."

"Hopefully, I'll make it through this procedure. See you then, I guess."

I stared at the phone for a minute after I hung up. I was surprised that I felt angry. What did my father expect from me? We hadn't talked in over a decade, and now he expected me to just drop everything and come see him.

"If you just learn a single trick..., you'll get along a lot better with all kinds of folks. You never really understand a person until you consider things from his point of view... Until you climb inside of his skin and walk around in it."

I looked up to see where the comment was coming from. The ghost of Gregory Peck's character, Atticus Finch, in *To Kill a Mockingbird,* was standing against the wall of the bar watching me.

His words, although well-meaning, actually made me angrier.

I was no Scout and didn't need Atticus's fatherly advice right now.

I gave Atticus my middle finger.

Jett had returned. He grinned and nodded in approval at my gesture as he pointed to Atticus.

"Who's he?"

"An iconic father figure in American Cinema."

I answered the question the way my father would have answered it.

"I'm not much of a movie fan, Honey. Never heard of him."

Jett shrugged as he said this. He then got up from his barstool, giving me a lingering look as he left the bar. Atticus watched Jett go. He turned to me.

"There's a lot of ugly things in this world. I wish I could keep 'em all away from you. That's never possible."

His eyes were kind.

I resisted the urge to give him my middle finger again and just nodded.

Atticus gave me a paternal look of understanding. He then waved goodbye and left the bar. I glanced at my watch. 12:30.

I pushed my coffee away and sipped my beer while I thought about my dad. My father had a passion for movies, especially musicals. Growing up, I had listened with interest as he had explained interesting backstory and facts on the movies we watched together, such as:

"*Singin' in the Rain* is a classic all the more for being one of the only movie musicals that isn't adapted from a Broadway musical," or:

"Stephanie, did you know that 'West Side Story' was originally going to be about a Catholic boy and a Jewish girl? Just like your mother and me."

I remembered these moments not only for the pleasure they had given me but also for the fact that they were the moments when my father truly felt like a father to me.

My dad had always seemed disappointed with life like he had just missed a plane ride to a fun vacation or had just lost a puppy he loved, and in a way, he had. My mother was depressed for most of my childhood and didn't give him much attention. He had taken his disappointment with life out on me to a certain extent, with his constant criticisms and emotional distance. But the problem with my father wasn't that he didn't love me. I know he did in his own tortured way. The problem was that my father was a lost little boy looking for love and didn't have the maturity to be a father figure.

My father had always dreamed of going on a road trip to Hollywood as if it was the Promised Land. But he never had ventured far from Michigan. Would my father have loved Hollywood if he had ever actually gotten there? Or would it have disappointed him just as much as everything else in his life?

I would never find out now.

I looked at the neon clock hanging over the bar. It was 2:30. I had sat at the bar and daydreamed for much longer than I intended. I had been nursing the same beer for some time, and luckily, I wasn't buzzed at all. I signaled to Joe that I was ready to cash out. It was time to meet Dennis for our pre-dinner status meeting.

CHAPTER 12

My pre-dinner meeting with Dennis had gone well. Dennis had put together an impressive roster of top media executives for the workshops we were going to have in LA in January. He had used his considerable industry expertise to assemble an interesting array of speakers and topics for the workshops as well. Dennis's technical savvy had impressed me since I first read his book. His ideas of how to scale video content were quite innovative. I was learning a lot from him. We had spent several hours going over all the details for the workshops and then had walked to Le Bernadin together.

As we entered Le Bernadin, I took a look around the restaurant. Stunning abstract art hung throughout the large open room. The tables had tea lights floating in bowls of water, and there were exquisite flower arrangements on each table with Orchids and other exotic flowers.

The receptionist was a thin, tall woman with light skin, blue eyes, and straight black hair cut in a vaguely Asian bob. Her eyes were made up dramatically with eyeliner. She walked us to our table and handed us small menus that were on parchment paper.

Dennis looked appreciatively at my outfit as he helped me into my chair. Even though I had just spent two hours with him in his office, now that we were together at the restaurant, the vibe had changed from a business meeting to a more intimate, social feeling. As Dennis's eyes grazed my body, my cheeks flushed with the hint of a blush. I gave him a nervous smile, relieved that he didn't comment on my low-cut sweater and tight leggings. As we waited for everyone to arrive, I ordered the first bottle of wine, an $800 bottle of white burgundy from France.

"Excellent choice," Dennis said as he nodded in approval.

"Only the best for you, Dennis," I said in a slightly flirty tone.

Once seated, I glanced around the room. Several large tables were filled with men of various ages in suit jackets and designer ties. Some had their hair slicked back; others had upscale haircuts that kept their hair in a subtle disheveled look where every hair was sculpted in place. All the suit jackets were hand-tailored and looked expensive.

The men at these large tables were laughing and toasting with glasses of red wine that their server was pouring from a large crystal decanter. I couldn't hear what they were saying, but by the way, several servers were hovering around the table catering to the men, my guess was that they were Wall Street traders toasting some sort of deal and spending an obscene amount of money.

A few tables for two had successful-looking middle-aged men in suits eating with younger women attired in fashionable dresses and full make-up. Each woman picked at their food and sipped white wine nervously. The men seemed to be eating their food and trying to enjoy their meals while their dates sat and made small talk with them, trying to look glamorous.

I could feel how uncomfortable these couples were as if eating at the restaurant was a job interview or even a job. At a few of the tables, the couples were finishing up their meals. The men ordered elaborate desserts while the women all ordered sorbet, taking tiny tastes. As I looked at each table, it felt strange to see everyone do the same thing, as if in an orchestrated dance.

When the sommelier came back with the wine, I went through the ceremony of tasting it and gestured to Dennis to also try it out and make sure it was to his liking.

As Dennis nursed his wine, my mind wandered back to our meeting earlier in the afternoon. In addition to the January workshops, we had discussed the streaming architecture for the Music and Video Awards shows. I had broached the subject of contracts, and Dennis had agreed to continue discussion towards closing the multi-million-dollar streaming deal by the end of the year.

With Michael all but banned from the account, I wasn't sure who should have these discussions with Dennis. It was a question I intended to ask Chris as soon as I had a chance.

A few minutes after the waiter brought our wine, the hostess returned to our table, escorting Chris and the MV1 executives. Rose and Tess were standing near the MV1 contingent. Dennis looked at me with proud pleasure as he introduced everyone to me. His chest was puffed out, and he had his hand on my back, giving the signal to the executives that he was vouching for me.

"Stephanie, I'd like you to meet Chuck, our President of digital content, and Andy, our President of subscription content. With him is Sam, who heads up our West Coast digital operations team, and Derrick, who is President for MV1 Europe."

It was quite an honor for an engineer like me to be having dinner with executives this high in rank. It rarely happened. I surreptitiously looked over at Chris to see if he was impressed, but he was busy shaking everyone's hand, his eyes focused on faces, most likely so he could match them to names.

Once we were all seated, the sommelier appeared again almost instantly. Chris ordered a red and a white wine that were each over $1,500 a bottle. Chris made a point of picking from the last page, pausing for effect so that the MV1 executives could see that he was ordering from the page that had the most expensive wines. Every executive at the table nodded in approval. Once everyone knew that they were being treated with respect, they all seemed to relax, and some side conversations began to take place while Chris finished the wine transaction.

"Always the same narrow people, the same mindless chatter."

Rose said this as she looked around the table.

"This dinner is an amazing opportunity. All these executives!" Tess didn't look up as she said this. She was intensely studying the menu, practicing the pronunciation of the entrees under her breath.

I ignored both ghosts, focusing my attention on Dennis instead. I looked into his eyes and pretended to listen with interest as he recounted a clothing mishap that one of the star performers had had last year at the Music Awards.

It was surprisingly easy to keep up with the conversation at the table because nothing much was being said. It was too soon after 9/11 to talk about current events, so the conversation was mainly about the food. As the tasting menu courses appeared, one after another, I oohed and aahed and nodded in agreement when Dennis made comments such as,

"The presentation is delightful. So vibrant and delicate."

Tess turned to me, pointing to her menu as she asked, "What's a yuzu-champagne emulsion?"

Rose gave Tess a look of disapproval but didn't reply.

During the third course of the tasting menu, Chris cleared his throat and tapped his wine glass to signal he wanted to make an announcement. We all turned politely to listen to him. Chris raised his glass,

"I'd like to announce that we're promoting Stephanie to account executive for MediaCom, effective immediately. Congratulations, Stephanie, on a job well done!"

Chris met my startled expression with an evasive one. He gave me a curt nod and a smile that was merely the upturned corners of his lips. As I looked into his eyes for an answer as to why I was being promoted, Chris took a sip of his wine, saying nothing more, his face a polite mask. Chris's behavior suggested to me that he didn't necessarily approve of my promotion. But if that was the case, why had he announced it at a dinner full of MV1 executives?

Chris's announcement completely caught me off guard. I had been doing most of Michael's work, so the promotion made a certain sense. But even as recently as my meeting with Chris earlier in the week, there had been no hint that I would be offered Michael's job.

I wasn't even sure I wanted Michael's job.

I smiled absently as everyone around the table congratulated me.

"Well done, Stephanie."

Dennis gave me a self-satisfied look and raised his glass in another toast as he said this. He didn't seem surprised at all at Chris's announcement. Dennis gave me a wink. He then leaned in towards me and spoke quietly so that only I could hear him.

"I've been in touch with Brett. We meet for scotch and cigars every couple of weeks. I suggested you would be a good fit as account manager."

How long had this been in the works? If Brett was meeting with Dennis directly, then why had he pressured Chris so much for the sales forecast? Why hadn't he simply asked Dennis himself?

Five years of being a solutions engineer had still not taught me the ritualistic mysteries of how men talked to each other to conduct business behind the scenes. Tonight I was as much at a loss for how to understand the mechanisms behind my promotion as I would have been on day one of my job.

Dennis had arranged my promotion for some reason. By the way he was looking at me with paternal largesse, I could tell that he assumed that I wanted Michael's job.

Whatever Dennis's motives for inserting himself in my promotion, I didn't have any time to think about it now. I needed to get gratitude on my face immediately, or I would be at risk of spoiling the tone of the dinner. As if reading my mind, Tess pointed to Dennis as she said impatiently, "What are you waiting for? Thank him! He's giving you your big break!"

Rose looked at Dennis, her eyes haunted by memories of her own, "I was put on the spot much the same way when Cal proposed to me at a dinner for twenty. It was impossible to say 'no' to him with everyone watching me."

I nodded. Rose was right. I couldn't refuse the promotion, at least not tonight. I took a sip of wine and turned to Dennis, leaning in towards him.

"Thank you so much for believing in me, Dennis. This is so exciting!"

My words seemed to satisfy Dennis. He gave me another wink. He then turned to Chris, his voice loud enough for the other executives to hear.

"I'll work with Stephanie on the streaming contracts. We should be able to wrap things up before we break for the holidays."

"Wonderful, Dennis! Thanks for all your help."

Chris raised his glass in a salute to Dennis as he said this, his tone one of polite deference and gratitude. I studied Chris quizzically. I had no idea how my promotion impacted him. Maybe I would now report to Michael's manager.

Although at the beginning of my career I would have had a preference who I reported to, a long series of mediocre managers over the years had caused me not to care either way at this point. One manager was as good as another to me.

The dinner dragged on. As the wine flowed, the laughter increased at our table, and talk of the World Series started to interlace in the conversation. Both Dennis and Chris shared the opinion that the Yankees should have won.

The Series had just ended a week ago. When I had watched the games on TV, half paying attention, I had noticed that there hadn't been much shouting, cheering, or any of the things you expected to see in the stands at a World Series game. The few times there was celebration in the stands, all the cameras zoomed in on it and lingered a bit too long so that it all looked forced to me. It made me uncomfortable to watch so many people trying so hard to have fun.

Everyone at the table had watched the games, and this made for an animated conversation as the West Coast executives showed some bias towards the Arizona Diamondbacks.

"Alfonso Soriano's error on Bautista's ground ball in game six was the clincher. It was over then."

Sam, one of the West Coast executives, said this animatedly, his arms reaching back to simulate a baseball error. Sam's face was flushed from the wine, and since everyone else was buzzed by now, his mimed baseball throw at the fancy dinner table seemed a perfectly natural gesture.

"That game was a tragedy. Witasick should have pitched better. It was embarrassing." Dennis insulted the Yankees pitching, and our table got louder as everyone chimed in.

I nodded when it made sense to and kept quiet for the most part. I took another sip of my wine, resisting the urge to yawn. The wine was making me sleepy. Dennis nodded to the waiter to refill both his wine glass and mine.

Tess pointed to Dennis and Derrick, who were still discussing the Yankees' win in game two.

"Make sure these powerful and important men know you can hold your own in the conversation. I always read the sports section of *The Daily News* just in case. You never know what you're going to need to know."

"This dinner reminds me of the Titanic," Rose said quietly, looking around the room with a melancholy expression. Dennis leaned in closer, his eyes holding my gaze, as he said, "Excellent work Stephanie."

We finally reached the final course of the tasting menu. The wait staff brought dessert and aperitifs. Derrick, the European President of Content, swirled the cognac in his snifter, taking an appreciative sip. He was in his mid-forties, and his curly blond hair was tossed with hair product, giving his curls an odd spiked look. He had on a large gold pinky ring that had a diamond in the center. Derrick was staring at a young woman sitting with her date at a table by the left wall as he sipped his cognac. After a pause, he turned to Chris.

"Where do people go to unwind after dinner here?" he asked.

Conversation quieted, and everyone turned to Chris for an answer. He glanced around the table, replying casually, "There are a few clubs in the area that have excellent scotch and cigars. What are you in the mood for?"

"I was looking for something a bit more, shall we say, 'personal' than a cigar and scotch joint."

Derrick smiled slyly at Chris. I heard a couple of chuckles, but I was too buzzed and unfocused to place them to individuals. I glanced around the table. Each man, including Dennis, was looking expectantly at Chris. Rose looked confused but intrigued. She asked me, "What are they talking about?"

Tess stared at Dennis with an indecipherable look on her face as she replied more to herself than to Rose.

"They want to go to a strip club."

Rose's eyes opened wide in surprise. Dennis reached over and refilled my wine glass. He pointed to it, urging me to take a sip. I took a larger gulp than I intended, nearly downing the glass.

Dennis looked down my neckline as he whispered, "You need more wine, Stephanie."

More wine was exactly what I didn't need. Dennis reached for the decanter again, filling my wine glass. I needed to focus my attention on Chris. Was he going to take the men to Scores? It was the only high-end strip club nearby. I stared at him, trying to get his attention across the noisy table. Chris finally met my questioning gaze with veiled eyes. We paused for a second; then he quickly looked away. He tapped on his glass to get everyone's attention and addressed the table.

"I have an early morning kiddie football league game that I'm coaching and have to get back to New Jersey. But Stephanie will be happy to take you to Scores. She's been there before and will make sure that you all continue your evening in style."

Rose looked at Chris with distaste. She then stood up from the table and turned to me, her eyes pleading.

"I think we should go now. Please leave with me."

"I can't."

I thought this to myself, but it was clear that Rose heard my thoughts by the way she looked at me with sympathy and nodded. My eyes were apologetic as I met her gaze, but I wasn't sure who I was apologizing to exactly.

"Don't worry. Stephanie can handle herself. She'll be fine."

Tess said this more to herself than to Rose or me.

Rose reached for my hand and squeezed it, looking into my eyes as she said softly, "Please take care of yourself tonight."

Rose then left the restaurant.

After an uncomfortable pause, Tess quietly added,

"I'm so sorry I can't join you at Scores. I've got speech class."

She looked down at her hands, picking at her nail polish.

Her excuse sounded as lame as Chris's.

She gave me a sad smile as she said quietly,

"Remember, you didn't make the rules."

Tess took one more wistful look at the MV1 executives as she left the restaurant.

As Chris signed the check, he was careful not to meet my questioning look. We all stood up to leave. Dennis kept his body close to mine as he put his hand on my back and guided me towards one of the town cars that the hostess had ordered for us. We split into three cars. Dennis and I were alone.

"Do you like Scores, Stephanie?"

Dennis turned his head to me and leaned in as he said this. I resisted the urge to pull back from the wine smell on his breath as I answered him.

"It's a very interesting place."

I didn't see the point in saying that Scores was a sad and tacky cliche.

Dennis had moved a bit closer to me, and I could feel the length of his thigh along mine. I swallowed hard, wiping the sweaty palms on my leggings as I continued,

"I think the girls are quite beautiful. I also like the way everything is so luxurious."

I didn't think the women who worked at Scores were particularly attractive. For the most part, they all looked like second-rate porn stars. As for the so-called luxury of Scores, the purple neon, harsh lights, red velvet, and labyrinth of ever more private rooms made the place seem just like what it was, a strip club.

But Dennis didn't care what I thought about the decor of Scores. It was clear from the way he was leaning in ever closer to me that he had only heard the first part of my statement.

"Do you like girls, Stephanie?"

My foggy mind raced, trying to figure out a fitting answer to Dennis's question. If I said I didn't like women, then that might bore him. But if I said yes, then Dennis would think that I was a lesbian.

As I opened my mouth to answer him, a new ghost appeared in the town car: the ghost of Elizabeth Taylor's character Gloria Wandrous in *Butterfield 8*. Of all of Elizabeth Taylor's movies. *Butterfield 8* was my favorite. It wasn't a great movie, but it was irresistible to me due to Gloria's character. Watching Elizabeth Taylor play an emotionally confused NYC call girl with a chip on her shoulder and mother and daddy issues always drew me in better than any soap opera ever could.

Tonight Gloria had on the dress slip and borrowed mink coat that she wore in the first scene in the movie. She winked at me and took a drag of her unfiltered cigarette.

"Answer Dennis's question, honey. You don't want him getting rough."

"What should I say?" I wondered silently, looking to Gloria for an answer.

Gloria blew smoke at Dennis and tapped her foot as she thought of the proper words for me to use.

"Tell him you like girls and have experimented."

Gloria took one last drag of her cigarette and then threw it to the floor of the town car, grinding it with her stiletto heel. She blew me a kiss and left.

I turned to Dennis and replied to his question in what I hoped was a tone worthy of Gloria Wandrous.

"I like men. But I guess it depends on the girl Dennis."

Dennis laughed appreciatively. He was about to say more, but we were at Scores.

CHAPTER 13

"Welcome to Scores! What can we do for you tonight?"

The maitre d' said this to Dennis as we entered the lobby. I was wobbly on my feet from the wine. Dennis's arm was on my back, helping me stand. Dennis pointed to me to let the maitre d' know that I was the expense account holder. The maitre d' gave me a slippery smile.

"We have a VIP package that includes a VIP room and tips for the entertainment."

He stressed the word "entertainment," and all of the men chuckled.

"Yes. Please start us out with a VIP package. I need to approve all charges beforehand."

The maitre d' nodded and gave me a knowing wink as I handed him my credit card. We walked past the main room, which was dark except for the bright lights shining on the current dancer, who was swinging around the dance pole and lifting a sequined cowboy hat off of her blond-wigged head. She had nothing on but a tiny sequined G-string and cowboy boots. Her implant-augmented breasts were bouncing to the beat of a Bon Jovi song. The maitre d' motioned to a woman wearing a tight black velvet dress and silver platform sandals.

"Come this way, gentlemen."

The woman gave Dennis a big fake smile as she said this.

"And lady."

The woman led us up two flights of stairs to a private room with a silky silver curtain covering the doorway. As we entered the room, we were greeted by eight women dressed in negligees. The room had a long red leather sofa that wrapped around so that the ends of the sofa faced each other. The lighting was softer than the neon stripes of lighting downstairs, but the room was still quite dark. There were wood cafe-style chairs scattered in the middle of the room. "Justify My Love" by Madonna was playing on the sound system.

A disco ball was hanging from the ceiling. Soft stage lighting made the ball flash patterns on the wall that looked like hazy stars. Chrome buckets for champagne were placed next to each end of the sofa.

"Welcome to the Champagne room, gentlemen. Please take a seat and get comfortable."

Our hostess pointed to the sofa, which was a cue for the women in negligees to come and help everyone take off their suit jackets. A stripper with red hair, purple glitter on her eyelids, and a fur-trimmed pink negligee started pulling at Dennis's arm. She was coaxing him to a corner seat on the sofa.

"I'm Roxy. What's your name?"

Dennis reluctantly let go of my waist and allowed himself to be pulled to the sofa by Roxy. I looked around the room at the strippers. They were all cliched caricatures of women. They were heavily made up, their breasts perfectly round spheres. Their hair was flowing over unfocused, heavily lashed eyes. They were all wearing see-through negligees.

"Don't call them 'strippers.' They're dancers."

Gloria scolded me playfully. She was standing behind the sofa.

I sat down. More women had appeared, and now there were two dancers for almost everyone in our party. Two waitresses, dressed in what I would describe as Playboy bunny outfits without the ears, walked around the sofa, taking drink orders. One of the strippers had attached herself to the pole in the middle of the room and was winding around it slowly while dropping the spaghetti strap of her negligee.

When we entered the room, the hostess had given each man several large packets of mixed bills, and Derrick tossed a couple of one-dollar bills at the woman on the pole. Roxy was kneeling before Dennis. She took his hand and put it on her perfectly round, silicone breast. Dennis didn't pull his hand away, but his eyes weren't on Roxy. They were watching me.

A stripper slowly walked over to me with a seductive smile. She was tall and blonde and was wearing a black negligee. Surprisingly, her breasts weren't augmented. Her hair had curls that looked like they had been created by a curling iron. Her eyes were focused and clear.

"Hi, I'm Angel."

Angel bent over me, giving me a full view of her smallish breasts. Her chest had silver glitter on it, which shimmered from the ceiling lights. I was still blurry from all the wine, and to me, Angel's words sounded like a waitress asking for my drink order.

"I'll have a vodka and tonic. Thanks."

"I'm not the waitress, but I'll let her know, honey. I'm here to give you whatever else you might need."

Angel brushed her breasts against me. Dennis stared at me with an intense, smokey gaze while Roxy sat on her knees in front of him and toyed with her breasts.

"Do you mind if I sit with you?"

Angel asked this in a breathy voice. I gave her a polite nod and motioned to the seat next to me.

"That's a pretty sweater. What's your name, honey?"

I wasn't sure if I should give Angel my real name. She hadn't given me hers. I turned to Gloria, who was watching me with an amused look.

"They have your name from the credit card anyway. Just give her your first name."

Gloria took a large sip of what looked like scotch on the rocks after she said this.

"Stephanie."

"You have beautiful eyes, Stephanie."

Angel leaned in closer to me. She touched the strap of her negligee.

"What brings you here, Stephanie?"

"I'm here with clients."

Angel nodded and gave me what looked on the surface like a warm smile.

"Would you like a back rub? It'll help you relax, honey."

Dennis was still looking at me. I'm not sure if his eyes had left me since we had been seated. Roxy was on her knees, with one hand rubbing Dennis's crotch in a circular motion. Dennis watched me watching him. His eyes dilated. He pulled away from Roxy, taking her hands off of him, and turned towards Angel.

"Hello, Angel. I'm Dennis."

"Hi, Dennis. You're so handsome, baby. I love that name. So strong."

Looking at me, Dennis said in a husky voice,

"Stephanie has had a long day. She needs help relaxing."

Angel's eyes took in Dennis. Even with a voice that was laden with wine and desire, Dennis's tone was authoritative. Angel gave Dennis a knowing nod. She turned back to me, leaning in closer.

"Let me loosen you up, honey. A backrub will feel good, I promise."

Gloria was leaning against Dennis's side of the sofa and was watching me. She absently took a drag of her cigarette.

I gave Angel a tired smile.

"Sure, Angel, a back rub sounds nice."

Dennis pulled money from his tip packet, mostly twenty-dollar bills, and handed it to Angel. Angel took the money from Dennis, keeping her eyes on me. She glanced at the money just long enough to see that it was a pile of twenties. She set the money down on the floor, and with two swift movements, she lifted her arms and took her negligee top off, and threw it to the floor.

Angel kept her eyes locked with mine as she caressed her nipples to make them hard. I could feel a blush creeping across my cheeks, but I didn't turn away. Angel leaned over me and started rubbing my tense shoulders.

"How does that feel, Sugar?"

Angel said this loud enough for Dennis and all the men to hear her. Dennis was watching me as Roxy sat in his lap and softly rotated her hips, her back arched to give her breasts maximum volume. He spoke to me in a guttural, throaty tone.

"Relax, Stephanie. Let Angel take care of you. That would please me."

All of the MV1 executives had nude strippers on their laps at this point, but they all turned to watch Angel get up from the sofa and stand in front of me. Angel took one more look at Dennis for guidance. He pointed to me, effectively giving Angel an order to dance for me.

There was a slow, mournful Prince song playing on the sound system. It was one of the songs from *Purple Rain*, and I think it was called "The Beautiful Ones." Angel pulled a chair in front of me, placing it, so she didn't block Dennis's view. She bit her lips in a display of passion and slowly looked me up and down as she moved around the chair.

Angel wiggled into the chair and sat down, facing me. She put her arms on her hips and spread her legs as she rolled her shoulders and arched her back. Roxy was grinding more intensely on Dennis's lap. Dennis ignored her. I looked at Dennis. Our eyes locked. I watched the flame of desire burning in his eyes.

"It's just a lap dance. It's a show, a fantasy."

Gloria walked over to me as she said this. She offered me one of her cigarettes. I shook my head. She shrugged and lit one for herself, letting her borrowed mink coat open up to reveal her dress slip underneath. She then walked back to Dennis's side of the sofa.

I could feel Dennis's desire pushing through the space between us. All of the MV1 executives were watching me expectantly.

I was still in my seat on the sofa, but that seat was now a stage.

I had gone through life up to this point telling the world that I was an engineer. I had worked hard and had just been promoted to account executive. But tonight, I was no account manager or engineer. Tonight my job was to entertain the MV1 executives. Tonight, Angel and I were coworkers, strippers, giving Dennis a private dance.

I had a choice to make. I decided to play out the lap dance.

I had nothing to lose.

There was no dignity and sense of self-righteousness waiting for me at home.

My only choice was no real choice at all.

If I left the strip club, I would only be in a downward spiraling career in an expensive, cruel city. Taking the lap dance was the convenient option, the easy way out.

I sat up on the sofa, ready to take Angel's lead.

It was show time.

I put on a shy smile as I nodded to Dennis and then looked down quickly with what I hoped was a demure expression. Dennis groaned. His voice was hoarse with desire.

"That's my girl."

Angel put her hands on my shoulders, giving me a smile that stopped just short of her eyes. Angel blew me a stage kiss.

"Come on, Stephanie honey. Let Angel take care of you."

Angel reached out her hand to help me to the chair. I took her lead. I was surprised that the Prince song was still playing. Or maybe it was another similar Prince ballad. My sense of time was completely skewed. I sat stiffly in the chair.

The Prince song ended, and the driving beat of "Closer" by Nine Inch Nails filled the room. Angel stood in front of me. She grabbed the waistband of her G-string and pulled it off, stepping out of it as she positioned herself on my lap, her naked hips grinding to the techno beat. She stroked my hair, her eyes looking beyond me to her audience.

I tried to ignore Dennis's eyes on me as I let the lyrics to "Closer" harness me to the chair. The words of the song: "Violation," "Desecration," "Complication," "Penetration" wove themselves around my rigid body, binding it to Angel and Dennis.

As the music pulsed on, I looked beyond Angel and saw a Hispanic man in the back corner of the room. He was wiping down tabletops and straightening chairs, trying not to look our way. But as Angel started to moan in a stage voice, his eyes met mine.

His look was the only expression in the room that was not greedy or expectant. It was the look of a brother or a friend. His eyes were asking me if I was ok.

Before I could answer him, the hostess tapped him on the shoulder with a stern look and pointed to the back room. He left, disappearing behind the black curtain, and was gone as quickly as he had appeared. Maybe he was one of my ghosts and had never been there at all.

Angel caressed my breasts above my sweater. She took my index finger and put it in her mouth, sucking on it. The combination of the music, the purple haze of the lights, and the rhythmic grinding of Angel's hips were all combined into one visceral sensation. I closed my eyes, and I surrendered to the moment.

Angel was doing her job. And I was doing mine.

Tomorrow business would be back to normal. Dennis would approve my technical recommendations. He would sign the contracts for the multi-million dollar streaming deal and would continue to sponsor me in the account. Tomorrow Dennis would tell Chris what a good job I was doing and sign on the dotted line.

Tomorrow I would be an account executive and an engineer again.

The song finally neared its end. Angel shuddered in a fake orgasm. She slowly stopped grinding.

Angel's moaning could be heard over the music by everyone in the room. She winked at me, her back to the men. She then let out a loud sigh of satisfaction as she looked around the room. Angel turned to face me one last time. She kissed my forehead and straightened my hair. She then slowly climbed off of me.

The dance was finally over.

I looked to Gloria, who raised her scotch to me in a salute. Angel reached her hand out to me to help me out of the chair. She led me back to the sofa.

"Thanks for the dance Stephanie, I really enjoyed it."

Derrick patted the sofa seat next to him. He already had a lap dancer on his lap.

"Come here, Angel. Show me how special you are."

"Sure, Precious."

Angel let go of my hand and turned to Derrick, walking over to him. I took a gulp of my watery vodka and tonic. As the music changed to "Sweet Jane" by The Cowboy Junkies, I watched the MV1 executives relax into the increasingly suggestive dance movements of the lap dancers. I tried not to look at Dennis.

With Dennis and the other MV1 executives occupied in their private dances, I was off the hook for entertaining them for the first time that long evening.

I motioned to the hostess to get me the bill. When she returned with a portable credit card machine, I signed for an additional several thousand dollars worth of sexual favors. I made sure that there was plenty of room on the bill for blow jobs, hand jobs, and any other private contact that the MV1 executives might want. I gave Angel a big tip.

The hostess walked over to Angel and handed her the credit card slip with my tip on it. Angel looked at the $300 tip while continuing to dance in front of Derrick, not missing a beat. She stuffed the credit card slip in her platform sandal and turned to me, giving me a wink and blowing me one last kiss.

"Thank you, Stephanie Honey."

She then turned back to Derrick, who was ready to go with her and the other lap dancer to a private room. My job was done.

I drained the remnants of my drink and got up from the sofa. As I took a last look around the room, my final image was of Roxy whispering in Dennis's ear as she led him to a private room.

I walked quickly down the stairs and through the long hallway, out the front door. The bouncer hailed me a cab. When the taxi pulled away from the club, I closed my eyes.

When I got inside my apartment, I tossed my purse on the dinette table and headed towards the bedroom. I didn't bother to wash my face or brush my teeth. I took off my clothes and let them fall randomly on the floor.

As I crawled into my bed, I thought I sensed a hand on my shoulder. I tensed, irrationally afraid that Angel had followed me home. But the hand belonged to Rose. She gave me a concerned look.

"I just wanted to make sure you got home safely."

Rose pulled the covers over my exhausted body. She stood by the side of my bed, watching over me. My fireman ghost was standing next to her, gas mask in his hand, ready for me if I needed it. Both ghosts watched over me until I quickly slipped into the dark escape of sleep.

CHAPTER 14

I looked over at my alarm clock. 10:00. My throat was parched, and my tongue was sticking to the roof of my mouth. I pushed my body out of bed and shuffled to the kitchen, where I grabbed a bottled water from my empty refrigerator. I took several long gulps, nearly finishing the bottle.

There was a hazy streak of sunlight coming in through the living room window. The sun streaming in from the mini blinds formed slat-shaped shadows around the room that made me feel like I was in a cage.

I needed a break from New York.

I wasn't supposed to go home for Thanksgiving until the end of next week, but there was no reason not to move up my visit. I logged into the Northwest Airlines website and picked the last available seat on an afternoon flight. Then, even though it was Saturday, I called Chris's cell number to let him know that I was going to leave early for the holiday.

"How did last night go?"

Chris didn't sound annoyed that I had bothered him during the weekend. He kept his tone neutral. If I had been a man, he might have sounded more amused, but with me, he made it sound like he was asking for my expense report.

"Great. Everyone had a good time."

I took the last gulp of water out of the nearly empty bottle and swallowed it, crushing the bottle and throwing it towards the kitchen.

"Temper Temper."

Phil from "Groundhog Day" was sitting at my dinette table. He gave me a mock reproachful look, pointing to the bottle on the floor. I looked at him with impatience.

"What do you want?"

"I'm here to give you the weather report. You're traveling today. I'm a weatherman, remember? You want a prediction about the weather? I'm going to give you a prediction about this winter. It's going to be cold, it's going to be dark, and it's going to last you for the rest of your lives!"

Phil's weather report was spot on. But it didn't matter.

I shrugged and turned away from him, focusing on my call to Chris.

"Listen, Chris, my father took a turn for the worse. I need to go home early for Thanksgiving. I'm leaving this afternoon, but I'll be reachable by cell and email if anything comes up."

There was a pause. Then Chris replied, "Family comes first."

He sounded tired. Why did sales managers always say that "family came first"? Most of them were too selfish to think of anyone but themselves. Phil pointed to the phone in my hand.

"Great mentor, that one."

I gave Phil a tired nod in reply. He turned to me, his expression gentle.

"Ciao Stephanie. I hope Ann Arbor gives you a new day."

Phil blew me a kiss and left the apartment.

"Stephanie, are you still there?"

I had forgotten I was still on the call with Chris.

"Sorry, my doorbell just rang. I'll be in touch."

"Go get your door. Keep me updated on MV1."

"Thanks, I will. Have a great Thanksgiving."

I looked over at the crushed water bottle on the floor. I sighed and picked it up, and put it in the trash. Maybe Ann Arbor would provide some answers. In Ann Arbor, there were people who loved me. I had never felt totally alone there, the way I did now. In New York, no one really cared about me.

I packed quickly, not stopping to think about what I was taking. I threw pretty much all of my casual clothes in a large suitcase. I then called my mother and let her know that I was coming home early.

PART TWO

CHAPTER 15

I looked out the taxi window and took in the small houses lined closely together on the bland suburban street. The taxi slowed down and pulled into the driveway of a modest red-brick ranch. White paint on the garage and the window shutters was peeling. There was a small concrete porch with cracks in the concrete. Soggy dead leaves cluttered the lawn.

My Mom had lived here for over a decade now, but I still kept expecting to come home to the house I knew from my childhood instead of this one when I visited.

I paid the taxi driver and got out of the taxi, taking my suitcase from the trunk. My mother was standing on the porch waving. As I walked closer, I was able to see her eyes. They looked tired.

"Hi, Mom."

I let my mother hug me. The hug was stiff and mostly involved our arms and shoulders, with no actual body contact. I pulled back first.

"You're so thin!"

My mother looked me over. I didn't say anything about the weight she had put on. She was about 20 pounds heavier than when I had last seen her. Her red hair was in a Dutchboy haircut with poorly cut bangs. It wasn't a flattering look. My mom was wearing a casual blue dress that had a large floral print and a scoop neckline. She had longish nails that had copper nail polish on them.

Lisa walked casually towards the porch, looking around the quiet street. She pointed to my mother.

"Is this your mom?"

I nodded in reply. Early last week, when I was feeling like I was going insane from the pressure leading up to the dinner with Dennis, I had re-watched *Girl, Interrupted*. In the movie, Lisa's mother had never visited her in the mental hospital. This had upset Lisa enough for her to mention it several times in the film and cry about it in her last scene in the movie.

I gave Lisa an uneasy look. Given her mother issues, I hoped that she didn't do something nasty to my mom. To my relief, she just shrugged and said, "I thought she'd be younger."

My Mother ushered us in. The front door of her house led directly to the small living room. Nothing much had changed since the last time I had been here over a year ago. Lisa looked around the living room, taking in the details of the house.

"It's a dump."

She walked over to Dan's recliner and plunked down in it, putting her feet up on the coffee table. I glared at her. Even though I was frustrated with my mother and ambivalent about my visit, I didn't want my mother to be the butt of Lisa's sociopathic cruelty.

Across from the brown velour recliner that Lisa was sitting in, was a worn beige plaid sofa. An old television and VCR player was housed in a shelving unit against one wall. The shelves were packed with curios and old family photos. A faded Toulouse Lautrec poster hung over the sofa. I rolled my suitcase next to the sofa and sat down.

"Are you hungry, Stephanie? We could order a pizza, or I could make you some eggs."

I was surprised at my mother's offer to cook. Holiday dinners with the whole family aside, I couldn't remember the last time my mother had cooked anything for just me. It was sometime long before I had entered high school.

"Pizza sounds good."

"Ok, Pizza it is then! Dan, can you order a large Pepperoni pizza from Hungry Howie's?"

My mother rummaged in her purse, pulled out a twenty-dollar bill, and handed it to Dan. Dan had entered the living room from the garage. He had a short-sleeve plaid shirt on with his white undershirt peeking out of the open collar. He was wearing navy Dockers that were slightly too short for him, showing his brown socks. He looked balder than when I had last seen him and looked like he had put on some weight. His potbelly had grown bigger. Dan came over and shook my hand, not smiling.

"Hello, Stephanie."

My mother sat down on the other end of the sofa. Lisa looked at the twenty-dollar bill in my mother's hand as if she was going to grab it.

"We could use that money for our road trip to Disney World."

Although I could empathize with why Lisa wanted to flee to Florida at the moment, I still gave her a disapproving look. She stuck her tongue out in reply.

"Make yourself comfortable, Hon. I want you to tell me all about New York and how things are going there."

Lisa was about to reply to my Mother sarcastically, but then she saw that my mother was talking to me, not her. She shrugged and pulled her cigarettes out, lighting one.

Dan looked at the twenty-dollar bill that my mother had handed him. He scratched his bald head as he said, "I don't know the number for Hungry Howie's."

"It's on a magnet on the refrigerator."

Dan went into the kitchen without saying anything further. My mother turned to me, looking me over.

"Are you doing Ok? You look pale. Why haven't we heard from you more?"

I wasn't sure how to reply to my mother. She was asking me questions like she was a daily presence in my life, and that suddenly I had stopped communicating recently. But noncommunication between my mother and I was the norm and always had been.

"Mothers suck."

Lisa said this more to herself than to me as she stared out the front window to the street beyond.

I didn't reply. I turned to my mother instead. My voice sounded polite but distant.

"I don't know, Mom...I guess I just really need some space to figure things out."

"Figure what out? Everything seems obvious to me. You need to leave that place."

My mother's voice had an edge as she said this. I could hear Dan puttering around in the garage. There was the sound of clinking and banging. I wiped my sweaty palms on my jeans.

"I need to figure out how it all happened and what's next, I guess."

"Who knows why, but it happened. You can't figure out all the reasons why. And as for your feelings, don't wallow in them. You're alive, and you made it out, and you have family who care about you. Here. In Ann Arbor."

My mother gave me a look that was a mixture of earnestness and frustration as she said this. Lisa had gotten up from the recliner and was pacing around the room restlessly. She took her lighter and put the flame up to her finger as if trying to set her finger on fire.

"Stop that! You'll hurt yourself!"

I thought this in alarm to myself as I stared at Lisa. Lisa must have heard my thoughts because she closed the lighter and shoved it back into her jeans pocket.

"Why doesn't my mother love me?"

Lisa whispered this, a haunted look on her face, as she stared out the window and twisted her arm like she was trying to break it.

For a sociopath, she was surprisingly vulnerable at the moment.

As for Lisa's question, who knew why mothers did what they did. After all these years, I had no insight into my mother's decisions and motives. She had never really made decisions that took my needs into account. I had forgiven her for this years ago.

As I thought about my mother, Lisa continued to stare out the window, twisting her arm, tears rolling down her face. After a few minutes like this, she abruptly turned to me.

"This place is depressing. I'm out of here."

Lisa didn't bother to wave goodbye as she left. I was relieved she was going. I didn't want her adding to the family drama. I turned back to my mother, who was watching me with concern.

"New York isn't good for you, Stephanie. They only care about money there. I bought you a book I want you to read. It's about grief, and I hope it'll give you some insight as to what's going on as you think about 9/11."

My mother got up to get the book. She handed it to me. I stared at the cover of the paperback book. The title was in big red block letters: *Growing through your Grief.*

I gave my mom a sad smile as I said quietly, "Thanks, Mom, I'll take a look."

We sat for a few minutes saying nothing. The doorbell rang. My mother shouted towards the garage.

"Dan, can you get the door, the pizza's here."

My mother turned back to me, distracted. "Hold your thought, Stephanie. I want you to tell me all about New York. But let's eat first."

The doorbell rang again.

"Dan, where are you? Come pay for the pizza!"

I could hear shuffling and banging noises in the garage. The doorbell rang a third time.

"Just a minute!"

My mother shouted to the front door. She got up and went towards the garage, but Dan appeared before she could get there.

"Where were you? The pizza guy is standing on the porch, breaking our doorbell!"

Dan shrugged, "I was working. Give me some money for the pizza."

"I gave you twenty dollars already! Don't start playing games with money again, Dan. Hand over that twenty dollars now."

My mother snapped her fingers and reached out her upturned hand to Dan to receive the money back. Dan reached into his shirt pocket and threw the wadded-up twenty-dollar bill at her.

He then walked away from my Mother and sat down angrily in the recliner. My mother picked up the wadded twenty-dollar bill and walked over to the door, and opened it. She put a smile on her face and handed the money to the pizza delivery man. She took the pizza and closed the door. "Let's eat," she said in a brittle tone.

She looked at the pizza suspiciously.

"I smell pineapple. What did you order?"

"They were having a special on the Hawaiian pizza. $10.99."

Dan got out of the recliner and sat down at the dining table as she said this.

"Hawaiian? Why would you change the order to something so unappetizing for a couple of dollars? Stephanie doesn't even like pineapple!"

Dan pulled a slice of pizza out of the box and took a big bite, ignoring my mother.

"If I had wanted Hawaiian pizza, I would have ordered it!"

My Mom opened the cupboard and pulled out three plates and three tumblers, and slammed the cupboard doors shut. She pulled a bottle of Diet Coke out of the refrigerator and set it on the table along with the plates and cups. She then poured me a tumbler of Diet Coke without asking if I wanted any. I was still sitting on the sofa where my mother had left me. The book was in my lap. I looked back down at it as I said,

"Hawaiian pizza is fine."

I set the book on top of my suitcase, walked over to the dining table, and sat down. I took a slice of Hawaiian pizza and put it on my plate. I took a small bite. It was disgusting. I glanced at my mother as I took a sip of Diet Coke to wash down the sickly-sweet pizza.

My mother met my gaze. When she saw the sad look in my eyes, my mother's eyes became glossy, as if she might cry. But a veil came over them instead.

It was a veil I was very familiar with, having seen it most of my life.

"How's the pizza, Stephanie?"

"It's fine, Mom."

"Good. I want this visit to be a pleasant break for you. Dan, stop picking pineapple off of the pizza!"

My Mother's small house always seemed suffocating to me when I interacted with her and Dan in it. This moment was no different. Their bickering was sucking all of the oxygen out of the room.

I just wanted a moment of peace.

I took one last bite of pizza and then wiped my mouth with a paper napkin.

"I'm going to go rest."

"Ok, honey. First bedroom on the right is the least cluttered."

When I entered the small guest bedroom, I shut the door and set my suitcase at the foot of the bed. The walnut nightstand, double-sized roller bed, and green floral bedspread were from the guest bedroom in the house I grew up in. The nondescript brass lamp with an accordion shade was from my childhood home as well. Seeing the familiar furniture from my childhood in my mother's house always made me feel like I was still a teenager when I visited. Today was no different.

I turned on a lamp and put the book my mother had given me on the nightstand. I didn't bother to pull the bedspread down as I climbed onto the bed and closed my eyes.

When I woke up, I had no idea what time it was. There was no clock in the bedroom. The lamp was casting a shadow over the folding doors of the half-closed, overfilled closet. Standing by the closet looking at me were two new ghosts: Shirley MacLaine's character, Aurora, from *Terms of Endearment*, and Ally Sheedy's character, Allison, from *The Breakfast Club*.

Terms of Endearment was one of my mother's favorite movies. She often wistfully referred to the strained and then redeemed mother-daughter relationship in the film when the topic of movies came up.

I don't think my mother had ever seen *The Breakfast Club*, however. In the movie, Allison was an awkward and alienated goth loner, and I had always identified with her the most of all *The Breakfast Club* characters. I had been both rebellious and disaffected in high school, choosing to hang out with punkers, theater types, and others that smoked pot in hidden corners and skipped classes.

But it had been fifteen years since I had been in high school, and I didn't see myself in terms of teenage social categories anymore. When I came home to visit my mother, I did feel labeled to a certain extent, however. She wanted to pretend that we were close and that I was the "loving daughter," a label that always made me either angry or mournful.

I couldn't ever remember being happy in my Mother's house. Growing up, I had moments of happiness, although they usually had nothing to do with my parents. But in this house, I always felt the strain of my Mother's poor choices and the weight of her expectations.

As I thought of my mother, I heard someone clearing their throat. I turned to look at Allison. She pointed to my purse and mumbled, "I stole your wallet."

Allison tugged at her black oversized turtleneck sweater. She reached into her bra and pulled out a driver's license, and read from it. The driver's license was from California and wasn't mine.

"Your middle name is Stephanie, as in puke, your birth date's May 25, you're 5'4 and a half, you weigh 120 pounds, and your social security number is 049380913."

"Why are you here?"

I asked this as I looked at Allison with curiosity.

Allison shrugged as she rummaged through my Mother's closet.

"I had nothing better to do."

After saying this, Allison put her turtleneck over her head and climbed into my Mother's closet, shutting the door.

"She needs help," Aurora said, looking at the closet in disapproval. She then turned to me and asked, "What do you think of Dan?"

I shrugged. What was the point of describing all of Dan's flaws? He was my mother's choice, and it was none of my business.

"Can you believe your mother left your father for that man?"

Aurora said this with a derisive snort. I shrugged again. Dan was a mess, but he was my Mother's mess.

"Ha!"

Allison shouted this as she jumped out of the closet. She raised her arms over her head, dancing with her eyes closed to music in her head. She stopped dancing and opened her eyes, turning to me with a serious look on her face.

"When you grow up, your heart dies."

I gave Allison a sad smile and nodded in agreement.

She was right.

All the grownups I knew had dead hearts. Except for my ex-boyfriend and long-time friend Arthur. He had maintained his intellectual curiosity and creative energy well into his 40's somehow. I grabbed my purse, which I had placed on top of my suitcase, and pulled out my cell phone. I flipped it open. It was 5:00. I listened to the message. It was from Arthur. I hoped the message was an invitation to get together.

Arthur didn't have a cell phone, so I had emailed him and left a message on his answering machine letting him know I was coming into town early. As I continued to listen to Arthur's longish message, I smiled the first genuine smile of my long day. It was just like him to be working late in the deserted office of *Mathematical Reviews,* the mathematical journal he had worked at since he had settled down in the seventies after his hippie years.

I was looking forward to seeing Arthur.

Aurora and Allison watched me as I used my cell phone to book a room at the Campus Inn on the U of M campus and then ordered a cab. The cab was going to take 30 minutes to arrive. That would just give me enough time to let my mother know I was leaving.

I needed some space and some quiet time to think about my next steps, and it was clear to me my Mother's house wasn't going to provide that. I had agreed to stay with my mother so that she could see I was okay and hadn't been damaged by 9/11.

But I wasn't sure if I was doing ok. This house made me feel like I was an angry, hurt adolescent. Besides, I usually stayed at the Campus Inn when I visited anyway, so hopefully, my mother wouldn't be too disappointed I was changing my plans. Either way, I didn't care. This trip was about taking care of myself, not her.

"I'm going to tell my shrink about you, the one I'm banging."

Allison pulled her black sweater over her head, leaving just her eyes showing after she said this to me. Aurora gave Allison a withering look as she said,

"What are you talking about? Do your parents know you're here?"

I turned away from both ghosts as I put my phone back in my purse. I shoved the book on grief into my suitcase and wheeled the suitcase, stubbing my toe on the bed frame as I struggled to maneuver around the bed and get through the small door.

"Your Mother is doing the best she can."

Aurora met my eyes as she said this. Her voice was somber and nostalgic.

"I know."

I replied quietly as I shook my leg out and left the bedroom. Aurora and Allison didn't follow me. My mother was sitting on the sofa watching the local news when I entered the living room.

"Did you have a good nap? Why do you have all your bags?"

"I'm going to stay closer to campus. It'll be easier."

"You just got here," my mother said, her tone neutral. She turned back to the television.

I put a thin smile on my face.

"We'll have plenty of time to catch up. I promise. Let's have dinner together tomorrow. Just the two of us."

My Mom gave me a melancholy look as she nodded in reply to my offer. We stood like that for a few moments. I was relieved to hear the horn of the taxi in the driveway. I reached over and kissed my mother's forehead as I wheeled all my stuff past the sofa and said, "I'll talk to you tomorrow."

I shut the front door behind me, leaving her sitting on the sofa, alone, watching the news. I hopped into the cab and gave the cab driver the address of the Campus Inn.

CHAPTER 16

Arthur was waiting for me at the front door of his office building. He gave me a big smile and a hug and ushered me in dramatically to the production room of the journal headquarters. The building was quiet. It was 7:15, and we were the only ones there. Arthur loved working in the journal building alone at night. He could walk the halls uninterrupted, humming or singing if he felt like it. Living a block away allowed him to come in whenever the mood struck him. Arthur liked to keep his life simple.

"The key to a simple life is to not have too many external frustrations."

He had said that to me on many occasions, both when we lived together and long after when we were friends. Arthur looked me up and down. I could see the concern he was trying so hard not to show.

"How are you? You look great. And your hair! I wish I had your hair."

Arthur looked at my curly hair with envy and ran his bony, ink-smudged fingers through his scraggly beard. Arthur was twelve years older than me, but the age difference had never mattered. He missed his younger days of long hair and had mentioned constantly that he regretted being bald. He tried to make up for it by having as much hair as he could grow everywhere else, and so his greying hair stuck out on the sides, and his beard was as long as he could get it to grow.

"It's great to see you, Arthur."

I felt a pleasant warmth as a genuine smile lifted my lips. I had missed Arthur and was truly glad to see him.

I wasn't surprised that Arthur was working in the production room instead of his office. Arthur hadn't used his office in years. His desk was buried underneath stacks of printed-out emails, math papers, discarded disposable coffee cups, and empty plastic Snackwell packets from his early morning trips to the vending machine. Arthur watched me fidget in a task chair I was sitting in. He looked at his beat-up Timex.

"Are you hungry? Let's go get something to eat."

We walked to the Old Town, a bar and sandwich place downtown and about a ten-minute walk from campus. The restaurant was busy. Arthur put his dog-eared Manilla folder filled with math papers on a booth by the window. Within a minute or so, a middle-aged woman with curly greying blonde hair, wearing a tie-dyed Grateful Dead T-shirt, came up to us. She gave Arthur a big smile.

"Arthur, how are you this evening! The usual? Hi, hon, the menu's right over there."

The waitress gave me a welcoming smile and pointed to the stained, creased menu held in place by a ketchup bottle and the salt and pepper shakers.

"Hi, Kathy. I'll have my usual. With spicy mustard. And a glass of Chardonnay."

Kathy nodded and waited for me to take a look at the menu. It hadn't changed since I had last been here the last time I visited Ann Arbor almost a year ago. In fact, it hadn't changed since I was in high school.

Back then, spending a lazy afternoon or evening hanging out downtown had been an enjoyable way to escape depressing parents and a tedious school workload. It had been a thrill when occasionally, I got away with ordering a beer. I gave Kathy a polite smile as I ordered the same meal I had ordered since I was 15.

"I'll have a cheeseburger with cheddar and grilled onions and a Blue Moon."

Kathy wrote down the order and turned back towards the bar.

After Kathy left, three of my ghosts approached our table. Allison, John Bender, and Andrew from *The Breakfast Club* crowded into the booth. John Bender was wearing his 1980's-burnout outfit of a Black Sabbath T-shirt, red flannel shirt, and denim jacket. Andrew was dressed in a letterman's jacket and jeans. Allison still had on her emo black outfit from earlier. They looked around the bar as they sat down.

"Fuck detention."

Bender said this as he pulled a joint out of the pocket of his red flannel shirt. He lit it and took a long drag. Andrew cracked his knuckles and glared at the joint in disapproval,

"Yo wastoid, you're not gonna blaze up in here."

Bender blew pot smoke in Andrew's face and didn't reply. Allison reached for the large canister of sugar that was near the salt and pepper shakers. She screwed the top off of the jar and poured a mound of sugar into the palm of her hand. She then started licking the sugar in her hand. Bender and Andrew ignored her.

I didn't react to any of them. Sitting here and listening to their banter was just one more reminder that I still felt like I was in high school when I came home to Ann Arbor.

I turned to Arthur and gave him a distracted smile. At least my memories of him were from adulthood. Arthur looked around to see if there was anyone he knew in the bar.

"I know those guys. They're physics postdocs. The one on the left is a visiting professor this semester."

I nodded. I used to try to understand what Arthur did, but I didn't believe in the central tenet of modern physics: that there was going to be a unified physical theory. This left me entirely on the outside of what interested Arthur intellectually.

"How can you think that these math puzzles that you are solving are tied to reality in any way?"

I used to say something like this to Arthur in the middle of a fight when we were together. Of course, this was never what I was really upset about. What I had been bothered by was how bored and suffocated I felt in a world that never changed.

Arthur had been patient with me during these fights, and they had always blown over quickly. I had known Arthur was right.

Besides, who was I to criticize academia?

My unfinished dissertation was on Hegel's theory of language. This subject had once filled me with excitement. But by the time I was almost done writing my dissertation, I came to disagree with Hegel's views. I took a computer class to clear my head of language theories, and do something tangible. I enjoyed the no-nonsense simplicity of learning a programming language. My new interest turned into a decision to get a second degree in computer science. My dissertation sat untouched as I took more computer classes.

Eventually, Yale sent me a letter giving me a deadline to finish my dissertation. I didn't reply. Three months later, I received another letter stating that I was being released from the Ph.D. program due to my lack of progress. When I read my dismissal letter, I felt like a failure. But I also felt relief. The decision was made.

Many of my first bachelor's degree credits were credited to my computer science degree, so I only had about a year and a half of courses to take to get the second bachelor's degree.

As I finished the last two courses for BA in computer science, I took a job working on a research team on campus. When a big software company bought the rights to the research project, I was given an offer to move to New York and work for the company. I jumped at the chance to change my life and move to New York. I saw it as a way of redeeming myself, of finally having a successful career.

Arthur had never come to see me in New York. He hated flying. He had dated here and there after we broke up, but he had never had a serious girlfriend again, at least not yet. I had not had another serious relationship either since leaving him.

I made it a point to keep in touch with Arthur. I usually came home for Thanksgiving, and because Arthur had no local family, he always attended Thanksgiving dinner with me. There were always mixed signals between us when we got together. The one or two times a year that I visited Ann Arbor, Arthur always invited me back to his place, and I always politely refused his offer. I had always believed that it would be easier for both of us if I kept our connection to a strictly platonic one. This visit, however, I was longing for closeness with Arthur.

I needed someone to care about me.

My thoughts were interrupted by Bender. He took a drag of his joint and then offered it to me.

"It'll help you forget."

I wasn't sure I wanted to forget. I shook my head. Andrew pointed to the joint in Bender's hand, his voice rising in anger.

"I told you not to smoke in here! If I lose my temper, you're totaled, man."

Bender stuck his tongue out, wiggled it between his fingers in a suggestive gesture, and gave Andrew a sarcastic grin. "I'm terrified."

As I watched Bender and Andrew interact, I felt the fifteen-year distance between them and me. I gave them an annoyed look and took a sip of my beer.

Allison gave Bender and Andrew a knowing look. She then poured the contents of the sugar container into a pile in the middle of the table and pressed her face into it, mumbling, "Ha!"

Andrew shook his head in disgust. Bender looked like he was about to laugh. Instead, he took a look around the table and stood up, saying to no one in particular,

"You know, I don't think that I need to hang with you fuckin' dildos anymore."

Bender gave me a nod and left the booth. Allison lifted her face out of the pile of sugar and followed Bender out, not bothering to wipe the sugar off her face. Andrew left as well. I was relieved to see the three of them go.

I didn't miss high school at all.

I took a furtive look at Arthur. He pointed to a table of men that ranged from mid-twenties to mid-thirties that were engaged in deep conversation.

"See the one with the red hair? He is up for a Taubman fellowship this year."

I nodded, giving Arthur a distracted smile. Our food arrived. Arthur reached for the pepper and unscrewed the top of the shaker. He poured a pile of pepper onto his plate. Arthur then opened the Grey Poupon mustard, spreading a generous amount on his sandwich. He put a large scoop of mustard on the side of his plate near the pepper. Arthur grabbed a fry and dipped the fry in the pepper and the mustard. He then took a bite of both the fry and his chicken sandwich.

I couldn't resist smiling as I watched Arthur eat. He had pretty much ordered the same sandwich and eaten it the same way the entire time I had known him.

Arthur licked his lips. I put some ketchup on my burger and cut it in half so that I could hold it. I took a bite. It was cooked perfectly. I let the juice from the burger drip onto my plate as I took another bite.

Arthur described the mathematical-physics research to me with excitement and animation, waving his hands as he described the 11 dimensions that would be needed to allow the supersymmetry of elementary particles.

Arthur's intellectual passion was for the mathematical proofs that described the details of the multi-dimensions and constructs of M-theory, or as laymen referred to it, the "theory of everything." I was surprised I still could follow along with what he was saying. It had been at least five years since I had read any string theory.

Arthur took the last bite of his sandwich. He wiped the stray crumbs in his beard with his napkin. His eyes focused on me.

"Stephanie, how are you doing? Are you ok?"

Arthur searched my face. I had no idea how to answer him.

I wasn't dying. I wasn't missing work—much anyways. I was drinking too much. My flashbacks came and went. Did this mean I was ok?

I gave Arthur a melancholy smile and forced myself to meet his worried eyes.

"I'm fine."

"You know, you don't have to stay there. You could always come back here."

"My job is there. I live there."

I said this apologetically as I reached out to touch his arm.

"Maybe it's too much to be there right now."

"It's not. I'm fine."

I kept my hand on Arthur's arm as he looked into my eyes, which were glossy but unable to shed any tears. He put his other hand on top of mine and patted it, and said nothing more. We sat like that for a few minutes. We were interrupted by Kathy, who came with the check.

"Is there anything else I can get you?"

Arthur shook his head and lifted his hand off mine. He took his worn-out wallet out of the back pocket of his jeans, pulled out three faded ten-dollar bills, and handed them to Kathy. Kathy laughed affectionately as she took the money.

"These bills look like they went through the washing machine."

Arthur grinned in response to Kathy's comment.

"Did you know that 10 was a sacred number to Pythagoras?"

Arthur put his index finger in the air to emphasize his question.

"No, what makes it sacred?"

"1 + 2+ 3+ 4 = 10, and Pythagoras thought those 4 numbers represent existence, creation, life, and the four elements. So that means that 10 represents everything, which makes it sacred. That's your friendly math fact of the day!"

"Thanks, Arthur, that's interesting. I might even put that up on the chalkboard by the bar as a fun fact!"

"Cheerio! Keep the change."

Arthur picked up his chardonnay and drained the last dregs from the glass. We both got up from the booth. I pulled a stray crumb that Arthur had missed out of his beard. I kissed his forehead. He stood still and accepted my kiss as he said quietly,

"Call me after you see your father tomorrow, and I'll meet you at Sweetwaters."

When I got back to the hotel, I turned on the TV to fill the room with noise. I usually would have watched a movie, but I didn't want to concentrate for that long. I climbed into bed and found a "Law and Order" rerun, and drifted off to sleep with the TV still on.

CHAPTER 17

The cab dropped me off at the main door of the hospital. I entered, not sure where to go exactly. The lobby was bustling. Families were heading to the elevators with balloons and flowers, and nurses and attendants in scrubs were walking to the cafeteria, laughing and talking amongst themselves. The woman at the reception desk was middle-aged and sour-looking. Her red hair was in a very bright bad dye job that clashed with her yellowish, wrinkled skin.

"Can you tell me what room James Willis is in?"

"Would you spell that for me?"

The woman at the desk didn't look at me as she asked this. I spelled out my dad's last name for her.

"He is on floor eight. Cardiac Intensive care."

"What should I do?"

The question just popped out of my mouth. It sounded more like a plea than a question.

"Go see him." The receptionist looked up and said this slowly, with annoyance, emphasizing each word.

When I got upstairs, my brother Steven was already there. He was sitting in the waiting area by the elevator.

"How is he?"

"He's sleeping. I thought I'd wait out here until you came."

I looked around the waiting room. There was a family huddled in one corner, with several adults talking quietly amongst themselves while a couple of young children concentrated on filling in Disney pictures in their coloring books. An older man sat in a chair, looking out ahead at nothing in particular. The television was showing a syndicated talk show, but no one was paying attention to it.

In the corner of the waiting room, standing next to the older man was the ghost of Gene Kelly. He tipped his hat to me and bowed. I nodded to him and then turned back to Steven.

"How long have you been here?"

"About an hour. I need a smoke."

Steven looked like he hadn't slept much. He had on a rumpled Megadeth T-shirt, a grey unzipped sweatshirt, and jeans. His hair was shaved close to his head, and his beard was growing long in a way you would expect to see a musician grow their beard long. Only Steven wasn't a musician. He worked the night shift at the Post Office and didn't seem to want much more out of his career. We didn't talk much, but that was more due to not having much in common than to any tension between us. I had always intended to invite him to New York to visit, but somehow I had never found the right time.

I wanted to check in with someone who could tell me what was going on, but I decided it could wait for a few minutes. I followed Steven downstairs and outside to the small atrium between hospital wings, where there were a couple of benches.

Steven lit his cigarette and took a long drag without saying anything. I could hear the gravel crunch under his feet as he shifted his weight.

He had the hoodie up on his sweatshirt, making it hard to see his eyes as I asked him how he was holding up. Steven answered my question with a question of his own. His voice was tinged with anger.

"Why didn't he tell us sooner this was going on? "

I shrugged. "You know how Dad is. He wouldn't have told me in any case. We don't talk. When was the last time you talked to him?"

Steven pulled down his hoodie and looked at me directly as he answered my question.

"It's been a while. A couple of months. The last time I talked to him, he was telling me I should stop smoking. We had lunch at Marks Coney Island. He hated the way I kept getting up from the table to smoke." Steven took a drag of his cigarette, looking down at his feet.

"Have you guys been getting together regularly?" I asked.

"Once a month or so. Mostly to have lunch. Why?" Steven looked at me curiously as he said this.

"What did you guys talk about?"

"Nothing much. He'd ask me how I was doing, and then he'd ask how Mom was doing. He gave me updates on how Aunt Chris and Uncle Gary were. Mostly we just ate. Why?"

I felt silly for asking Steven about his visits with Dad. It was none of my business, really. I looked over at Gene Kelly, who had followed us downstairs. He raised an eyebrow and gave me an amused smile. He twirled around in a circle, dancing with his arm extended as if he were holding a woman in his arms. He then pointed to Steven. I nodded and asked the question that was echoing in my head.

"Did he ask how I was doing?"

Steven looked towards the hospital door as he took the last drag of his cigarette and threw it to the ground before stubbing it out.

"No, you never came up."

I wasn't surprised.

I thought of the decades that my father and I hadn't had a real conversation. I thought of everything my father didn't know about me and the missed milestones and life markers we hadn't shared.

We hadn't talked even on 9/11. He had heard that I was in one of the towers from my brother. In some ways, I was facing my father's death without ever having shared his life.

I was seven years old when my brother Steven was born. My mother suffered from postpartum depression after his birth. The depression didn't go away. She had seen a series of therapists, but the only result of all her inner work had been that she had grown increasingly detached from my father, Steven, and me.

When I was in high school, my mother finally began to snap out of her depression. But her renewed energy was focused on living a separate life from us, going out with her work friends, and seeing other men. In my first year of college, she finally left my dad for Dan.

During the years of my mother's depression and emotional abandonment, my father had become ever angrier. By the time I was in my junior and senior years of high school, I had become the recipient of a lot of his frustration.

I hadn't understood at the time why my father was always angry and upset with me. It wasn't fair, and I'm sure if he had had insight into his behavior at the time, he probably would have made better choices in regards to me.

The result of my father's misplaced anger had been that he and I became increasingly distant with each other. Our alienation had turned into complete estrangement when I went off to graduate school. My father hadn't approved of my long-distance move. He had called me selfish and immature. I had cut him off, and we had never fully recovered.

It all seemed so silly and pointless now that he was in intensive care.

I looked over at Gene Kelly. He was doing a quiet soft shoe on the gravely pavement. He tipped his top hat, looked at me with sympathy, and then knelt on one knee, placing his hat on his chest.

"You dance love, and you dance joy, and you dance dreams."

I wasn't sure what Gene Kelly was trying to tell me, but it sounded like something he would say in an interview.

My father would have loved this quote. He had said to me repeatedly over the years that the dancing in Hollywood musicals was an expression of the most profound emotions of the characters in the movie. He had mentioned to me one time when we watched *Singin' in the Rain* together, "If you want to understand the characters in this movie, watch how they dance."

Gene Kelly had made my father smile many times with his jumping over couches and dancing in the rain. In fact, he had created many of the moments of enjoyment and closeness that existed between my father and me.

I gave Gene Kelly another nod to acknowledge his quote and then turned to my brother and said, "Let's go upstairs and see if he's awake yet."

When we got back to the cardiac ward, a doctor was heading out of my father's room. He was tall and thin with neatly slicked back black hair. He had a Mediterranean complexion and looked like he was in his mid-forties.

"How is he doing?"

The doctor looked at me quizzically, trying to decide who I was and how much he should tell me. Steven spoke to the doctor before I could say anything.

"We're his children."

"Your father's heart is stopping intermittently. He's too weak for a second operation. We're relieving his pain with medication and are monitoring the situation. We should discuss moving him to hospice care."

Hospice care. That meant that they didn't expect my father's heart to recover.

The doctor's voice was calm and professional, and his eyes were looking directly at us to make sure that I understood what he was saying.

"Ok, thank you."

The doctor acknowledged my thanks with a quick nod and then turned from me, heading to the next room on his checklist.

As we entered my father's hospital room, he was talking to a nurse as she refilled his IV bag. My father had a tube going through the vein in his hand to the IV and was hooked up to a catheter from his groin. His skin was a pasty grey, and he looked small and fragile in his hospital gown. The nurse turned around as she heard my brother and me approaching and greeted us with a hearty false excitement. She had dull blond hair, clipped back in a ponytail, and was wearing a pink nursing uniform with pink track shoes to match. Her skin looked overly dry, and tiny wrinkles formed near her eyes and mouth when she smiled. She looked about ten years older than me, but it was difficult to tell.

"Who do we have here?!"

"Hi, Dad." I forced myself to smile as I said this. I didn't answer the nurse immediately.

"Hi, Stephanie! I'm glad you could come."

My Dad sounded excited to see me but very weak. It was jarring to have him welcome me into his emergency cardiac hospital room the same way he would have welcomed me to dinner at his home.

I turned to the nurse and replied to her, introducing myself and Steven, glad for a minute to gather myself and work the emotion out of my voice.

"That's great! I was just trying to get your father to order some lunch. Would you like some food now, Mr. Willis?"

The nurse turned to my father, her voice never wavering in its shrill optimism. My father had bags under his eyes. Even his curly grey hair looked tired and was flattened to the sides of his temples more closely than usual. The skin on the top of his head had liver spots. My father looked thin and frail, and I wondered if he was eating much.

As if echoing my thoughts, my father shook his head in reply to the nurse and looked up at her with a familiarity that suggested that she was now one of his immediate family.

"No thanks. Maybe later."

Steven was shifting back and forth on his feet and looking like he wanted to flee the room. Gene Kelly went to the left side of my Dad's bed and started doing knee bends as if he were warming up for a dance number. Having him here in the hospital room with my father reminded me of the final hospital dream-death scene from Bob Fosse's *All That Jazz*, one of my favorite movies. I wanted to ask Gene Kelly if he had ever seen that film, but I looked at my dad instead.

"Are you sure, Dad? I can help you order something from the menu."

The nurse looked first at my dad and then at me as she stood in the doorway, ready to go on to the next patient.

"No, I'm fine."

My father fussed with one of the tubes on his chest.

"Ok then, let me know if you need anything. Have a good visit, you guys!"

The nurse belted this out with a singsong good cheer and didn't meet any of our gazes as she quickly left the room.

With her gone, the room was still and quiet. The only sound was the slow background beeping and pumping sounds of the machines my dad was hooked up to. The machines kept their steady drone and didn't start pumping to a rock beat as they did in the final number of *All That Jazz*.

Gene Kelly sat down in a chair facing my father's bed. He quoted a line from *Singin' in the Rain* as he looked at him.

"Dignity. Always dignity."

Steven sat down in the chair by the window. There was one more seat on the other side of the bed, but I was too anxious to sit, so I stayed where I was. Gene Kelly took his hat off and hung it on my father's IV drip stand.

"You dance love, and you dance joy, and you dance dreams. And I know if I can make you smile by jumping over a couple of couches or running through a rainstorm, then I'll be very glad to be a song and dance man."

Gene Kelly was finishing his quote from earlier for me. I gave him a tired smile to show my appreciation for his words. He gave me a courtly bow and continued.

"The way I look at a musical, you are commenting on the human condition no matter what you do. A musical may be light and frivolous, but by its very nature, it makes some kind of social comment."

This was precisely something my father would have said as we watched a musical together. Even though it had been years since I had watched a movie with my father, I could still see it from his perspective and view the stylized dancing as a metaphor for ageless themes of hope and love.

This was probably an overly academic way to look at movies that were produced for entertainment, but I had never challenged my father's views on musicals and saw no need to now.

"How are you feeling, Dad?"

I asked my father this as if we had been in touch daily as if our many years of estrangement hadn't existed.

"I keep getting shocked by my defibrillator. It's very painful. They tried to disconnect it, but it didn't fix things."

He sighed after he finished talking as if the effort of answering me had already exhausted him.

"Are you comfortable right now? Can I get you anything?"

It seemed like such a silly and small set of questions to ask him in light of the circumstances.

"I'm fine."

My father was wasting away. His eyes, which were looking at me expectantly, stood out against the pallid skin of his face. They seemed so much larger than I expected them to be.

I looked into them. His gaze was so different from the angry, critical glares he had always given me during our many fights when I was an adolescent and a young adult.

When I looked back on my childhood, the images that came to mind were my mother, her face puffy, and eyes red, as she stared into space and cried, and my father, his face contorted with anger, as he yelled at me for disobeying some random edict of his.

Growing up with no mother to speak of and an angry father, I had parented myself for the most part. My father hated my burgeoning independence. This resulted in even more frequent fighting between us by the time I was a teenager, with brief periods of reconciliation.

As we fought more, we stopped watching movies together. I had tried to duplicate the experience with my friends, commenting on the artistry or the social significance of certain scenes, but they had just laughed at me and told me to "lighten up."

My father and I had had yet another big fight right before I moved to Yale for graduate school to begin my Ph.D. program. We had barely been talking for over six years at that point. I had asked him for some financial help with the move, and he had accused me of being selfish.

"You're just using me for money, Stephanie. You're always asking for something."

I was hurt that my father said this to me. I had never asked him for anything.

In hindsight, it probably shouldn't have mattered at that point. I was 22 years old and could have seen myself off to graduate school just fine.

But it did matter. I wanted one of my parents to act as a parent and support me in my move. I cut my father off in a huff of self-righteousness.

He didn't reach out to me either. The years went by, making our estrangement worse. I never made it a priority to reconcile.

And now my father was dying.

I had no idea what to say to him. I looked directly at him, my eyes softening.

"I'm glad you called Dad."

Gene Kelly looked at my Dad and then at me. He gave me a friendly salute, encouraging me.

My dad's eyes welled up with tears.

Steven leaned forward in his chair. Although my father had never fought much with Steven, he hadn't spent much time with him either. Steven's eyes were focused on my dad as if my dad's reaction would somehow spill over to include him too. But my father kept his focus on me.

His voice cracked as he said, "Me too, Stephanie. It's good to see you."

"I'm sorry it's been so long, Dad."

And I was sorry. Our estrangement seemed ridiculous to me at the moment. Why had it been so important to me that I not talk to him all these years?

"You know I'm very proud of you. I admire what you've achieved and accomplished with your life."

My dad looked at me expectantly as he said this as if he had handed me a gift and was waiting to see me open it up and react to it.

I stood awkwardly and received my father's heartfelt words. His intense gaze made me self-conscious, the same way I always felt when I opened a gift in front of an audience. I stood there, feeling all those fatherless years. I wanted to feel healing wash over me. I wanted to feel a sense of vindication and completion.

But I didn't.

I was glad my father had gotten a chance to say the words to me before he died, but they didn't make me feel any better.

Gene Kelly glanced over at me. Seeing my discomfort, he got up from the chair and grabbed on to the side of the bed as he put his hand on his chest and started singing a verse from *Singin' in the Rain*—the one about laughing at clouds and with the sun being in his heart, being ready for love.

I should have been appalled at the irreverence of the song at a moment like this, but it made me smile. It was perfect.

Steven was watching my Dad. His eyes were cloudy, his expression moody and distant. He got up from the chair and started pacing as much as he could in the small patch of space between his chair and my father's bed. Gene Kelly was now swinging around the vital signs monitor stand, performing the same steps he did when he danced around a streetlight in the rain. As I watched him improvise his iconic dance number, I thought about my father's words.

I felt like I had just been gifted the Ultimate Barbie doll that I had asked for at Christmas when I was nine years old and had never gotten, and yet I was receiving it as an adult now, all gift-wrapped and shiny and presented with fanfare.

But what was I to do with a Barbie doll now?

I closed my eyes to ward off my father's intense stare.

I looked within myself and imagined myself standing across from my father in a field of lavender. We both were young and healthy. The lavender smelled sweet and refreshing, and there was a gentle breeze blowing.

My father stood in the lavender field, patiently waiting for me to talk. I bent down to pick a handful of blossoms. I then straightened back up and smiled, reaching out my hand to my father to offer the bouquet of lavender.

"I forgive you."

I said this to my mind's image of my father. He smiled, and we moved closer to each other in the purple field. Our reconciliation melted away the past and opened us to a future of promise and redemption.

We were both set free.

I opened up to receive words to take with me from the field behind my closed eyes, back into the hospital room. But as I stood waiting to capture the right words, my father coughed a short nervous cough, and the beeps and slow pumping of the hospital machinery made their way back into my consciousness.

The image of my young father receded. The sweet smell of lavender was replaced by the astringent and slightly musty odor of the hospital room.

I opened my eyes. I was standing in an ICU room, with my frail, dying father eying me expectantly.

I opened my mouth to speak. But my words were just words.

I tried to say them with as much feeling and gratitude as I could muster.

"Thank you, Dad. That means so much to me."

My father silently pleaded with me, his focus on me unwavering. My only concern at that moment was to ease his pain and suffering.

Gene Kelly did one last twirl around the IV stand and then sat back down in the chair by the window. He watched my father and me waiting to witness our big reconciliation moment.

I certainly forgave my father for his inability to give me the love I had needed as a girl and a young woman. And I even felt concerned that he was in pain and grief that he was dying.

But I didn't feel close to him. I couldn't erase the many years of estrangement as much as I wanted to.

Forgiveness would have to do.

I moved towards my father and hugged him, careful not to upset any of the tubes and wires connected to him. I stepped back from the hug after a moment, and, taking my lead, my father reluctantly let go.

"I love you, Dad."

I looked into his eyes with compassion. I was grateful that I truly meant it.

"I love you too, Stephanie."

My dad had tears in his eyes. I could see his relief that we were ending on good terms. Gene Kelly looked on, holding his hands up to frame the scene as if he were a director. He shouted to an invisible film crew.

"Cut. Print!"

Steven watched us, his hands resting awkwardly at his sides. We all held the moment. Even the beeping and pumping of the machines seemed to fade into the background.

My father broke the silence first. He glanced at the television and said,

"What time is it? I don't want to miss Oprah. She's on at 4."

My father was trying to sit up in his bed but was having trouble.

"It's only 1:00. Do you want me to check what else is on?" I looked around for the remote as I said this but then realized it was part of the bed controls.

My father shook his head.

"*Oprah* is the only good show on in the afternoons. Sometimes she has excellent movie directors and actors as guests."

My dad's eyes lit up as he said this. I was truly surprised. But then I realized that this was his world now.

"I'll let the nurse know you don't want to miss the show."

I smiled at him as I pointed to the television, but the smile didn't quite reach my tired eyes. My dad looked like he wanted to sleep. I wasn't sure if I should wait for the nurse to return or leave him to rest.

"I'm going to go downstairs for a smoke."

Steven said this to no one in particular. My dad looked over to him and gave him a wan smile.

"Take your time. I'm just going to rest for a few minutes."

My dad laid his head on the pillow and closed his eyes after he said this. My visit with him was ending.

"I'll go downstairs and let you rest too, Dad."

I said this gently. I knew I would be leaving once I got downstairs. My dad gave a slight nod with his head still on the pillow. I looked at him lying there: his eyes closed, his body curled up in the fetal position he had begun his life in, his tubes flowing oxygen and liquid in and out of his frail body.

"Get some rest, Dad. The nurse should be here soon."

My father opened his eyes but didn't lift his head from the pillow. I gave him a last lingering look, and then I turned around to leave the room.

I could hear his shallow breathing and knew that he had closed his eyes again.

I was relieved to see that Gene Kelly had decided to stay with my dad while he slept. He was sitting in the chair closest to my father's bed and was humming *Singin' in the Rain* softly so that it sounded like a lullaby.

I waved goodbye to Gene Kelly and stood in the hallway for a moment, feeling the death and sickness all around me.

I then continued my walk to the elevator.

CHAPTER 18

On the cab ride back to campus, I thought about my visit with my father. This was the last time I would see him. Even though we had put the past behind us during the visit, I still felt alone the way I had growing up.

I expected Phil from *Groundhog Day* to show up and lecture me on "living in the moment" and "forgiving the past." But I was alone in the cab.

I pulled out my cell phone and called Arthur. He was at work waiting for an update. Although in all the years I had known Arthur, he had never met my father; when I had told him about my father's condition, he had been concerned.

"How did it go?"

"Ok, I guess. He doesn't have much time left. They're suggesting hospice care."

Arthur said nothing and listened. It felt strange to talk and be heard. I wasn't used to people genuinely listening to me anymore. It left me nowhere to hide.

I told Arthur that I was too drained from the hospital visit and that I would meet him in the morning. When I got to my hotel room, I ordered a burger from room service and searched pay-per-view for a movie I could watch as I cleared my head of the hospital visit.

There were no classic movies available, but one recent musical, *Moulin Rouge* with Nicole Kidman, seemed like a fitting tribute to my father. I ordered the film, and as I watched the saturated, over-the-top dance numbers, I found myself quietly singing along and enjoying the spectacle.

As I watched the finale dance number, a Bollywood-style extravaganza, I took a sip of my white wine and then raised my glass to my father.

"Mazel Tov."

I closed my eyes and using the literal translation of the Hebrew toast, I wished my father a "constellation of good stars and destiny."

CHAPTER 19

The lights flickered again. I looked at the ceiling, my annoyance clearly showing on my face.

"Stephanie, it'll pass. I'm sure they're working on fixing the problem."

My mother absently tapped her finger against her empty water glass and looked around the restaurant as she said this. Her nails were freshly manicured, and her auburn hair had just been cut and colored. She was wearing a floral-patterned green silk dress and a rust-colored cotton blazer. She was more dressed up than I was. I hadn't packed work clothes for my visit to Ann Arbor and was wearing a simple grey wool tunic sweater and black leggings. Someone finally came and filled our water glasses. I took another look around the dark dining room and sighed.

I had no idea why I was so angry.

"This trip home is supposed to be relaxing you. You're overreacting. This is a celebration. What's wrong with you?"

"I'm just hungry." I glanced around the restaurant restlessly as I said this.

"Why are you looking for a fight? You're ruining the evening."

I was surprised that my mother was being so direct. Usually, we didn't discuss any tension between us.

As I was thinking about how to reply to her, a young waiter in a poorly fitting suit finally came to our table. He looked like he was an undergrad at the university. He had blond hair that had product in it to make it stick up in peaks. His complexion was fair and flushed from the heat of the restaurant. He handed us menus. I kept my face buried in the huge parchment menu until he left. The lights had stopped flickering, and the dining room was now fully lit.

"What are you thinking of ordering, Mom?"

"Probably pasta."

I had no idea what my mother meant by ordering pasta. This was an Italian restaurant. Everything on the menu was pasta.

"I might just have a salad."

My mother shook her head and leaned over and pointed firmly to the ravioli listing on my menu.

"Why don't you get the ravioli? That looks good. If you didn't want Italian food, you should have spoken up when I suggested this restaurant."

"I hoped that we would try someplace different. We always come to this place."

"No, we don't. We only come here for special occasions." My mother said this in an irritated tone, not looking up from her menu.

Our waiter approached our table. Whether I had been here two times or a thousand times before, I was here now, and there was no point in upsetting my mother.

"I'll have the ravioli in mushroom sauce."

"I'll have the fettuccini with meat sauce."

The waiter nodded, jotted down our orders, and took our menus. When he was gone, my mother turned back to me.

"I hope they bring us bread. I'm starving."

I just nodded. I took another look around the restaurant. The patterned rug looked faded. The paintings were the same prints of famous Renaissance paintings that had adorned the walls since the restaurant had first opened twenty years ago. Sitting here, you could never imagine that 9/11 had happened only two months ago. Or at all.

"How does it feel to be back for your first visit home after 9/11?"

My mother's question startled me. I had no idea how it felt to be back. In some ways, it felt like I had never left.

"It feels good."

I gave my mother a strained smile. She took a sip of her water and then said, her voice brittle with the effort to sound cheerful:

"You know you don't have to stay in New York. Why don't you come back home."

"New York is my home, Mom."

"Things change."

"My career is in New York."

"Can't you find a job here? I didn't bring you up only to have you move so far away. You have no family in New York, Stephanie."

I raised an eyebrow in response to my mother's comment. Her parenting skills were a topic we usually avoided discussing. Surely, my mother was self-aware enough to know that mentioning how she raised me wasn't going to steer the argument in her favor. I looked away from her so she wouldn't see my face flushing with anger.

When I felt my annoyance was under control, I turned back to my mother, intending to tell her again that I needed to be in New York for my job. But she spoke first, a wistful look in her eyes.

"I wanted to see the world too when I was your age."

I looked at her with surprise as I said, "What stopped you?"

"I had two kids, and your father wasn't the traveling type."

My mother's gaze shifted beyond me to the entrance of the restaurant, as if a world of lost possibilities existed just outside the door. She turned back to my questioning eyes and gave me a sad smile.

"Anyway, that was a long time ago. The point is, I understand the draw that New York has for you. But you could live here and still travel, Stephanie. I wish we could spend more time together. Family is important."

"She's right. Family should be a priority."

Aurora had arrived. She pointed to my mother as she said this.

I didn't reply to Aurora. Frankly, I didn't know how close a mother-daughter bond I could achieve at this point. Too many years had gone by. But I wanted to try at least to give her some of the connection she was yearning for. While I was here anyway.

Our food arrived. My mother toyed with her fettuccine while she looked longingly at the celebration across the restaurant from us. A large family was sitting around a long table. There were grandparents, parents, and several noisy children that were dressed up in fancy outfits and had spaghetti sauce all over their happy faces. The family was eating and laughing, clearly enjoying themselves. They looked like an advertisement for the restaurant.

Aurora glanced at the happy family as she said, "You don't have to be an advertisement for the restaurant. Start with forgiveness."

Aurora's tone was sympathetic, and in spite of myself, I nodded in response.

My mother had said that family was important. But I had never had much of a family to speak of. Ever since I had left Arthur and moved to New York, I was used to being independent and, for the most part, alone.

I took a small bite of my mushy ravioli, and turned back to my mother, and asked, "How's your fettucine?"

My mother had barely touched her food. They never had brought her the bread that she had wanted.

"It's a little salty." She looked around the table nervously to see if anyone had heard her complain. "Not that it isn't delicious. It's just saltier than I remembered from last time."

To negate her critical comment, she took a big forkful of her fettuccine.

As I watched my mother, my frustration with her dissipated. She was doing the best she could.

As if reading my thoughts, my mother said shyly,

"We've had a lot of good times together. Haven't we, Stephanie?"

My mother's eyes pleaded with me as she nervously waited for my answer.

"Yes, we have Mom," I said gently.

Aurora was standing over the table. She nodded in approval at my comment, as she said,

"She's your mother, Stephanie. She loves you."

Aurora wiped a tear from her eye.

"Enjoy your time with your mother. She's the only mother you'll ever have." Aurora's voice cracked as she said this. She waved a hasty goodbye to me and left the table.

My mother and I sat in silence for a few minutes, eating. I took one more bite of my inedible ravioli and then pushed the plate away. My mother had stopped pretending to eat her fettuccine as well. She couldn't take her eyes off of the large family celebration. I pointed to the children, who were now eating slices of cake, and said, "Let's order dessert tonight."

My mother's eyes lit up at the thought of something sweet to finish her meal. I signaled to the waiter, and he brought the dessert cart to the table.

"Everything looks so delicious! What should I have? Help me decide."

"You like carrot cake, Mom."

The waiter pulled our chosen desserts from the cart and set them down on the table, along with fresh forks. He then wheeled the overloaded cart away. My mom took a big forkful of carrot cake. I took a small forkful of my flourless chocolate cake, dipping it in the raspberry sauce. The cake was dense and chocolatey, and good.

My Mother watched me savor the cake. Her face softened.

"Your cake looks delicious. I wish I could eat chocolate."

I smiled in reply, my first genuine smile of the evening. I was relieved we had found something to connect over, even if it was just a piece of cake.

"Yours looks good too, Mom."

As I watched my mother enjoy her dessert, I thought about how quickly my week in Ann Arbor was flying by. It was already Thanksgiving tomorrow. I asked my mother if she wanted me to bring anything to dinner the next day and had her bring me up to speed on everyone who would be there. We took our time enjoying our dessert. When we were finished, I signaled the waiter for the check. I walked with her to the parking lot.

When she was in her car, she asked, "Are you sure you don't want me to drop you off at the hotel? It's still raining."

"No, I want to walk off some of that heavy food. I'll call you tomorrow when I'm on my way to your house."

"Be careful walking back. Cars don't look where they're going in this weather. Turkey will be served around 2:00. See you tomorrow Hon."

My mom gave me a wan smile and started her car. I gave her one last wave, and turned around, and headed towards my hotel.

CHAPTER 20

"The cranberry sauce still has the ridge shape from the can, Mom."

Steven handed the cranberry sauce back to my mother.

"Sorry, honey. Bring the other bowl of cranberry sauce out, the one with the berries in it."

My mother swapped bowls with Steven and handed me a large bowl of mashed potatoes with the butter melting in a pool on top.

"Take this out and set it with the other food. Dan, are you done carving the turkey yet?"

Dan was trying to carve the turkey on the small table that was across from the sink. He was using an electric carving knife, but it needed sharpening because it was not cutting clean slices of turkey but was instead shredding the turkey to messy slivers.

"I'm having trouble with the knife. It's not cutting the turkey."

"What did you expect? You bought it at a garage sale for a dollar. Use a regular carving knife. The turkey's going to get cold."

My mother opened one of the utensil drawers with a jerk and pulled out a large knife with a serrated edge. She came around the kitchen counter to Dan, handing him the knife.

"I can get this to work. Give me a few minutes. You're so impatient."

"Use this, or I'll cut it myself."

Dan ignored my mother's outstretched hand and continued chipping at the turkey.

"Go sit down, Dan. I'll finish." My mother pointed to the dining room.

Dan set the carving knife down and shrugged. My mother looked like she was gritting her teeth as she unplugged the knife with a yank of the cord.

"Go join the others, Stephanie. I'll bring out the turkey in a minute."

My mom started efficiently cutting the turkey with the manual knife. I nodded and went to the dining room.

Everyone was already seated at the table. My Mother's sister Alice, her husband George, and their college-age daughter Dawn and twelve-year-old son Alex were there, along with my brother Steven, Dan, and Arthur. A couple of my ghosts, Atticus from *To Kill a Mockingbird* and Aurora from *Terms of Endearment*, were sitting at the table as well. I took a seat next to Arthur.

Apart from my ghosts, Arthur was the only non-relative at the dinner. Since Arthur was single and Canadian and had no other family to spend Thanksgiving with, I continued to invite him each year even after we broke up. My family liked Arthur, and he was always welcomed warmly.

My Aunt Alice was the only one who had dressed up for dinner. Her black hair was clipped into a bun. She was wearing a green silk blouse paired with a red blazer that had a holiday wreath brooch pinned to the lapel.

My cousin Dawn had her brown hair in a shag of sorts. She was wearing a Powerpuff Girls T-shirt and jeans and was picking cashews out of the bowl of mixed nuts she had brought to the table from the living room, putting them into a small pile in front of her, creating her private stash.

My Uncle George was talking with Steven. George looked quite professorial in his khakis and a navy crew neck sweater with a light blue button-down shirt under it. Since he was over six and a half feet tall, he was sitting on the end so that he could stretch his legs. His straw-colored hair was parted on the side, and his beard was trimmed much closer than Arthur's.

My Mom had put a fall-themed tablecloth with a leaf pattern on the table. She was using holiday china that had a mistletoe pattern around the edges. The table was filled with platters and bowls of food. There were two types of canned cranberry sauce, broccoli, asparagus, mashed potatoes, one of those disgusting green bean mushroom soup casseroles, and canned yams with burnt marshmallows on top, all lined up in the center of the long dining table.

Arthur gave me a reassuring smile as I settled into my chair. Steven continued his discussion of the Lions game with my Uncle George.

"We should have gone to the game. It's the last season the Lions are playing in the Silverdome."

My uncle laughed and shook his head.

"No point in going out in the cold to watch the Lions lose again."

"It's close; they could win this one. Two field goals, and it's early."

Steven said this as if he were trying to convince himself. The Lions had had a losing streak that extended back into my early childhood.

Arthur looked ready to join the football talk. He liked sports, and his mathematical mind made him very good at remembering all the statistics in a game. By the way he was leaning towards George, I could tell that he was going to start chiming in with numbers that demonstrated just how bad the Lions were.

My mother came out with the turkey before he could say anything.

"Here we are! Dan, can you make some room in the center of the table? I hope everyone is hungry!"

My Aunt Alice and I assisted Dan and reached over and rearranged the bowls on our respective sides of the table to make space for the turkey.

My Mom was wearing a rust-colored casual cotton dress that went well with her auburn hair. The dress had a rhinestone turkey pinned to the collar. She seated herself next to Dan before reaching over and handing the platter of turkey to her sister Alice. She started passing around the other dishes as well.

The food was traveling counterclockwise around the table, and it got to Arthur first. He took a few pieces of turkey for himself and then served me a couple of pieces of white meat. He did the same for the potatoes and stuffing. When the sticky yams came by, I shook my head vehemently when he raised the serving spoon to offer me some. Once everyone had food on their plates, my Mother cleared her throat and looked around the table.

"Happy Thanksgiving, everyone. I just want to say that I'm grateful that Stephanie got out of The Towers on 9/11 safely and is here with us to celebrate Thanksgiving."

Everyone at the table turned to look at me. I gave what I hoped looked like a smile.

"Thank God!"

My Aunt Alice said this and raised her glass. Everyone nodded and raised their glasses as well, toasting me.

"To Stephanie!"

Aurora was watching me. She gave me an amused look.

"They certainly are a sentimental bunch, aren't they?"

I nodded. Then the first dreaded 9/11 question came my way.

"What was it like getting out of the Towers on that day?"

My Uncle George asked this. Aurora wrinkled her nose in distaste as she looked at the mushy green bean casserole on my mother's plate. She turned back to me, her voice sympathetic.

"You don't have to wow them with the perfect answer. Any information you give them is more than they'll be able to understand."

I didn't have an answer for them.

I tried to think of a benign image from that day, something that wouldn't be so morbid that it would cast a shadow over the dinner.

As I was working on an answer, Atticus set down his fork and cleared his throat. "Courage is more than a man with a gun in his hand. It's when you know you're licked before you begin, but you begin anyway and see it through no matter what."

Aurora turned to Atticus, shaking her head.

"Don't be so defeatist, Atticus."

She then turned back to me.

"Any images will do, even ones borrowed from the newsreels."

I nodded absently as I tried to think of some image that I could relay back to my family.

"It took a long time to walk across the bridge. There were people on every inch of it."

Everyone at the table listened to my answer, including Atticus and Aurora. Dan was the only one that continued to eat.

"Were people walking on the bridge while they were hurt?"

My cousin Dawn asked this. She had tears in her eyes.

"Some were probably hurt. All of us were mostly in shock, I guess."

I thought of all the people who had walked across the Manhattan Bridge with me on that sunny September day. We had all been marching quietly like an army of zombies.

"A mob's always made up of people, no matter what."

Atticus quietly quoted his line from "To Kill a Mockingbird." He seemed deep in thought as he stared out towards the living room.

The next question I faced was I was from my cousin Alex, who, at twelve, was the youngest at the table.

"Were there cops and firemen on the bridge with you?"

I thought about how the cops and FBI agents downtown had made the crowds more hysterical as they had screamed for us to run and outpace the dust cloud. But there were very few cops on the long walk back to Brooklyn. There was no panic on the trek across the bridge. The march was slow and deathly quiet. I didn't evade Alex's question, but I didn't go into detail either.

"There weren't any cops or firemen that I could see."

Alex nodded solemnly.

I tried to turn back to my turkey, hoping that that would end the questions for a while. I wanted to get a bite before it got cold. Too late. I resisted the urge to spit the cold, dry turkey meat out in my napkin. Aurora pointed to my water glass, suggesting I take a sip to clear my throat. I shook my head.

"Are you ok?"

Arthur was looking at me with concern. He asked this quietly and close to my ear so that no one else could hear it. Before I had a chance to answer him, Dan chimed in.

"Damn Arabs. They've been planning this for years. We're too weak."

Dan looked around the table angrily at no one in particular.

"We can't blame all Arabs for the actions of a few."

My Uncle George said this to Dan like he was lecturing a child.

"We cater to them and coddle them, and we should have thrown them all out years ago!"

Dan took a large gulp of his beer, finishing the mug. I looked at Dan in distaste. Who in their right mind would blame all Arabs for what happened on 9/11 except some reactionary wingnut?

"Charmer, isn't he." Aurora pointed to Dan and rolled her eyes. I didn't reply.

"As a beacon of freedom for the world, we have a responsibility to be tolerant."

My uncle said this to Alex and Dawn as if they were still young children, and he was teaching them manners. Dan snorted and shook his head as he shoveled a sticky mouthful of yams into his mouth.

I had resisted all the political conspiracy theories that had been making the rounds on talk radio and news shows. 9/11 was a human tragedy to me, not a conspiracy. Dan was politically conservative, and I tried never to get into a political conversation with him. My Dad, for all of his other faults, at least was a liberal. Or had been. I had to get used to thinking of him in the past tense. I wondered how he was doing in intensive care on a holiday. Alone. Were they serving turkey in the hospital?

Everyone was staring at me, including Aurora and Atticus. I had no idea how much time had passed. Clearly, by the look of worry on everyone's face at the table, it had been more than a few seconds. My Aunt asked me another question.

"We saw all these pictures on the news of people covered in dust. Were you like that, Stephanie?"

My Aunt's eyes were riveted to me as she absently ate her green bean casserole.

The dust had been everywhere. Everyone and everything was covered in it. I was no exception. My clothes had been completely covered in dust. It was in my hair. It was a film on my skin. It was a coating in my throat choking me.

"Yes, I had dusty clothes."

My voice cracked as I answered my aunt. I pictured the hazy heat of that day and the dust and ashes that had settled on me, making me a living mummy on the long trek back to Brooklyn.

I looked at all the expectant gazes around the table. I felt trapped. I turned to Aurora. She approached me and pointed to my wine glass, saying one of her lines from *Terms of Endearment*.

"Grown women are prepared for life's little emergencies."

I took a sip of the dry, acidic wine.

"How long did it take you to get across the bridge?"

Young Alex asked this. I didn't have an answer. Even though I had had a watch on, I had never looked at it once that long day.

"I'm not sure."

I picked up a forkful of food and put it in my mouth, trying again to signal that I needed a break from the questions. Aurora watched me, saying nothing. Atticus was smoking his pipe and looking around the table as if trying to figure out what his jury was thinking. Arthur seemed to be the only one besides Aurora who understood my signal. He was about to say something to try to change the subject, but Dan interrupted him.

"They should have locked down and secured those bridges. What if those Arabs had blown the bridges up? We need to secure our country!"

"We're a free country. With the freedom to go where we please. Dad understood that." Steven said this, looking defiantly at Dan. He turned to my mother, his eyes filled with scorn.

My Mother held Steven's gaze for a moment. She then looked down at her barely touched plate of food. Dan shook his head, saying nothing, as he poured some wine into his mug without bothering to wash out the remains of the beer that he had just finished.

"I think they've secured the bridges and tunnels now. I was listening to talk of that on NPR. Apparently, there's a security coding system now."

George stated this as if we were having an academic colloquium at the university on the relative merits of locking down a city during a terrorist attack.

I lived with endless daily security checkpoints into every building, tunnel, bridge, and meeting place in the city. I lived with Downtown Manhattan, which was a war zone, secured by tanks, marines, warplanes, and armed soldiers with machine guns guarding the huge mountains of melted steel and ashes that used to be the Towers.

I thought of all the scared eyes I looked into each day as yet another siren went off, all the exhaustion on everyone's faces as we all were stopped for another search. I thought of the sniffer dogs, the men in hazmat suits, the guards. None of this was academic to me or up for a pleasant cerebral debate. It was my life.

My hands were shaking, not from nervousness, but with rage. No one seemed to be able to tell that I was angry except Arthur. And Aurora. Even Atticus didn't seem to notice my rage. He was still smoking his pipe and looking thoughtfully at Dan as if Dan were a witness he was trying to understand.

Arthur was looking at me worriedly. Aurora's eyes held sympathy. She gestured to my wine glass again.

I took a sip of wine to try to calm myself. How dare they talk about the inconveniences, the heartache, the misery, the human suffering, as if they were a topic for a Barbara Walters or Oprah interview?

They drove in their cars to their jobs in their small safe towns that were completely in another world from New York. They watched the tragedy on television like it was a disaster movie made by the same producer as *The Towering Inferno*. Then if they got bored, they changed the channel on the TV and watched *Wheel of Fortune* instead.

Before I could stop myself, I shouted, "I don't think any of you should be discussing what you don't understand!"

Everyone stopped talking and turned to look at me in shock. Arthur placed his hand on mine, which was on the table and now balled into a fist. Aurora raised an eyebrow but didn't comment on my outburst.

"The best way to clear the air is to have it all out in the open."

Atticus turned to me and gave me an understanding look as he said this. He put his pipe in his jacket pocket and stood up from the table.

"I've got to get to the courthouse. Happy Thanksgiving."

Atticus waved goodbye to Aurora and me and departed.

My brother turned to me and spoke. He looked genuinely confused at my rage.

"We're just discussing what was on the news. Why are you so angry?"

"Because none of you have any idea what you're talking about!"

My voice still sounded angry. Everyone at the table stared at me in discomfort.

"We didn't mean to upset you. I'm sorry our discussion is striking a raw nerve."

Alice, who was a social worker, said this calmly and slowly like she was trying to placate a patient who was having an outburst in the psychiatric asylum. Everyone nodded in agreement with what my aunt was saying.

"Let's change the subject to something happier. Dan, could you change the television to TNT? I think *A Christmas Story* is running non-stop today."

My mother said this in a forced cheerful tone. She was looking at me in concern.

"Al Qaida should be eradicated!"

Dan mumbled this as he got up and changed the channel. No one responded. *A Christmas Story* started playing in the other room.

Aurora was still looking at me sympathetically.

"Just survive the conversation. Tomorrow it won't matter."

Her advice was surprisingly comforting.

"They just want you to know that they care. Just concentrate on taking care of yourself, Stephanie. Life is precious, and you never know how long you have."

Aurora gave me a sad smile and then stood up from the table. She dabbed at her eyes with a napkin. She gave me a nod as she left the dining room. I watched her go, sorry that I had inadvertently opened her raw wound.

"Are you getting up early to do some shopping on Black Friday tomorrow, Stephanie?"

Alice asked this with polite curiosity. She was watching my face carefully. My look of rage had shifted to one of embarrassment, which seemed to satisfy her. She turned to my mother.

"I'd like to hit the outlet malls tomorrow if you're up to it."

My mother nodded absently.

"I want a Game Boy!" Alex said enthusiastically. "Walmart is selling them for half price and on TV. They showed people already lined up to buy them tomorrow!"

"I don't understand what the big deal is with all of those games. They certainly aren't worth sleeping in the cold for."

George made this remark with an amused smile on his face, and everyone laughed. The moment was over. For them.

Arthur turned to me. "Want to get out of here soon?"

I nodded and smiled gratefully.

"Who wants pie? We have pumpkin, apple, and chocolate cream."

My mother got up from the table and turned towards the kitchen as everyone chimed in their preferences.

I looked around the table at everyone talking and enjoying the last few bites of their dinner. My outburst was forgotten. I got up to help my mother clear the plates.

"Great dinner, Mom."

I handed her the dirty plates that I brought with me into the kitchen.

My mom looked me over to see if I was ok now.

"Thanks, Hon. How are you feeling?"

"I'm just tired. Arthur and I are going to head out after dessert."

My mother nodded. We stood there for a few minutes in silence as she put the dirty dinner dishes in the dishwasher.

"Have you read that book I bought you yet, the one about grief?"

"I've started it."

"I know we've had our disagreements Stephanie, but I'm here if you want to talk. Let me know if you want to come Black Friday shopping with Aunt Alice. We'll probably get an early start."

My mother turned to me as she said this. I was taken aback by the longing I was feeling. I wanted my mother to somehow dust me off and make me all better as if my grief were a scabbed knee I had gotten from playing outside, which could be healed with a kiss and a Band-Aid.

I thought I had long ago gotten over yearning for my mom to be the mother I had wanted so desperately as a young girl. My mother and I had never found closeness or intimacy in all these years. Maybe she was finally ready to provide it. I allowed myself to hope for a second.

But as I stood there, my eyes open and yearning, my mother, broke our locked gaze and looked away. She handed me a pumpkin pie and a can of Ready Whip.

"Here, honey, take the pumpkin pie out to the table. I'll let people put their own whipped cream on their pie."

"Sure, Mom." I kept my voice neutral as I said this. Like I had since I was a child.

My mother didn't meet my eyes as she handed me the pie. She buried her head in the open refrigerator, rearranging the shelves to fit the leftovers.

The only noises in the quiet kitchen were my mother's shuffling of leftover containers and the humming of the refrigerator. I turned to go back to the dining room.

As I was about to leave the kitchen, my mother called out to me.

"Stephanie...Hold on just a sec, hon."

I paused at the kitchen doorway. I figured she had another pie to hand me. But when my mother turned to face me, her hands were empty, and her face looked forlorn and lost.

Her expression was one of a small child in need of a hug. It was not the face of someone who was going to fix my scraped knee or fix me breakfast when I got up for school in the morning or show up for my high school graduation. My mother's countenance was one of a lost little girl.

Someone had to be the parent. At least for a moment.

I went to her and kissed her on the forehead. Her eyes held both gratitude and an apology. I nodded, accepting both emotions from her. My mother then smiled sadly as she said, "Let's get these pies out to the table."

She picked up the chocolate and apple pies she had set on the counter and headed towards the doorway, calling out with false cheer to everyone at the dining table.

"Who's ready for some dessert!"

CHAPTER 21

Arthur and I held hands in the back of the cab. If we had still been together as a couple, I would have rested my head on his shoulder. But even though it felt natural to do that, I resisted the urge.

"How are you doing?" Arthur looked me over.

"Relieved. I thought we'd never get out of there."

"Did the questions bother you?"

I looked at the pine tree decal that was hanging from the rear-view mirror. It was one of those car air fresheners and was faded from being exposed to the sun. The cab smelled more like leftover Chinese carryout than evergreen. I continued to stare at the air freshener as I answered Arthur's question.

"Everyone's so removed from what it's like in New York. I feel like I'm on a different planet."

"They don't live in New York."

"They live in a bubble. Their lives will never touch anything close to what I deal with every day. They have no idea what the real world is about. Life isn't television!"

My voice rose. I looked wildly around the cab. There was a smudged green towel draped on top of the passenger seat. I focused on it. The towel had grease marks like it had been used to clean oil in the engine. I looked down at my trembling hands in shame. My family hadn't done anything wrong.

Arthur didn't say anything in reply to my outburst. He just watched me, his eyes scanning my face as I continued.

"Everyone here is carrying on as if 9/11 was all just a movie on TV. I don't know how to talk to people that are so safe that they can't understand what it's like to live constantly with guns and police and endless security checks!"

The cab driver turned the radio down and spoke with awe.

"Were you in one of the Towers on 9/11?"

I turned my eyes back to the greasy green towel in the front seat of the cab.

Aurora was now sitting in the passenger seat. She looked at the greasy towel with distaste and addressed my escalating thoughts about the cab driver.

"He's just curious. He doesn't mean any harm, even though he's a nosy slob."

I was glad to see Aurora. I decided to answer the cab driver's question if only to end the conversation more quickly.

"Yes, I was there that day."

"What was it like being there?"

I looked to Aurora for guidance as to how far I should go. She looked the cab driver over.

"Cut him off after another answer. He needs to focus on the road."

"It was intense."

I answered in a tone I hoped conveyed that I didn't want to discuss the matter further.

"Did you see people jumping?"

The driver turned to look at me, nearly swerving out of our lane. The truck next to us beeped its horn, and the cabby quickly turned his attention back to the road.

"Ok, Bandit, the stunt car driving is over."

Aurora pointed to the road as she addressed the cab driver. Arthur was watching me. Whether I answered the driver's questions or not, I was still going to be trapped in this cab until we dropped off Arthur at his apartment. I decided to continue. It didn't matter.

"I saw people jumping. Many hung out the windows begging for help. Some jumped."

My voice was a whisper. The cab driver wasn't even pretending to watch the road. Aurora listened intently to what I was saying. She wiped a tear from the corner of her eyes. She then turned to the cab driver and pointed to the road.

"Do your job and watch the road!"

The cab driver, of course, couldn't hear Aurora. Arthur opened his mouth to tell the cabby to stop asking questions, but the driver spoke first.

"I can't believe you were there. Did anyone try to help the trapped people?"

I hadn't gone to help anyone.

I hadn't moved from my spot on the pavement until the FBI and police had screamed for all of us to move because the Towers were collapsing. I had then watched the Towers get shorter and shorter in the skyline until they had disappeared, taking the screams, help signs, and jumping bodies with them until all that was left was an enormous dust cloud that tried to consume us all.

I shook my head. No. I hadn't gone back into the building. I had done nothing.

Arthur cleared his throat and spoke to the cab driver.

"My friend Stephanie needs to just sit back and relax for the rest of the drive. I'd feel better if we concentrated on the road."

The cab driver shrugged and turned the radio up. The white metal angst of "In the End" by Linkin Park filled the cab. The driver turned his attention back to the road.

As we drove the last couple of blocks to Arthur's place, I let Arthur keep his arm around me. I kept my eyes closed so I didn't have to talk to him or the cab driver.

We finally arrived at Arthur's apartment, which was the top floor of an old house near campus. It was the same apartment I had lived in with him from about age twenty-four to when I left for New York. Arthur got out of the cab. He took the rubber band off his wallet and pulled out a twenty-dollar bill, and paid the driver quickly so that the driver wouldn't ask any more questions.

As I got out of the cab, the cabby's eyes lingered on my face.

"Take care now."

He looked like he wanted to say more, but he looked over to Arthur and shrugged instead. The cab drove away, the rumbling muffler making the only noise on the quiet street. Arthur squeezed my hand. I didn't pull away.

"Want to come upstairs?"

I knew what he was asking me. And I knew what a "yes" answer would mean to him. I had avoided moments like this for the last five years since moving to New York, although the offer had been made by Arthur almost every time I saw him. But today was different. Today I craved connection. Even if I would pay a price for it later. Today, a part of me longed to get in a time machine and go back to when I felt safe and loved. Right now, every cell in my body craved to travel back to the years when Arthur and I were truly happy.

Maybe that was possible. Time seemed to stand still in Ann Arbor. Perhaps I could erase the past five years and forget they ever happened.

After my long struggle to escape the bubble of Ann Arbor, it was ironic, but maybe an insulated fishbowl was what I needed right now.

I nodded affirmatively in answer to Arthur's question. He looked both pleased and surprised at my response. He blushed, and a shy smile crept up the corners of his mouth. Arthur fumbled in his pockets and pulled out his house key, which was on a keychain that doubled as a small flashlight. I could hear the crunch of the dead leaves under my feet where I was standing. A cat was lounging on the grey wooden porch swing. It had long, well-groomed fur and yellowish almond eyes, which were staring at me as I walked up the rickety porch steps.

A mix of emotions hit me as I waited for Arthur to open the door. I felt melancholy. I also felt remnants of the anger that had overwhelmed me in the cab and at dinner earlier. But the strongest emotion I was feeling was a bittersweet yearning.

I followed Arthur up the familiar staircase. Even the creaks that the stairs made as we walked up them sounded familiar. Once we got up to the front hallway, Arthur took my coat and hung it in the small, mostly unused closet at the foot of the stairs.

"After you." Arthur gestured to the living room. I stood in the entranceway and took a long look around the dusty, cramped living area. Nothing had changed since I moved out of the apartment five years ago. It was messier, but for the most part, everything was just where I had left it.

There was a frayed, overstuffed turquoise sofa and a brown wood coffee table in front of it, which homed a thirteen-inch television with a cable box and VCR attached to it. Across from the sofa was a large mustard-colored armchair that had math papers stacked on the cushion. The side wall had an enormous glass and chrome entertainment unit that was being used to stack books, miscellaneous unopened mail, math papers, and VCR movies, mostly classic musicals and film noirs.

The art on the walls consisted of the same framed posters that I had left behind. A Picasso print of abstract figures dancing around in a circle around a dove hung just to the right of the sofa. There were several Dali prints as well. Somehow my old posters looked at home in Arthur's cluttered living room.

Arthur motioned to the sofa. "Make yourself comfortable."

Once seated, I glanced at the stack of movies near the VCR. *Double Indemnity* and *Strangers on a Train* were out of their boxes and sitting by the TV. I had spent many a night on this sofa with Arthur, watching Hitchcock, noir films, and old gangster movies (such as Cagney in *White Heat*). I had forced Arthur to watch some musicals with me too, such as the inevitable *Singin' in the Rain,* or classics such as *Gypsy* and *West Side Story.*

Being a good student of my father, I pointed out to Arthur the artistry in the dance numbers and how dance and music were used to communicate key plot movements and character development. Arthur had been an open-minded pupil to my teachings, and we had enjoyed the musicals together.

I thought of my last night in Michael's sterile apartment and its troubled combination of bland modern design and rancid trash. Arthur's apartment was so different. Arthur's apartment felt like his home.

There was a used napkin on the arm of the side of the sofa where I sat down. It had coffee stains and math equations on it. I smiled. This must be the side of the sofa that Arthur usually sat on.

"Would you like some wine?"

Arthur usually had white wine in the refrigerator that he purchased at Trader Joe's on his monthly cab trip to stock up on cereal, wine, and vanilla sandwich cookies. When I lived with him, I used to drive us there.

Arthur handed me a tumbler filled halfway. I had bought this glass at the main kitchen accessory store in town, Kitchen Port, when I had moved in with Arthur and discovered that he had no plates, cutlery, or glassware to speak of. He had been eating on paper plates and cups and had one or two chipped and stained coffee mugs, and that had been about it.

I had enjoyed picking out a cheerful set of plates and cups and a sturdy set of forks and knives. Playing house with Arthur had made me feel rooted and safe back then. I looked at Arthur. He smiled at me shyly. I found myself smiling back with the first genuine expression of enjoyment I had felt all day. I wanted to feel grounded again. Maybe it was possible.

I took a sip of the cold, utilitarian wine. It was oddly comforting to be drinking alcohol that had not been purchased on an expense account.

Arthur took a long sip from his tumbler and sighed in satisfaction. We sat for a few minutes quietly sipping our wine, saying nothing. Arthur broke the comfortable silence first:

"Does this place feel the same as when you were here last?"

I nodded in answer. The last time I had been here was when I had moved out. Even though I had seen Arthur numerous times in the last five years, we had always met at the cafe, his office, or one of his other hang-outs. I had never come upstairs. I had hoped that if I avoided any awkward attempts at intimacy, Arthur and I could transition successfully from our breakup and remain good friends.

Although Arthur hadn't changed any in the five years since I had left him, maybe I had changed enough for us to work out somehow. Maybe I could find a quiet haven here, a retreat from my vodka-soaked evenings and stressful, work-oriented days. I longed to find faces that would look at me with expressions devoid of grief, anger, or suffering.

Maybe I would now feel that it was ok to live in a bubble. Perhaps I could even be healed and renewed in the never-changing air of Ann Arbor. In leaving for New York five years ago, I had left a piece of my youth and innocence behind. I wanted to try to reconnect to the part of myself that enjoyed cafes, colloquia, and abstract ideas. I wanted to be idealistic again. Maybe Arthur could lead me back to my former self.

My thoughts were interrupted by a loud growl from my stomach. I looked down at it in annoyance like it belonged to someone else. I hadn't really eaten any of my Thanksgiving dinner. I was starving. I turned to Arthur and gave him a sheepish grin.

"I'm hungry. Can we get something to eat and watch a movie?"

"How can you be hungry after all that food? I don't have any food in the apartment, and nothing is open for delivery except maybe Chinese carryout or pizza."

Arthur shook his head in amusement as he said this. I shrugged, still grinning. I thought of the horrible Hawaiian pizza I had had at my Mom's when I first arrived in Ann Arbor. I wasn't ready to repeat the experience.

"I didn't eat that much at my Mom's. I was too busy answering everyone's questions. Chinese sounds great. Do you have menus?"

"They're in the kitchen on the refrigerator door. I don't know which places are open, though. If no one wants to deliver, I can go pick up the food. To be honest, I didn't eat much at your Mother's either. I was worried about you."

Arthur went into the kitchen and pulled the menus off of the refrigerator door. I took a quick look at the Dinersty menu. Dinersty was one of the few Chinese places where the kitchen was open until midnight. The food was unremarkable, but it wasn't horrible. Arthur and I had had our first date there. We had sat side by side at the stools that faced the large picture window looking out on Liberty Avenue and had eaten dinner and then gone to a movie at the now-closed theater down the block.

The irony of choosing to eat at Dinersty now didn't escape me. I stared at the creased menu, waiting to see if I would feel any melancholy or sadness from reading the familiar dishes. I waited for the significance to wash over me. But the moment held no deeper meaning. It was just food. I turned to Arthur as I said:

"Let's order from Dinersty. Do you want Kung Pao chicken?"

Arthur nodded. I walked over to the phone and dialed the number on the menu. It rang a few times. I was relieved when someone answered. I placed our order. They were quoting an hour for delivery.

"I'll go pick it up."

"Thanks. That would be great." I gave Arthur a grateful smile.

He grabbed his navy blue LL Bean ski jacket. I stood in the stairwell and watched him go. When I heard the click of the lock, I headed back to the living room, where I sat down on the sofa, curling my legs up under me.

I looked around for the remote on the cluttered coffee table. It was on top of some completed and yellowing New York Times crossword puzzles that were stacked haphazardly next to the television. I turned on the TV. Footage of the Macy's parade filled the 13-inch screen. I flipped through the channels, passing through Lifetime, TNT, and TBS, which were all showing sickly sweet holiday specials or movies. I looked at the clock near the entertainment unit. It was almost 8:00.

I left the TV on AMC. *Miracle on 34th Street* was on, with a special about Miracle on 34th Street playing after that. Groundbreaking programming for Thanksgiving.

Before long, I heard the sound of Arthur's key in the door.

"I'm back. They gave us an extra egg roll for free."

I followed Arthur into the kitchen. We filled our plates with Chinese food.

"Want some more wine?"

Arthur topped his glass. He pointed to my tumbler. I nodded as I picked a piece of broccoli out of my General Tsao's chicken and nibbled on it. It was a comforting combination of sweet and peppery, with an aftertaste of grease.

Arthur had heaped most of the kung pao chicken on his plate and had taken the extra egg roll as well. He had a skinny build, with well-toned legs from all the walking that he did around campus. He could afford to eat the extra egg roll.

We sat in silence for a few minutes and took a few bites of the greasy Chinese food. It was a comfortable silence, blanketed by the familiar holiday music and dialogue of Miracle on 34th Street.

"It's good."

Arthur said this with food in his mouth. He bent over his plate and shoveled the food in his mouth quickly, which he only did when he either really enjoyed food or was very hungry.

He probably had been nervous during the 9/11 conversation at dinner and hadn't eaten much. I took a salty-sweet-peppery bite of chicken and agreed.

"It's perfect. Thanks for going and picking it up."

Neither one of us wanted to watch a Christmas movie. I let Arthur choose something else to watch. He chose DOA, a classic Film Noir that was one of the best of its kind. I was relieved that he hadn't chosen a musical. It would only have reminded me of my father dying in the hospital.

I let Arthur hold me as we watched the movie together. I rested my head on his shoulder. When I looked over furtively at him every now and then, I saw a beautiful and kind man that was truly happy in that moment.

Midway through the movie, Arthur leaned in closer, his lips parted, ready to kiss me. Part of me wanted to lead up to this moment gradually, perhaps finishing the movie, and part of me wanted to dive in and get it over with. I had no idea how I would react to Arthur's advances after all these years.

I took one more sip of my wine and set my glass down on the coffee table next to the remains of my General Tsao's chicken. Arthur set his wine down next to his dirty dinner plate. He moved in closer to me, and I didn't pull away.

Arthur put his arms tighter around me. He brushed my lips with his, and I felt the tickle of his beard on my cheeks and chin. I opened my mouth so that he wouldn't think that I was resisting his kiss. I kept my tongue in my mouth. Arthur's lips were moist from wine. His kiss was more earnest than probing. His tongue ended up in my mouth too quickly for me to respond naturally.

I relaxed my throat and tongue so that I wouldn't gag as his tongue jabbed deeper into my mouth. I put my arms tighter around Arthur to keep my balance. He took this as me responding to his kiss and started kissing me with more urgency. He pressed his hips against mine. His eyes were looking into mine to make sure that I was still ok with him proceeding.

I had forgotten what it was like to be asked for consent.

I ran my fingers through his hair affectionately as I moved my hips to encourage his erection, which was rubbing against me through his black jeans.

Arthur started to fumble with his belt buckle and the fly of his jeans. I pulled back and kissed his forehead.

"Let's go into the bedroom, so we have more room."

Arthur and I climbed clumsily off the sofa and headed towards the bedroom, which was at the back of the apartment. Arthur held my hand as we walked single file down the narrow hallway.

The bedroom was a mess. There was a queen size-futon that was in the open position. The sheet was off the futon on one corner, and the blanket and top sheet were in a tangled mound at the foot of the bed. Arthur had a bunch of dirty clothes in a pile near the closet, and a few items were hanging on hangers that had been there since I pulled my stuff out of that closet five years ago.

My eyes rested on the small nightstand by the side of the futon. A paperback mystery and a mostly empty tumbler of wine were resting on it, along with a small table lamp whose beige shade was slightly askew. I noticed a scattering of sandwich cookie crumbs on the surface of the nightstand.

There was a small dresser on the other wall next to the closet. It was a three-drawer chest with scratched reddish wood. It had been painted at one point a bright yellow, but the paint job had only been half-finished, and some of the yellow paint was peeling off the side. Arthur had gotten the dresser for ten dollars at a garage sale across the street. I had always intended to paint it a bright blue or put some sort of decaled pattern on it, but I had never gotten around to it.

There was one lone poster in the room. It was on the wall near the closet, hanging over the dresser. It was a poster from a Grateful Dead concert when they had come to town some years ago. The poster was of a skeleton with a headdress of roses. The skeleton was holding roses as well, and the band's name was in a fancy script font, in red, at the top of the poster. I had bought the poster for Arthur for one of his birthdays and had it framed. The Grateful Dead was one of his favorite bands, and even though he didn't take acid anymore and only smoked pot occasionally at a party here and there, Arthur still very much loved the music from his hippie days.

A wave of warmth flushed over me as I looked at the poster. There was so much that was good about Arthur. He was so comforting to me in so many ways.

The lyrics to an old Cat Stevens song, another favorite musician of Arthur's, ran through my head. The song was called *Father and Son* and was about a son telling his father he was leaving to follow his dreams.

Although the song was a dialogue between a father and a son, it always reminded me of the struggle between Arthur and me. Arthur was settled into his life in Ann Arbor. And he was happy. But I had always wanted a bigger life. I had had no idea what that had meant, really, but I had always known that whatever Ann Arbor had to offer me, a bigger life wasn't it.

But now, I was tired of my life in New York. Maybe this was momentary malaise due to being in the middle of the misery and suffering of 9/11. Perhaps once all the dust settled in New York, my career would start mattering to me again. But right now, I just wanted some peace. Arthur had always been a solace to me. He was stable and reliable. I could trust him.

I let Arthur lead me to the futon. He let go of my hand and straightened out the tangle of covers.

"Sorry, the room's such a mess."

He kissed my forehead. I smiled, again feeling genuine affection and warmth for him.

In all the years I had known him, Arthur had never fully made a bed. Once the covers were laid mostly flat on the futon, Arthur quickly undid his belt buckle, unzipped his jeans, and pulled them off. He kicked at them when they were at his ankles, finally removing them. He then quickly stepped out of his underwear and unbuttoned his shirt.

As Arthur was undressing, I started to remove my clothing as well. I quickly took off my jeans and pulled the tunic sweater I was wearing over my head. I tossed my clothing over towards the pile of Arthur's near the closet. I unhooked my bra quickly so that Arthur wouldn't try to remove it. Over the years, I had found Arthur to be clumsy at removing my bra, and I preferred to just do it myself.

I quickly stepped out of my grey cotton bikini underwear and sat on the bed, watching Arthur pull his T-shirt over his head. The T-shirt was a cloudy grey color instead of its original white. Arthur never separated his whites from his darks when doing laundry, which had made all his underwear take on a greyish hue over time.

When Arthur was fully undressed, he approached the bed. I laid down on the side of the futon that was against the wall, making room for him on the other side. Arthur pulled me close up against the length of his body. His erection was still intact, even though it had taken us a few minutes to get undressed. I was leaning on my side facing Arthur, and I opened my legs to let his erection have room to rub me as we kissed. There was a little bit of liquid coming out of the tip of Arthur's penis, and that helped me feel less dry as he rubbed against me.

I could tell by Arthur's heavy breathing that he was very aroused. I tried to relax and catch up with him. Arthur grabbed my breasts and started squeezing them, and brushed my nipples with his thumbs. I had never liked direct contact with my nipples like that. It hurt. I bit my lip and used my concentration to keep from pulling back from Arthur's hands. Arthur took me biting my lip to signify that I was aroused, and his kisses grew more urgent. His tongue pushed back in my mouth, almost to the back of my throat. I felt like I was choking. I tried to relax my throat so that I wouldn't make a gagging sound.

I didn't want to disappoint Arthur.

He had been so kind and understanding these past few months and for all of the long five years since I had left him. I didn't want to ruin his sexual experience by pulling away or gagging.

I let Arthur draw me closer to him. His hips were grinding into me. His chest, with its curly, greying hair, was beaded in drops of sweat even though the room was chilly. Arthur's eyes had been closed when he was kissing me, but now he pulled his head back and opened them to see if I was ready for him to enter me. I looked into his eyes and took my arm, and stroked his curly greying hair. He looked at me with a mixture of expectation, tenderness, and desire. It was a look of love.

I absorbed his gaze, taking in his need. I would have rather died in the moment than let him down. He would have his sex, even if I had to give the best acting performance of my life to give it to him.

I kissed his nose and finished stroking the sweaty hair off of his glistening forehead. I turned on my back and pulled him towards me. I wanted this moment to be romantic. I wanted to use it to communicate that I appreciated him and his steady presence in my life. I wanted to use the moment to make us closer.

I wanted to let Arthur know that I hadn't moved away from him when I had moved to New York. I wanted Arthur to know that I loved him.

But Arthur was too far gone into his sexual release. He didn't see what was in my eyes. He clumsily nudged his penis between my open thighs, guiding it with his right hand while he grabbed one of my breasts with his left hand. He wasn't looking at me, so he couldn't see what I was trying to communicate to him. His eyes were closed as he groaned and dug into me.

I wanted nothing more than to go back to a time before Ann Arbor had made me feel boxed in and bored. I wanted to be fully connected to Arthur.

But as Arthur's thrusts grew more urgent, my body betrayed me. I couldn't get into the sex no matter how much I wanted to. I moved my hips so that Arthur wouldn't know I wasn't really into what was happening. I groaned every now and then, and I even twisted and turned in feigned intense anticipation of a climax. But the truth was, I wasn't responding at all to Arthur's movements.

I kept my eyes closed for the most part so that I wouldn't have to see his longing and his need. I felt utterly inadequate. I would have liked to think that my lack of enjoyment was momentary and situational, and therefore fixable. But it wasn't.

The ghost of the fireman was patiently watching me. He touched his helmet in a greeting. I met his eyes and silently asked him if he could some-how rescue me back from the ashes and the ruins of New York so that I could have a renewed life with Arthur here in Ann Arbor.

But the fireman shook his head. He couldn't help me. The part of me that could live a happy life in Ann Arbor had perished five years ago, long before the dust and debris of 9/11 had consumed her last traces.

I had changed and could not change back. The fireman offered me a blanket and some oxygen. I shook my head and gave him a melancholy smile, silently thanking him for his time. He gave a salute and waved good-bye. His job in Ann Arbor was done.

I opened my eyes, and Arthur started jerking in a way that let me know he was almost ready to come. I looked around the room that hadn't changed at all since I had moved out five years ago. My eyes rested on the Grateful Dead poster and scanned the clothes piled up on the floor. This was the room of a student, or at best, a single, absent-minded professor. It wasn't the room of a person that was in the same place and time I was. It was a room from my past.

Arthur was fully into the sex and was sweating and groaning as he pushed hard into me at a rapidly increasing speed. I couldn't join him in his pleasure, but at least I could make sure that he had a decent orgasm.

I moved my hips faster to urge him along, and I groaned and shook my body so that he would think I was having an orgasm too. I called out his name.

I was relieved that at least the longing and the depth of emotion in my voice as I called out his name was real. I tried to stretch my voice to reach him across the abyss of time that separated us. I called out to him with all of my longing for reconnection. I called out to him in love.

Arthur moaned in response, and then he came. I felt the hot stream of his semen fill me and then trickle in a sticky trail down my thigh. When Arthur was done, he opened his eyes and looked at my face. There were tears in the corners of my eyes as I met his gaze. Arthur thought that they were part of my fake orgasm, and he tenderly wiped them away. He kissed my forehead.

"That was amazing."

Arthur kissed my lips softly after he said this. I nodded and smiled sadly.

"Yes."

I turned on my side and laid my head on his chest so that he wouldn't be in a position to look at my somber expression. I wanted him to be happy. At least for the rest of the time, I was here.

Time would show that I had other priorities. There could always be some new project at work that could be used as an excuse to keep me in New York.

Of course, this line of reasoning totally ignored the fact that by having sex with Arthur today, I was sending a signal to him that I wanted to reconcile. I hadn't figured out how to handle any questions he was sure to bring up about my moving back to Ann Arbor. I could lie and say I wanted to move back, and then I could let my move always be a dot on the horizon that never seemed to get any closer.

Sooner or later, I would have to be honest with Arthur. This would hurt him. Again. And I just couldn't face hurting Arthur this weekend.

"I'm sorry."

I thought this with every fiber of my being. But I didn't say it out loud. I was going to lose something precious to me when I finally lost Arthur for good.

There was no happy course of action for me to play out with Arthur. All I could do was tie up the loose ends of our relationship and hope that somehow, some way, I would still be able to keep him in my life and remain friends with him.

Arthur held me and quickly drifted off to sleep.

But I was wide awake. I thought about what faced me in New York and LA.

Even though I couldn't reconnect with Ann Arbor, at least this visit had given me some clarity. Regardless of where I lived, I needed to somehow stop my downward spiral.

I needed some peace. I had no idea how I was going to find serenity, but at least I was going to try to make a few cosmetic changes in my life that might lead to breathing room.

I stared at the ceiling, my thoughts tumbling over each other as Arthur snored next to me. His air went in and out in a gentle brushing sound, punctuated by the occasional yawn or short gasp for air. I looked over at him, feeling protective. I brushed a few stray, sweaty hairs off his forehead and pulled the blanket and sheet back over him where he had kicked them off. Then I turned to my side, with my back to Arthur, facing the wall.

All I could feel was the quiet of a night that was more than half over and the gentle sounds of Arthur's rhythmic breathing next to me. I finally drifted off to a restless sleep.

CHAPTER 22

The next morning Arthur asked the inevitable question as we drank our coffee and waited for my taxi to pick me up. I needed to go back to my hotel and quickly pack and then proceed to the airport.

"Have you given thought to our discussion about moving back?"

Arthur asked this casually, but he was making sure that he could watch my expression as I answered.

"I need a change. And of course, I really enjoy being with you. I just need to get through these workshops with MV1 in LA in January. Once those are done, I'm going to focus on making changes."

I cringed at my words. They had sounded so practical and reasonable to me when I had laid awake last night coming up with them. But now, in the hazy daylight, they sounded like I was reciting a memorized speech.

To my surprise, Arthur didn't push back. But I died inside when I saw sadness in his eyes. And disappointment. He deserved a better answer than the one I had just given him.

I had known Arthur for ten years. I knew that he didn't like feeling emotional pain. I believed it was best to give him the gift of denial.

Arthur searched my eyes, and by my sheer force of will, he saw no final goodbyes there. He relaxed.

"Yes, of course. You need to wrap up loose ends."

He gave my hand one last squeeze. The taxi blared its horn from the driveway, and we both rose from the sofa and headed downstairs.

I left Arthur with a kiss as I climbed into the taxi.

Arthur's expression was pensive as he said goodbye. I kept my head turned to him while the taxi pulled out of the driveway. When I no longer could see Arthur, I closed my eyes.

PART THREE

CHAPTER 23

My flight home went smoothly. As soon as I stepped out of the terminal at LaGuardia, I felt relief to be out of the bittersweet nostalgia of Michigan. My visit to Ann Arbor had made it clear to me that moving back there was out of the question. For all its flaws, New York was where my life was located now.

As my taxi inched its way along the BQE, I put my headphones on. The song *Road to Nowhere* started to play. I opened the window a crack and let my mind wander.

A part of me felt that I was heading on the road to nowhere. I was heading towards my Brooklyn apartment, but was that really home?

I was 33, and I was exhausted.

I looked at my watch. 12:30. Now that I was back in New York, I needed to get some work done. I had a meeting with Dennis on Monday to plan the January executive briefings. That gave me today and tomorrow to prepare. I had more to discuss with Dennis than just the executive meetings, however. We needed to discuss his expectations of me.

Chris had made it relatively clear that now that I had been promoted, I would be expected to build relationships in the MV1 account. I would also be expected to flirt if necessary to build those relationships.

But how far beyond flirting was I expected to go?

No one would ever answer this question. I needed to figure out a plan myself for doing my job. The problem was, I wasn't clear just what my job was anymore.

Gloria was sitting next to me in the cab. She burst into laughter.

"You could call yourself a 'model' like I called myself if that would make you feel better." Gloria winked.

"I'm an engineer, not a call girl like you." I didn't say this out loud, but Gloria heard me anyway. She shrugged.

"Stephanie darling, you're about as much of an engineer as I am. Dennis isn't interested in your video streaming architectural flow charts. Unless, of course, you wrap yourself in them and wear them to bed."

Gloria stubbed her cigarette out with her stiletto heel and turned to me, her hand on the taxi door handle.

"You're clear-headed about Dennis's motives. Men are so easy to please. If you give Dennis what he wants, you can write your own ticket."

Gloria then opened the taxi door and left.

Gloria was right. Where Dennis was concerned, I knew exactly where I was going. I wasn't an engineer anymore. I was now an account executive, and my job was to please Dennis and the MediaCom executives enough for them to spend millions of dollars on Sun Microtek hardware, software, and services.

Dennis had big plans for me in LA. I knew those plans led to a hotel suite in Beverly Hills with a king-sized bed we both would share. If I was going to sleep my way to success, at least I would have liked to have some sense of what being successful meant to me. But I had no idea.

The rest of the taxi drive home was uneventful. When we got to my apartment, the taxi driver set my luggage to the curb and gave me an enthusiastic exclamation of thanks when I gave him a decent tip. I nodded in reply, giving him a tight smile that didn't reach my eyes.

When I got upstairs, I set my suitcase against the dining table and looked at my watch. 1:00. I pulled my cell phone out of my purse. I had forgotten to turn it back on when I landed. I had a message. It was from my mother. My father had passed away early this morning. The message said that there were no funeral details yet, but it didn't matter. I knew I wouldn't be attending anyway.

I had been back in New York for less than an hour and was confronted with death again already. I looked around my small apartment. My father had never gotten to see it. Or New York.

I needed some air to clear my head and process his death. It was nice outside, cool with a hazy late-fall sun. It was perfect weather for a walk. I grabbed my purse and headed back out my front door, which I hadn't bothered to close yet.

When I got outside, without thinking too much about where I was going, I headed towards the general direction of the Promenade. As I approached the waterfront, there were still remnants of 9/11 altars leaning against fences and street lights. The candles in the makeshift altars had burnt wicks and hardened wax. The flowers were all completely browned and dried.

Even though the altars were decaying, they weren't forgotten. Not by me anyway. I carefully walked around them.

The Promenade was relatively empty. There were a few couples walking arm in arm or holding hands, and a bike whizzed by as I sat down on one of the empty benches facing the river. A puff of ever-familiar dust wafted across the river, giving contrast to the shiny mirrored surfaces of the downtown buildings that had survived. I stared at the bruised Manhattan skyline, with its two empty spaces where the Twin Towers used to be.

As I sat on the bench looking out at the skyline with its gaping wound, Rose joined me. She pointed to the gaping hole in the sky.

"So many people, not enough boats."

Rose wiped a tear out of her eye with her gloved hand. She pointed to the ghosts of those that had died in the Twin Towers, who were now floating above the chilly river watching us. Ghosts with help signs, ghosts that were burnt and bloody, and ghosts that had broken bodies from jumping, were staring at us, saying nothing.

Although he had never stepped foot in New York, my father was also amongst the silent ghosts.

I met their solemn eyes and whispered, "I'm so sorry."

It was such an inadequate response.

I looked away from the river specters. I didn't want to offend their silent, mournful faces. My thoughts were horrible, even if true. I looked down at my hands in shame.

Rose looked out at the gap in the skyline, her eyes haunted, as she quoted one of her lines from *Titanic*.

"1,500 people went into the sea when the Titanic sank from under us...6 were saved from the water, myself included...Afterward, the 700 people in the boats had nothing to do but wait. Wait to die, wait to live, wait for an absolution that would never come."

Rose turned to me, tears in her eyes.

"Remember when we were sitting on this bench two months ago, and I asked you to promise me that you would never let go and never give up?"

Rose's voice was ardent. She touched my arm, her eyes pleading.

Just like the first time she had implored me, I still wasn't sure I could make that promise.

I looked at the specters in the skyline. My eyes filled with tears.

"I'm sorry."

I tried to repeat my earlier apology out loud, but when I opened my mouth, no words came out.

I was sorry my father had died without ever having really lived.

I was sorry I couldn't promise Rose that I wouldn't give up.

I was sorry I hadn't saved anyone on 9/11.

I was sorry I had hurt Arthur.

I was sorry that I was about to sleep my way to the top.

I was sorry that I couldn't feel more sorry.

"I'm sorry!"

I said this in a tormented whisper as I started to cry, tears streaming down my cheeks. I jerked as a hand touched my shoulder. I turned around abruptly in the direction of the hand, thinking it was one of my ghosts.

"Are you all right?"

An older woman in a lavender puffer vest, jeans, and walking shoes was looking at me with concern. I blinked to get the tears out of my eyes. I closed my mouth when I realized it was wide open. Had I been crying out loud just now? I had no idea. I must have been making quite a scene for someone in New York to break the unwritten code of privacy and reach over to see if I was ok.

I looked at her in embarrassment and wiped the trails of tears off my cheeks with a brusque swipe of the back of my hand. I met the woman's concerned stare. My voice was shaky as I said, "I'm fine."

The woman scanned my face, looking completely unconvinced. She pulled her hand off of my shoulder and gave me a nod. She then turned away, continuing her walk down the riverfront.

I watched her lavender puffer-vest recede to a small purple dot in my field of vision. When she was completely gone from my view, I turned to the task of cleaning up my tears. I wiped my blurry eyes with my jacket sleeve. When I could see the Manhattan skyline clearly again, all my ghosts were gone.

I looked around the Promenade. A flock of gulls flew over the river, forming a regimented V shape in the late November sky. I shivered even though the sun was shining on me. It was time for me to go.

I gingerly rose from the bench. I didn't turn around to look at the river or the Manhattan skyline as I left the promenade, but I could feel its presence behind me, letting me know that it had witnessed my tears.

CHAPTER 24

"How was your Thanksgiving?"

Dennis asked me this as he stood near the large picture window in his office. He was looking out at the Midtown skyline. The view displayed several flashing marquees from Broadway theaters, a bunch of billboards, and many tall office buildings. I was sitting in one of the leather chairs that faced Dennis's desk. He motioned me over to the window.

"You have to see this. If you look from just the right angle, you can see a chorus line of Santa and his elves performing on top of the Virgin Records sign. They're dancing Rockette style on top of a billboard. Come take a look."

I walked up to the window. I didn't see anything at first, but then Dennis pointed to the Virgin Records billboard, and I saw the red fur-clad dancers at the top of the lighted sign, on a ledge usually reserved for the painters and workers who put up new billboards. They must have been filming a commercial because no one would have been able to see them dancing up there from the street.

"See them?"

Dennis moved closer. His arm was now around me with his hand pressing into my back, a familiar habit he had developed over the last couple of months. It was a hand positioned to start rubbing my back at any second. I concentrated on keeping my body relaxed.

"I see them now. Cool!"

I gazed up at Dennis. When I replied, the tone of my voice must have been just the right mixture of awe, deference, and gratitude to satisfy him. He turned back to look out the window. I stood there, with his hand on my back, and waited for him to speak.

"Are you ready for LA?"

Dennis's fingers moved lazily back and forth across my back as he said this. I swallowed hard and nodded, focusing on not recoiling from his touch. I forced myself to relax.

Dennis moved closer and turned directly to face me. He pretended to remove a stray piece of lint off my blouse, allowing his hand to brush against my breast as he said, "I'm staying at the Beverly Wilshire. It's very close to Spago. I want us to have dinner there with Derrick and some of the other executives. I think it would be easiest for logistics if you booked there too. You know what a nightmare LA traffic is."

Although Dennis had mentioned the Beverly Wilshire hotel casually, it was clear to me by the possessive look in his eyes that his words were a command.

If this had been a movie, a little devil conscience and a little angel conscience would have appeared in respective mini flames or white puffy clouds and whispered in my ear to represent the two sides of my dilemma with Dennis. The two consciences would have given me advice on how to handle the situation.

"Go for it!" the devil conscience would have said to me, shaking his pitchfork for emphasis.

"Take the moral high ground. Leave the meeting now!" my angel conscience would have said self-righteously, as a choir of angels emphasized her words.

The camera would have zoomed in on my face and would have shown my inner struggle as I succumbed to Dennis's increasingly intimate gestures.

Then the camera would have panned back, allowing a full body shot of Dennis and me standing very close together, his arm around me, caressing me against the panoramic view of Times Square. Dennis would have grabbed me and started kissing me.

How I would have responded to Dennis at that moment would have depended on what genre the movie was.

If the movie was a romance, I would have been swept off my feet to the sappy crescendo of violin music. Dennis and I would have held each other for a long time and kissed passionately, two soul mates that had finally found each other in the hurly-burly of Manhattan.

If the movie was a drama, I would have slapped Dennis's face and stormed out of his office, vowing to myself that I would go to law school and become a labor lawyer so that nothing like this ever happened to any woman again. The last shots of the movie would have flashed forward to a future shot of me in a somber business suit and scholarly glasses, representing another manhandled female client in court, a supreme court judge nodding sympathetically from his esteemed bench.

If the movie was a comedy, either Dennis or I would have slipped and fallen while coming closer to embrace, or someone would have burst into Dennis's office and said something funny, ending the moment between us. The kiss would have happened later in the movie after several slapstick false attempts.

And lastly, if this had been a porn film, Dennis would have kissed me roughly and pushed me on top of his desk, tearing both my and his clothes off. We would have highly choreographed sex with close-ups, and a lot of loud moaning, as a beat-driven disco song played in the background.

But this wasn't any of those movies. This was my life, and I was getting exhausted from trying so hard to look relaxed. I turned to the ghost of the fireman, who had entered Dennis's office and was watching us to see if I needed assistance.

I gave my fireman ghost a brave look tinged with bravado and shook my head when he lifted his fire extinguisher and pointed to Dennis. He nodded and touched the brim of his helmet with his gloved hand as a gesture of goodbye. He then turned to depart, saying nothing. I watched him go, wishing I could leave with him, safe in his arms as he carried me out of Dennis's office.

"I'll have my admin Stacy make the Spago reservations."

Dennis's words startled me. I looked up at him in surprise. Dennis stepped back from the window and walked towards his doorway. I followed him. When he was at his doorway, he shook my hand, holding it a moment too long, his eyes lingering on my breasts, as he said: "This was a productive meeting Stephanie. I'll see you next week."

"Thanks so much for your time Dennis."

I looked up at Dennis and smiled with fake gratitude. Actually, I *was* grateful. I was appreciative that the exhausting meeting was finally coming to a close.

When I got into the elevator, I closed my eyes, relieved to finally be alone. I had just finished what all my peers and management would consider a successful meeting with Dennis. They would all call it a win for the account.

But I didn't feel like I had triumphed. The only winner in that meeting had been Dennis.

I hailed a taxi and climbed in. I knew in my heart that it didn't matter whether my new promotion made me feel like a victor or not. Account executive, or solutions engineer, lap dancer, or private escort, my role in the MV1 account didn't matter. It was all the same. There was no success for me to chase after.

I had success, and this is what it looked like.

As I settled into the cab, I noticed that the ghost of Holly Golightly from *Breakfast at Tiffany's* was already in the back seat. She was in a casual outfit of a white crop sweater and black capri slacks. Holly picked up her dime store guitar and started singing "Moon River." As she strummed her guitar and sang, tears formed in the corners of my eyes.

My huckleberry friend. Arthur had been that at one time.

Before I had changed.

Holly Golightly continued to croon her soulful ballad as I grieved for my dreams of success and a high-powered career in New York. The woman I had been five years ago had pursued a dream of a happy, fulfilling life in New York. She had chased her rainbow's end. But that woman was dead.

I was on my own now.

I closed my eyes and thought about Dennis and the choices I was making to get on with my life in New York amidst the ruins. When I opened my eyes, Holly was gone. She had left her guitar on the seat, abandoned. I sniffled and wiped away my tears.

As the cab driver drove me back to Brooklyn, I thought about my next steps. What happened in LA didn't matter. Whether I slept with Dennis or somehow managed to keep him at bay, I still needed to find a way back to joy and a sense of purpose in my life. I still had to find my rainbow's end. I still had to find a home.

CHAPTER 25

I left baggage claim and headed for the taxi line at LAX. It had been two weeks since my last meeting with Dennis right before Christmas. The holidays had gone by quickly and had been uneventful. I had spent them alone, watching movies in my apartment and preparing for these workshops.

Once outside the terminal, I looked at the palm trees that were lining the road. They seemed so tall and out of place amidst the low, boxy, aging airport. December had gone by so quickly. As much as I had reservations about this trip to LA, I was relieved it was finally 2002, a new year and hopefully a new beginning.

I eagerly looked around for the famous Theme Building that hovered over the airport. It wasn't hard to spot. It looked like a giant flying saucer. I loved mid-century modern design and architecture, and the Theme Building was a monument to mid-century modern aesthetics. It looked like something out of a Jetson's cartoon with its futuristic arches perched above the rest of the airport. I was disappointed the building was closed to the public due to security concerns after 9/11. I had wanted to go to the new restaurant and lounge at the top and get a panoramic view of LA.

I had purchased a disposable camera at the Newark Airport gift shop before boarding my flight to LA, just to get a picture of the Theme Building. I quickly took several shots and put the camera back in my purse. I then made my way to the taxi line. I couldn't believe how perfect the weather in LA was. Sunshine and sixty-eight degrees. It was like every movie cliche that I had ever seen about the city.

Once I was in the taxi and inching along the 405, LA's main North-South highway, I thought about the week ahead. The executive briefings were going to be four days of presentations and project roadmap planning. Executive priorities for upcoming projects would be discussed. Chris was joining the meetings for a couple of days as well.

The MediaCom executives attending this week's briefings controlled all content and technology decisions for MV1, VideoNetwork1, KidsNetwork, Paramount, NBS, and BEN. They were in charge of the purse strings for new projects. If I impressed them, I could potentially sell tens of millions of dollars of Sun Microtek hardware, software, and services to MediaCom. Presenting to these men was a tremendous opportunity. It was the pinnacle of my career up to this point.

Dennis would be attending all meetings and dinners, and it was my job to keep him happy this week. I had met with Chris a couple of days after my last session with Dennis. In that meeting, he had seemed pleased that Dennis had taken such a liking to me.

"Congratulations, Stephanie. You're doing a great job in the account."

Chris had not met my eyes as he complimented me.

Chris would never mention it out loud, but he knew what entertaining Dennis probably entailed. Dinners, drinks, and most likely another strip club, perhaps one of the famous Sunset Strip clubs that had frequently been the scene of so many heavy metal videos in the 1980s.

Of course, Dennis was expecting more this trip than a voyeur's seat at my next lap dance. I kept telling myself it didn't matter what I did with Dennis, that it was just the price I had to pay for so much success in the account. I kept trying to be like Gloria.

But Dennis made my skin crawl.

I had come to New York five years ago to advance my career. I had believed that working hard, and being willing to sacrifice for what I wanted, would lead to the holy grail of Success.

And here I was, five years older, in LA, on my way to a week of high-profile meetings with powerful and influential executives. When I had first begun my career, I would have been excited and grateful to be included in such a strategic and important set of workshops.

But something had changed in me. To be honest, I had started to grow estranged from my career even before 9/11. But the death and chaos of that day, followed by the strange interlude with Michael and my promotion to an account executive, had only made me feel more alienated from the hopeful zeal I formerly approached my career with.

Frankly, I wasn't sure I wanted a career in sales. Pleasing the client and cultivating account relationships at any cost was definitely not what I had signed up for five years ago. My recent victories felt hollow to me somehow.

At this point, I had no idea what I was chasing anymore as I drove in a taxi down I-405 towards Success.

I knew it was an unwritten rule that I could never bring up the sensitive subject of Dennis's sexual interest in me. Account executives were usually men, and it was understood and unspoken amongst all of them that if a bit of fun had to be had to secure a multi-million dollar deal, then whatever the client desired would be arranged.

But I felt uncomfortable trafficking in human flesh to close a deal with MediaCom and MV1, especially when the flesh was my own.

I sighed, hoping a deep breath of the temperate Los Angeles air would clear my misgivings about Dennis and my Sun Microtek management. I was almost to the Beverly Wilshire, and I had a busy afternoon ahead of me. Dennis, Derrick, and a couple of other MediaCom executives wanted to drive out to Burbank this afternoon to conduct a visit to the KidsNetwork studios.

Burbank was about eight miles outside of central Hollywood and was where many game shows, cartoons, live variety shows, and soap operas were filmed. KidsNetwork was a MediaCom subsidiary, and most of their content was filmed in their Burbank studios. The MediaCom executives were especially interested in live streaming KidsNetwork content and wanted me to take a look at how things were produced in the studios.

I had always wanted to get insight into how television shows and movies were made. I was looking forward to the studio visit and the video production meetings. As my taxi approached the Beverly Wilshire, I looked out the window at the stately entrance of the hotel, with its multinational flags and its striped awnings adorning the windows. The hotel reminded me a lot of the Waldorf Astoria back in New York. It had the same dignified, stately presence.

I paid the taxi driver and hopped out of the cab, letting a bag porter take my luggage. The bag porter looked like he was in his mid-twenties, and by his perfectly coiffed hair, suntan, and whitened teeth, I got the impression that he was probably a wannabe actor.

I went to the front counter to check in. I looked around the polished marble lobby with its soft lighting. There was a colossal flower arrangement in the center of the entrance near the elevators and an enormous chandelier hanging over the flowers, giving them a soft luminance. The hotel had the refined vibe of a place that hosted many meetings and business power lunches. My room had been upgraded to a one-bedroom suite on the ninth floor with a balcony view of Rodeo Drive.

The clerk handed my room key to the luggage porter. When we got to my suite, the porter stepped in before me. He flashed his whitened teeth in a practiced smile as he opened the curtains of my balcony view of Rodeo Drive with a flourish and began reciting all the upgrades and features that the room possessed as if he were at an audition for a hotel commercial. The porter was about to demonstrate the wonders of the minibar when I cut his demonstration short. I handed him twenty dollars, which was double what I would have normally given as a tip. I wanted to be alone.

The porter got the hint. He quietly left, closing the door behind him. I walked over to the balcony and looked out at the palm tree-lined Rodeo Drive.

The sunny open vista of Rodeo Drive was so different than the somber grey of New York. There was sun everywhere in LA. It warmed the pavement, lighted the sky, and gave everything a warm glow.

There was no dust anywhere, not even in the hotel room.

I looked out my window at the upscale designer shops, and I thought I saw Julia Robert's character from *Pretty Woman*, Vivian, walking down the street in her tasteful brown dress with the white polka dots that she had worn to the polo match in the movie.

She had gloves on and a wide-brimmed hat with a matching polka dot ribbon. I remembered that the Beverly Wilshire had been the hotel depicted in *Pretty Woman*. Vivian looked happy and confident, much as I had always imagined I would look once I had made it in New York. She looked successful.

I walked out to my balcony and waved to Vivian. To my surprise, she stopped and waved back. I motioned her closer. Without looking to see if there was oncoming traffic, she crossed the street, and before I knew it, she was at my front door. I let her in, and we walked back out to the balcony.

"Nice room! What's up?"

Vivian took a look around my hotel suite from her position on my balcony.

I had called her over to get her advice. She would understand how to handle a man like Dennis. I took a deep breath and asked the question that was on my mind.

"Were all the nameless johns and compromised situations that you endured worth it?"

Vivian didn't seem surprised at the directness of my question. She looked down at her polka dot dress and looked out towards the designer shops. She then turned back to me.

"Love is always worth it."

I was surprised that Vivian's tone was defensive as she said this. She continued:

"You mean if Edward hadn't turned out to be my prince charming? I still think it was worth it. A nice hotel suite, new clothes, a chance to get off the streets. What's not to like?"

I nodded, saying nothing more. Vivian had found a way to stroll the streets of Rodeo Drive in elegant designer clothes, desired by a wealthy man who could provide for her and give her security and status in a hostile world.

She had found her version of Success. Who was I to question that? I changed the subject.

"I could use some tips on how to handle Dennis this week."

Vivian nodded, a look of relief on her face as my question touched on a safer topic.

"Tell him you're going to treat him so nice, he's never gonna let you go."

"No, that's not what I mean…"

"You want to know how to give Dennis what he wants but also keep him at bay. I don't have an answer for that. I always delivered on the services I was paid for."

Vivian shrugged.

"I could give you tips on how to avoid the streets, but that's just geography. Dennis isn't that bad. I've had much worse. Listen, I have to go. Edward is waiting for me. Polo match."

Vivian looked out towards the designer shops of Rodeo Drive as she said this, her eyes wistful. She then shook her head, smiling to herself.

"My advice is, you stay, you kid."

Vivian gave me a pensive smile and turned towards the door, waving goodbye. Once she was back downstairs, I watched her continue her stroll down Rodeo Drive.

Her advice had not helped much. I took one last look at Rodeo Drive and stepped away from the balcony.

Vivian had her destiny, and I had mine.

I looked at my watch. It was almost time for the KidsNetwork studio tour. As I grabbed my purse and headed towards the door to head downstairs to the hotel lobby, my cell phone rang. It was Chris.

My interactions with Chris had been strained before my promotion. Now they were even more so. Since early December, Chris had been giving me advice on how to work with the legal department to get the MV1 contracts processed and how to work with our accounting department to get the MV1 deal recorded against my new quota. Chris was impatient with me as he explained the finance process. Yet because he wanted the deal closed, he called and met with me far more frequently than he had when I had just been an engineer.

As Chris started talking, I could hear a lot of noise in the background on the phone. It sounded like he was on the plane already.

"Just checking in before my flight takes off. I want to catch up on the account before dinner. Let's meet in the hotel bar around five."

I had no desire to meet with Chris one on one today. He would grill me about all the executives at the studio tour. I needed some time to plan my week with Dennis, and I wanted to put off Chris's questions for now. If I postponed debriefing him until right before dinner, it would allow me to give him as brief a recap as possible.

Since my promotion, Chris felt more like an annoying peer than a manager to me. He didn't seem to have any wisdom to impart to me on how to be a successful account manager. Chris liked to appease his clients and keep them happy by giving them whatever they wanted. He had moved into management by inheriting a longstanding account from someone that moved to another company.

Chris's main claim to fame at Sun Microtek was that he was very good at statement-of-work and purchase-order paperwork. If I wanted to get some solid advice on managing Dennis, I would most likely have to look for a new mentor when I got back to New York. Perhaps Brett, Chris's boss, would take me on as a mentee.

But here in LA, this week was more about Dennis than Chris. It would be relatively easy to minimize contact with Chris if I said I was spending that time with Dennis. I decided to blow Chris off as politely as possible.

I made my voice sound cheerful as I replied to him.

"Let's make it 7:00. Dinner's at 7:30, and it's across the street, so there's no traffic."

"That's fine. My flight's taking off. See you then."

I stared at the phone for a moment after Chris hung up. Although Chris was, for the most part, harmless, and meeting with him wasn't that big a burden, I preferred the former lack of interest and distance he had always shown me when I was merely the engineer.

In distance, there was privacy, and I craved some space right now to settle into my new role with Dennis.

CHAPTER 26

I left my hotel room and went downstairs. Dennis was sitting on an olive-colored silk sofa in the visitor's area of the lobby, with Derrick and another man I hadn't met yet. Derrick had a much darker tan than when I had seen him in November. His hair was sun-streaked to a light frizzy blonde. He was wearing a royal blue golf shirt and beige khakis, much like Dennis, only Dennis's shirt was green.

Dennis had shaved his beard, and his face was already sunburned, making his blue eyes stand out. Dennis stood up as he saw me approach. He let his eyes wander up and down my body and then put his hand on my back possessively. He introduced me to the other executive sitting with Derrick.

"Stephanie, this is Robert Billings. He's the Vice President of Strategy, New Business, and Digital Content for KidsNetwork. He was out this way for another meeting this morning, so he came to pick us up and give us the tour of the studios."

Robert shook my hand. He was younger than Derrick or Dennis and looked a couple of years older than me. He was tall and slender, with a fashionable haircut that accented his sideburns. His eyeglasses had funky red plastic frames, and one of his ears was pierced and had a small gold hoop in it. He was wearing a shirt that looked like a vintage bowling shirt, a light grey linen blazer, black jeans, and expensive-looking purple track shoes.

"I'm psyched about the design sessions. We have so many ideas for expanding our digital properties. Kids will be interacting a lot online, and I want KidsNetwork to be a go-to portal for kids."

As Robert spoke about his vision for KidsNetwork, he waved his hands in the air in front of him enthusiastically. He inadvertently leaned in closer to me. In reaction, Dennis moved closer to me as well and started rubbing my back with his left hand. I smiled at Robert and nodded in response to what he was saying.

Ironically, if I had been in a room with Robert alone, I would have gone to the whiteboard in his office or whatever conference room we were in, and I would have started outlining my ideas enthusiastically. I was interested in what Robert was talking about. I agreed that digital platforms and streaming video would be a growth area moving forward, especially for properties like KidsNetwork that catered to the youth market.

But I couldn't get into a technical discussion with Robert right now. It would annoy Dennis. Dennis would see it as me taking charge of the discussion.

So I kept quiet and let Robert finish his thought. With no one to continue the discussion on digital programming for KidsNetwork, the conversation soon turned to the safe topics of the planned dinner later and the weather. Dennis mentioned that we were having dinner at Spago.

"Reservations are for 7:30. They're preparing a special tasting menu for us, with wine pairings from California wineries. It should be quite a dinner."

Dennis said this to Robert, with a glint of excitement in his eyes, as we waited for the valet parking porter to retrieve Robert's car, which was a shiny silver Mercedes convertible.

Derrick went to the passenger seat, leaving the tiny back seat for Dennis and me. We all climbed in, and Robert pulled out of the hotel drive. Derrick was the first to break the silence that had settled over us.

"Stephanie, have you been to a production studio before?"

"No, not a real one. I've been to the fake ones at the Universal Studios theme park in Florida, and I've been to live studios like the *Saturday Night Live* set, but not a full production studio."

"The Florida theme park is also a full studio. We do some KidsNetwork production out there, although not as much as we used to."

Robert said this as he cursed at a blonde woman in a white convertible that cut him off while he tried to merge onto the highway. I thought of *American Graffiti* and Richard Dreyfuss's character, Curt's, quest to find the blonde in the white Thunderbird convertible. He spent the whole movie searching for her.

Only her car was a white Porsche, not at T-Bird, and this woman didn't smile suggestively in a come hither way to Robert as Suzanne Somers had smiled to Curt in *American Graffiti*.

Instead, the blonde in the white Porsche gave the finger to Robert and cut him off a second time. Robert cursed and slammed on the brakes, sending Dennis and me flying towards the front seats. I grabbed onto Derrick's seat back for support, and Dennis put his arm in front of me protectively so I wouldn't slam into Derrick's seat.

"Are you ok?"

Dennis turned to me with concern. I adjusted my blouse, which had pulled back as I had flung forward, revealing a glimpse of my bra. Dennis's eyes instinctively went from my face to my chest as I adjusted my blouse. I sat back in the seat.

Dennis continued to stare at my chest. Somehow in all of the confusion of the hard stop on the freeway, his hand had ended up on my leg. Dennis's hand felt warm and sweaty, resting on my thigh. I steeled myself to endure his hand for the rest of the car ride. It was just a hand on my thigh. It didn't matter.

Derrick looked pointedly at Dennis's hand on my thigh and gave a knowing glance to Dennis. They exchanged quick grins before Derrick turned to me. Derrick's tone was professional, but it had a tinge of familiarity now that he saw Dennis's hand on my leg.

"What's the *Saturday Night Live* studio like? Did you ever go to a live taping?"

I had attended a taping. My coworker Jeff had been the architect on the NBC account and had gotten seats for a show, and I had gone with him last year. I had been shocked at how small the actual theater was.

Jeff had been excited to see Bon Jovi perform live. They didn't disappoint and performed two of their iconic '80's hair metal songs. I had enjoyed the show.

Jeff was happily married with two kids and lived in Yorktown, a Westchester suburb of New York. He had initially planned on giving me both tickets so that I could invite someone, but when he found out that Bon Jovi was the musical guest, he had kept one of the tickets. We had gone for a beer after the taping.

Having a fun evening out with Jeff had made me feel very lonely. The truth was, I wouldn't have had anyone to go to the show with me if he hadn't wanted to go.

I had expected to make a lot of interesting friends when I moved to New York. In all the movies I had ever seen about New York, the main characters always had an exciting social life. I had expected the same and was bewildered why I had ended up so alone.

It was an odd memory to have as I was sandwiched in a car, slowly inching towards Burbank with Dennis's hand on my thigh.

"The studio was so small. But I got to see a pretty good taping. Lou Reed was on that night, although he didn't sing."

"Who sang?"

Robert asked this as he started to inch towards our exit lane.

"Bon Jovi. I remember that show because I watched it live and also taped it to watch again later. I love Lara Flynn Boyle. She was hosting that week."

Dennis said this before I could answer Robert.

"Isn't she the actress in that movie *Threesome*?" Derrick asked Dennis in a teasing tone as he gave me a suggestive look. Dennis chuckled and nodded. He squeezed my leg again.

"Lara Flynn Boyle was in *Twin Peaks* too. She's a pretty good actress. Don't judge her by that one movie."

Robert said this matter-of-factly as he slowed down and turned onto Olive Avenue and the animation studio lot.

The KidsNetwork studio was a long warehouse-shaped building. It was white, with the words "KidsNetwork Animation" painted in puffy red letters across the side. Many of the cartoons were produced for KidsNetwork here. Sitcoms and live-action shows were produced at the Hollywood studios.

"Albie Hecht designed this studio. Albie designed it to be like the chocolate factory in Willie Wonka and the Chocolate Factory." Robert pointed to the building as he said this, much like a tour guide would point out an attraction on a bus tour.

"I think you're going to love it here, Stephanie," Dennis whispered in my ear, his lips brushing against my earlobe. Before Dennis could say anything more, Robert opened the driver's side door and got out of the car.

"This way."

Robert pointed to a door in the middle of the white and red building and headed towards the entrance with Derrick close behind him. Dennis and I quickly got out of the car and followed.

When all of us were in the lobby, Robert started pointing out some of the highlights of the animation studio.

"We currently house 200–300 employees here, and we can accommodate up to five simultaneous productions. We do post-production here as well."

Robert smiled proudly as he recited the studio facts. The central area where we were standing looked like it could have been the set for one of KidsNetwork's shows. It had purple, red, and bright green lounge chairs and a fountain that spouted green water. The hall was a wide-open expanse with production rooms lining the walls behind a row of closed doors. Robert motioned us forward, leading us down a bright green hallway.

"Up ahead is the indoor basketball court and screening room. Let's have a quick look."

Robert opened the door with a flourish.

"Games are hosted here weekly for our employee league, and we also have pick-up games whenever there's interest."

The basketball court could have been any high school basketball court anywhere, except for the movie screen and fancy projection equipment. It had bleachers, a typical wood basketball floor, and large screens on both sides of the stands, as well as in the front of the court so that you could watch what was being played from any seat. Robert was about to go into more detail about the court, but Dennis interrupted him and turned to me.

"Want to play a one-on-one pickup game, Stephanie?"

Dennis said this loudly enough for everyone to hear him. He must have thought he was being funny because he looked around the room for a reaction. No one was looking in our direction. Dennis pressed his body closer to me. He then put his arms around my waist and picked me up off the ground.

Derrick finally turned to look at us, and as Dennis put me back down but kept his arms around my waist, Derrick gave me a once-over and laughed.

"That's a game I can't wait to watch, Dennis."

Since I first met him in November, Derrick had reminded me of a European Beavis from *Beavis and Butthead*. This was especially true today. His long face, squinty eyes, and frizzy blonde hair bore a vague resemblance to Beavis. But the fundamental similarity was his smirk and his laugh. Derrick's laugh as he watched Dennis pick me up was the giggle of a thirteen-year-old boy hoping to cop an accidental feel of a stray breast during gym class.

I expected Dennis to respond to Derrick's comment and play Butthead to his Beavis, but he just chuckled, saying nothing more.

I looked across the basketball court, trying to avoid Derrick's smirk. Robert was looking at me with discomfort. I would have loved to think that Robert's discomfort was because I was being made the butt of an adolescent joke between Derrick and Dennis.

But Robert looked more like a novice actor on stage, who had forgotten part of his prepared speech, than someone who was appalled by Dennis's behavior.

I considered my options of how to respond to Dennis.

If I reacted in anger, I would be jeopardizing my standing in the account. If I acted like I enjoyed Dennis's comments and arms around me, I would be seen as open to more of the same moving forward. If I did nothing, I would be ignoring Dennis, which as an account executive, I couldn't do. And lastly, if I put Dennis in his place with a reciprocal joke, I would be seen as insulting the client.

Dennis still had his arms around me, and he was squeezing all the oxygen from my lungs. I called out to the ghost of the fireman for help. He responded and appeared in full firefighter battle gear. He had an oxygen mask on, covering his mouth. He took it off and handed it to me, motioning for me to put it on. The mask looked too complicated to handle myself. I gave the fireman a helpless look. He put it on for me.

I took in the oxygen. When I was breathing steadily, the fireman took the mask off me. He gave me a wave and then put the oxygen mask back on his mouth and left the basketball court. I turned back to Dennis.

I decided to try my hand at a joke that wasn't insulting.

"Why look at you, Dennis, trash-talking, and the game hasn't even started yet!"

I made my voice sound teasing and seductive as I said this. I also pasted a big smile on my face, and I touched Dennis's arm lightly for emphasis.

Dennis grinned and nodded appreciatively in response to my comment. He looked down at my hand touching his arm, and his pupils dilated, showing me a small flame hiding beneath them. I pulled my hand away slowly and looked down with what I hoped looked like a shy look so that I could avoid the heat of his gaze.

Derrick grinned and said,

"Watch out for those penalty points, Dennis!"

"Ok, let's go, everyone. We need to meet everyone in studio five."

Robert looked at Derrick and Dennis as he said this. I wasn't sure exactly what the power dynamics between Derrick, Robert, and Dennis were, but I knew that Robert was the highest rank executive amongst them. This made Robert's suggestion effectively an order.

I let Dennis's hand resume its position on my back, and we both stepped back into the hallway. Dennis held the door for me, and I somehow ended up pressed against him when we both walked through the door.

"You excite me, Stephanie."

Dennis whispered this in my ear, his lips grazing my earlobe in a combination nibble and kiss. I felt my throat clench and my armpits moisten with panic sweat.

I hadn't expected to field Dennis's physical advances until later tonight. But the workshops hadn't even officially started, and Dennis was acting like we were already in his hotel room alone.

I looked up at Dennis and gave him what I hoped was a look that implied that his machismo and charisma left me nervous and aflutter. I then pulled away from him to enter the animation studio.

The studio looked like a living room. There were cushy armchairs and ottomans in purple, gold, red, and blue scattered around the room. There was also a huge plasma movie screen and several smaller plasma screens as well. The work tables were on wheels and could be pushed to form a larger conference table. Three large rolling whiteboards were positioned around the armchairs. Two men around my age and a young woman were huddled around one of the whiteboards, discussing some notes that someone had put on the whiteboard.

"Stephanie, I'd like you to meet Alex, our Director of Long-Form Content, Mark, our manager of digital content, and Beth, our new content engineer. They will be responsible for working with you to come up with a solution for streaming a preview and series of web advertisements for the new *Rugmice* movie we're producing."

Robert walked towards the whiteboard where Beth, Mark, and Alex were sitting. All three of them came over to shake my hand. Mark and Alex each gave me a friendly smile as they introduced themselves. Beth also smiled, although she seemed shy. She looked like she was in her early to mid-twenties. She had long black hair with bangs and blue eyes like me. She was wearing a simple white button-down blouse and black jeans. The outfit made her look like a waitress or bartender in a trendy restaurant.

Beth kept looking down and kept wiping her palms on her jeans. There was an eager light in her eyes as she nervously shook my hand.

"I've heard a lot about how you're going to lead this project, and I'm very excited to get to work with you."

Beth continued to hold onto my hand as she said this. When she realized what she was doing, she gasped and pulled her sweaty hand away.

I tried to hide my amusement as I wiped my palm on my leggings to get Beth's sweat off them. Beth ran her fingers nervously through her straight black hair. The look of admiration in her eyes caused me to pause. She seemed to be looking up to me. I was definitely not anyone to revere. I wondered if Beth would think so highly of me if she saw me taking a lap dance for Dennis.

I saw Derrick give Beth an appraising look as he continued to talk to Dennis.

"Alex, Mark, you've met Dennis and Derrick before. Let's get started, shall we? We'll start with the concept we're trying to digitize, and then let's work on a high-level plan. Lunch will be brought in. I want to try to get clear next steps today and an overall approach. Everyone, please take a seat."

Robert said this in a tone of authority as he glanced at all of us and then sat down in one of the chairs. Dennis and Derrick nodded and started to move to a couple of arm-chairs.

I focused my attention on Alex and Mark, who had started putting several tables together to form a conference table. They both looked like most of the engineers I worked with. They had on casual long-sleeved pastel blue shirts with the sleeves rolled up and expensive jeans. Their hair was styled in almost identical neat haircuts that were slicked back slightly with hair product. They looked like twins, except that Mark was shorter than Alex.

Beth was still standing in front of me. She turned around when she heard the wheeling of the tables. She looked mortified that she wasn't helping her management with the setup.

"Excuse me!"

Beth turned to help Mark and Alex. I stood and watched her awkwardly try to find a way to help. Mark and Alex ignored her, and with no direction from them, she made a flash decision to pull one of the armchairs over to the makeshift conference table. But the armchair wasn't on wheels, so she was making a spectacle of herself trying to push a chair that wasn't meant to move. Alex looked at her with annoyance.

"We'll be using the big screen, and the chairs are all positioned already to see it. Mark and I are setting up the tables for lunch. It should be here shortly."

I watched Beth's face flush. She looked around the room to see if everyone was watching her mistake. Derrick and Dennis were seated next to each other, quietly chatting. While they were talking, Dennis was looking at me. His eyes motioned subtly to the chair on the other side of him. I nodded and turned my eyes back to Beth. Derrick also turned his eyes to Beth and appraised her again, his eyes roaming up and down her body.

My eyes were on Beth. I could see her mortification. I had stumbled through my first meetings as a solutions engineer five years ago, making many similar errors to the one that Beth had just made. She would probably run this mistake over and over in her mind, torturing herself with her faux pas.

Derrick interrupted my thoughts. He motioned to Beth.

"Hey...what's your name again? Beth? Come sit on the other side of me. Mark and Alex can finish setting up for lunch."

Derrick winked at Beth and patted the seat next to him. Dennis and Derrick shared a brief amused look between them. Then Derrick turned back to Beth.

"Don't be scared, honey. I won't bite. At least not until later tonight."

Derrick patted the chair again. Alex looked over at Beth and then tilted his head in the direction of the chair, effectively giving her an order to sit there. Mark didn't look up from his task of adjusting the height of one of the rolling tables to match the others. Robert was talking on his cellphone.

I turned to Beth. Her eyes were gently pleading. She searched my eyes for a clue as to how to proceed.

In my mind, I advised Beth that Derrick was a classless pig and that she should run. In my imagination, I pulled a chair up for her far away from any hand pats, back rubs, or winks. In my internal dialogue, I told Beth to say "no" now or forever hold her peace.

But in reality, my mouth stayed shut. I said nothing.

With Dennis here, I was the entertainment. I was the show.

And because I was on stage, I couldn't help Beth. Not any more than an actress or stripper on stage can help someone in the audience who is having a personal crisis during the show. There was an invisible wall between Beth and me.

I had to concentrate on my own performance.

When Beth didn't find the guidance and support she was looking for in my eyes, she turned away. I could feel her disappointment.

Beth shrugged and turned to Derrick. She sat down next to him, and almost immediately, his hand was on her knee as he leaned in close to her and said loud enough for all of us to hear.

"See, I told you I didn't bite!"

I walked over to the seat that Dennis had designated for me and sat down.

"Ready to wow me?"

Dennis leaned over and whispered this in my ear.

I was thinking of a reply when Robert spoke first.

"Alex or Mark, can you give Stephanie an overview of what we're trying to accomplish with the *Rugmice* streaming project?"

Alex nodded and pointed to the whiteboard.

"We're in the middle of production for the third *Rugmice* movie, *Rugmice go Wild*. Its release date is mid-2003. This movie is going to be a crossover piece with *The Wild Thornberrys*...."

Robert interrupted Alex.

"We want to see more cross-marketing and reuse amongst our content, especially movies. My hope for the Digital Division is that we plan cross use from the getgo and build it right into our approach."

Robert looked over at me. He was waving his hands enthusiastically, and his words were tripping over themselves, trying to get out. Robert clearly had a passion for this plan, and I found myself nodding as he spoke. I leaned forward with interest towards Robert. I had a soft spot for anyone with creative passion, and Robert's ideas made perfect sense. He was onto something.

"If we can get properties cross-marketed through coordinated live streaming events, for example, streaming several shows live in a coordinated event, we should be able to streamline costs while increasing content views."

Robert's eyes flashed with excitement as he said this. I thought about the possibilities of having coordinated live streaming events and how relatively simple it would be to combine content and do combined promotions and previews. As I leaned in to listen more intently to Robert, Dennis increased the pressure of his hand on my thigh.

I forced my body to pull back in my chair, and I turned to Dennis and gave him an excited smile, gesturing to the whiteboard to let him know I was excited about the technology, not Robert. When Dennis saw that I was merely enthused about video streaming, I felt him relax his grip on my leg. He turned to Robert.

"This is great stuff. My team in New York and LA will provide whatever IT support is needed to support this venture. Network changes, extra encryption, and security, just let us know what you need."

Robert nodded absently, turning to Alex.

"Alex, can you please explain my concept to everyone. And make sure you mention the Apple angle."

"We want to be able to show previews of the new *Rugmice* movie live on our websites. We want to create content-specific websites as well and live stream from those sites. We've also been talking with Apple. They're telling us that they're planning on launching a new application to purchase and stream music called iTunes. Video will follow a year or so afterward. The goal will be to sell their customers videos much the way they plan to sell music next year. We want to be ready to add our properties to this iTunes player and store when the time comes."

With the mention of Apple, even Derrick perked up and turned to look at Alex. Since they had released their digital music player, the iPod, Apple was the hottest company around. If they were going to be putting movies and television content into a music and video player, that would be a substantial new revenue stream for KidsNetwork and all the other MediaCom divisions.

I looked over to Beth to see if she understood what Robert was saying and to see whether she was showing any of the enthusiasm that I would have shown at her age. Beth wasn't even looking at Robert. She was looking down at her hands as Derrick stroked her leg and whispered something in her ear. She looked miserable. I turned my eyes away from her. I needed to stay focused.

"What do you think of this strategy, Stephanie?"

Robert asked this, looking at me directly. Dennis turned to me as well. He didn't look happy that Robert was addressing me directly.

I wasn't expecting Robert to ask me such an important and key question. I had two options on how to reply to him. I could answer in a vague but amicable manner and tell him that I would "follow up with Headquarters." That would be what Chris would do.

Or, I could let Robert know what I really thought.

I thought about my new role as account executive. My job was to sell. To close the deal.

But what was I selling exactly? And to whom?

I had never wanted to sell my attention, my body, or even my ideas. I would much rather give of myself freely. By choice.

Chris had advised me repeatedly to keep quiet and let Dennis do all the talking during these briefings. But I was sick of keeping my mouth shut.

Besides, even though my Macintosh laptop and iPod were brand new, I was already sick of Steve Jobs and the Apple hype. I turned to Robert, my words taking on a volition of their own as I said:

"I think if you can get Apple to help you now, that's great. But Apple tends to think of Apple first."

"Why do you think Apple won't help us?"

Robert looked intrigued by my comment. I knew I should just retreat from my remarks and move on, but I wanted a real conversation: even if that discussion ruined my career. I took a deep breath and smiled at Robert before continuing.

"I think Steve Jobs is a narcissist. I read a book on NeXT, the company that Steve Jobs formed when he left Apple, and it said that Jobs always does what's in his interest. That's all fine if what is best for KidsNetwork aligns with Jobs. But if not, you might be disappointed."

I gave Robert a smile that looked far more assured than I felt. My voice was shaking.

I could feel how annoyed Dennis was at my growing dialogue with Robert. His hand was no longer on my leg as if this was some sort of punishment for me. He was tapping his fingers restlessly on the table next to his chair and looking at me with displeasure.

Usually, upsetting a client would have made me feel terror that I was doing a bad job. Strangely I felt calm. Except for my anger at Dennis. Why did I have to be his personal sock puppet that sat on his lap and only spoke words sanctioned by him?

The promotion and the money weren't worth it to me.

"How do you know what traits a narcissist has, Stephanie? Are you one yourself?"

Dennis said this in a way that was meant to be a joke, but his frustration with me gave his voice an edge. I breathed inward and swallowed my rising anger. This was not the time to fight with Dennis. What would be the point? I would be the only one hurt. I tried to think of a reply. Robert interjected first.

"She works in sales, Dennis. I think she's met her share of over-inflated egos."

Robert winked at me, and I smiled in gratitude.

Robert continued his eyes on me, drawing the conversation back to Apple.

"You have a point, Stephanie. I know not to trust Apple completely. They have their own agenda to be sure. But it's still more cost-effective to distribute our content on their platform than to try to create our own."

"Apple can provide the audience through their video player when it launches, but if they're going to take a huge fee for each download, it may end up being a bad deal to use their platform."

My voice sounded more excited than I expected as I said this. I looked at my hands and noticed they were gesturing in front of me with the same enthusiasm that was in my tone.

It was bittersweet to feel passion for my work again. What place did passion have in my new role as an account executive and Dennis's plaything?

Nevertheless, I felt the magnetic pull of Robert's words and leaned in towards him as he replied.

"It's always about money in the end. But if we have to spend millions to drive eyeballs to an untested platform, I don't see how Apple's fees could end up surpassing that. It's worth further exploration from both sides."

Robert stood up after he said this, and that was everyone's cue to do the same. I felt the angry heat of Dennis's glower as I stood up. I didn't care.

Even though I was now standing and facing Robert, I could still feel the imprint of Dennis's hand on my leg. I kept my eyes on Robert.

I was sick of worrying about Dennis. When I looked at his irritated, possessive face, and I thought of just how much more he planned on extracting from me in exchange for setting up these meetings, my face flushed in anger.

The price for these meetings had simply become too high for me.

"Stephanie, is something wrong? Do you need to sit down?"

Dennis's tone held a mixture of fake concern and sarcasm. He was clearly angry that I had spoken out. I should have kept my mouth shut and let him take the lead, as Chris had advised in one of our one-on-ones.

Fuck, Chris.

I was sick of keeping my mouth shut. Even though it was a mixed blessing to feel excitement for Robert's ideas, at least I felt alive when I listened to them. I turned to Dennis.

"No, I'm fine. Thanks for asking."

It took complete focus to make my tone sound neutral. I couldn't quite manage a smile, however, so I concentrated on not letting my expression turn into a grimace.

I had come to LA this week knowing that I would be Dennis's geisha girl during the workshops. But the sight of Dennis's petulant expression, with his arms crossed in sulky discontent, and his mouth pursed in a frown, was making every cell in my body suddenly stand in resistance and scream "NO."

I didn't want to be Dennis's lap dancer.

I wanted to flee this meeting and find a safe place where I was free of his pawing hands and suffocating expectations of me.

I couldn't leave, however. There was nowhere to go.

I refocused on the room. My hands were shaking, but not from a passion for Robert's ideas. My hands were shaking in anger.

Fuck Dennis.

I had planned on keeping myself numb to get through the week, as I had for months with Michael and even Arthur. But now, I suddenly found myself angry and alert.

"Sit down for a minute, Stephanie, if you need to. We don't want you to be uncomfortable."

Dennis didn't bother to keep the edge out of his voice when he said this. Everyone turned to look at him, including Robert, who scanned his face curiously. Robert then looked me over. I'm not sure what he saw in my tense expression and shaking hands, but he nodded to himself before turning back to Dennis.

"She said she's fine. I have a suggestion. Let's save the rest of the workshops for tomorrow. Stephanie, are you ok with moving them?"

"That would be great. Thanks, Robert."

The words left my mouth before Robert had even finished talking.

"Perfect. Let's break for now and reconvene at dinner, shall we? Stephanie, do you have a few minutes to meet one-on-one with me right now to go over what we just discussed? Now that we've freed up some time, I would like to capture a few points while they're fresh in my mind."

Robert nodded goodbye to Dennis and the rest of the team and motioned for me to follow him as he started walking towards his office.

I could feel Dennis glaring at me, and I knew I would have to deal with his anger later. As I walked with Robert and Dennis faded behind me, I stopped caring about the repercussions of taking this meeting with Robert and postponing the rest of the workshops. A meeting with an executive could always be explained. And besides, I was intrigued as to what was so crucial that Robert wanted to discuss it now.

CHAPTER 27

"After you."

Robert motioned me into his office, which was a sizeable loft-like room. There were floor-to-ceiling windows that overlooked a palm tree-lined view of the KidsNetwork campus. A huge plasma television was mounted to a wall decorated in graffiti of slogans from KidsNetwork shows such as "A baby's gotta do what a baby's gotta do" the famous Tommy Tomato line from *Rugmice*.

On the left side of the office was a coffee bar with an elaborate espresso machine and a small refrigerator. A turquoise leather sectional filled the middle of the room, and a modern teak desk lined the right wall. Scattered around the office were several intriguing statues of various KidsNetwork characters. A statue of Sponge-Rob was being used as a coat rack, and one of the Rugmice was holding up yet another plasma television. A small basketball net hung in the back right-hand corner of the office with some crumpled paper wads scattered on the floor around it, suggesting that Robert had thrown them through the hoop at some point.

"Have a seat anywhere, Stephanie."

Robert pointed to the leather sectional. I sat down. He took off his linen jacket and hung it on Sponge-Rob.

"Can I get you an espresso or something to drink?"

I didn't want to distract from the purpose of the meeting by having Robert tinker with what looked like a highly complex coffee maker.

"I'll have some bottled water if you have it, thanks."

Robert pulled a Pellegrino water out for himself and then walked over towards the sectional. He handed me an Evian and sat down a couple of cushions away from me. When he opened his Pellegrino, the hissing fizz echoed in the quiet room. I was surprised that a room that was so colorful and vibrant could be so still.

Robert set his water down on the table and turned to me.

"Are you happy working for Sun Microtek?"

I was startled at his direct question. I tried to mask my surprise by opening my Evian and taking a slow, careful sip.

I looked around the office, buying myself a moment before I answered. In the corner, by the basketball net, Vivian was standing in her street hooker clothes. It was the first time I had seen any of my ghosts since my brief interlude with the fireman at the basketball court. Vivian pulled off her Walkman headphones, letting them hang around her neck. She gave me a friendly smile before she spoke.

"You've got a great hotel room at the Beverly Wilshire, and two guys are interested in you: one for your brains and one for your body. Sounds like a good problem to have."

Vivian adjusted her spandex micro mini skirt. She then straightened her blond wig and sat down on the sectional. She pointed to Robert.

"Don't let your new john get away. Answer his question about whether you are happy working at Sun Microtek, but remember to protect yourself. Safety first."

I turned to Robert, who was observing me earnestly. There was something in his eyes that made me want to answer him honestly. I gave Vivian a slight nod of acknowledgment before I answered Robert.

"No, not really."

"Why?"

I looked beyond Robert to Vivian, who was also watching me. She had grabbed a handful of jelly bellies from a jar on the table and was picking out the purple ones.

"Purple reminds me of Prince. I just love Prince."

I thought of Gloria fleeing New York in *Butterfield 8*. At the end of the movie, she had driven her car off a cliff and crashed it as she tried to escape to a new life in Boston. No matter how much she had wanted to change, there was no way out for Gloria in *Butterfield 8*. She died a call-girl, alone, at the bottom of a ravine.

I wanted to escape my present situation with Dennis as much as Gloria had wanted to flee her life in the movie. I wanted my life to change. And although it was unlikely that my fate would be identical to Gloria's if I told Robert the truth, I could still wind up ending my career, if not my life.

I still wanted to take the chance. If I answered Robert honestly, he would at least know that I wasn't a soulless salesperson or a mindless account executive.

"Tell him the truth. Sometimes a prince charming can save you."

Vivian said this as if she were trying to convince herself as well as me. I turned to Robert. I decided to give him a bit of truth. But when I opened my mouth to speak, more than just a bit of truth spilled out.

"I'm sick of sales and account management. I'm sick of pretending to like ideas I don't. And. . . people I don't. I want to create something cool with technology. But I feel like I'm getting further and further away from that."

I thought about how Dennis was expecting sexual favors from me. Why had I even bothered to go back to school and work so hard after quitting my Ph.D. program? My hard-earned knowledge was useless.

I glanced over at Vivian, who was moving in her seat to the beat of a Prince song blaring loud enough to be heard from her Walkman headphones.

216

Perhaps not. Maybe being better educated made me a better candidate to capture the attention of men like Dennis. Maybe Dennis liked the "Naughty Nerd" stripper/hooker stereotype.

I felt trapped. I expected to feel claustrophobic by my lack of choices. But instead, I felt reckless and giddy.

I grinned to myself as I surrendered to my metaphorical cliff. I quickly put my hand over my mouth, hoping Robert couldn't see my strange reaction, but it was too late.

"What's so funny?"

Robert was looking at me with curiosity. Vivian turned to look at me as well.

To explain my grin to Robert, I would have to explain the entire sordid account pecking order and client entertainment rule book. But given that Robert had been around a while, I'm sure he knew perfectly well what went on at client dinners and after-dinner outings. He needed no explanation from me.

I had no idea if he approved of such goings-on or not.

"I was just thinking about how so much of my job lately has been about entertaining and pleasing Dennis, but how little of my ideas are required or desired to please him."

"Why is that funny?"

Robert said this thoughtfully. He leaned in closer to me, but it didn't feel like he was invading my personal space or being suggestive. Vivian was leaning towards me as well. She looked interested in what I was saying.

"It's not funny. It's the opposite of funny, frankly. I want to provide interesting solutions to content streaming problems. But lately, I've been spending more time entertaining Dennis than solving any technical problems. I think I grinned just now because it felt both refreshing, to be honest with you, and reckless as well."

I reached for my bottle of water after giving the longish answer, taking a big gulp. My guess was that other account executives never used a meeting with Robert as a de facto therapy session. I felt quite audacious.

My whole mood at the moment was much like the end of a movie where the hero throws up her arms and walks away from her car or building just as it's about to explode and be consumed in flames. It was easier to walk away from the fire, even if it ended up being the death of my tenure at Sun Microtek.

As Robert paused to consider my words, Vivian stood up. She checked the safety pin on her patent leather boot.

"Interesting thoughts Hon, but I need to make rent this month, so I'm going to get to work. Maybe Robert's your prince. Give him a chance. You take care of you kid."

After she said this, Vivian exited through the office door, giving Robert a thoughtful once-over before she turned away and left.

Robert stroked his goatee as he took in my words, which made me feel like he was sincerely trying to understand what I was saying. I could hear my heart beating in the quiet of the office.

"Dennis does like his fine dining."

Robert said this neutrally. He took a sip of his Pellegrino water. Before I could stop myself, I blurted out what I was thinking.

"He likes his lap dances as well."

My words hung in the air. I didn't put my hand over my mouth or apologize for saying them. I felt an odd wave of relief as I held still under Robert's surprised gaze. I had now truly done the worst that I could do. I had just accused my executive sponsor of liking back-room pussy.

To my total surprise, Robert grinned.

"Touche."

My hands were shaking from a mixture of adrenaline, fear, and defiant self-destruction. I clasped them in my lap. Robert looked pointedly at my hands.

Why do you think being direct with me is a risk, Stephanie?"

"Talking with any executive is a risk."

"I can assure you, there's no risk in talking to me. I believe in innovation, and that requires honesty sometimes."

If Dennis had said these same words, they would have had an air of pomposity about them. But there was something in Robert's relaxed, introspective expression and his earnest tone that made me feel like he might actually mean what he was saying.

"On that note, you're probably wondering why I asked you to this follow-up meeting. I inquired about whether you were happy at your current job at Sun because I have an opening on my team to lead the Apple iTunes content project, and I think you could be a good fit for the job."

Robert's eyes brightened with enthusiasm as he mentioned the iTunes project.

"We have a chance to open up content distribution and reach a whole new audience, perhaps internationally. Imagine being able to watch a show anytime, anywhere. I think this is the future."

As I listened to Robert talk about the job, his enthusiasm was infectious. A small flame lit itself within me. My excitement hurt, but the pain was cleansing, like when antiseptic was poured on a scraped knee. Robert continued.

"I've heard excellent feedback about your meetings with Dennis and his technical staff. He gave me a briefing in December about the work his team is doing with you, and I think you have the skills that this project is going to need."

I was surprised at what Robert was saying. I had been so focused on my obligation to entertain Dennis this week and Chris's advice to keep quiet and let Dennis shine that it had never occurred to me that I might have anything to offer to any of the other executives.

"Don't you have anyone internal working on the project?"

"I'd like to hire someone who comes from outside the MediaCom food chain and has a broader point of view. My goal will be to use Apple as a springboard for distributing our content on other platforms as well."

"Yes. If we let Apple control format, we'll be hamstrung from exploring other opportunities."

We. I was taken aback by my presumptiveness. I knew very little about Robert, other than he had a cool office. What if he turned out to be another Dennis? There would be no point in uprooting myself and moving to the West Coast if my life would be the same as it was in New York.

To be fair, I had no cause to believe that Robert would be a jerk. He seemed like a pretty decent guy. Besides, I had no job offer yet or even the hint of one. I should at least let Robert explain his thoughts before I started looking for reasons to shut him down.

"What do you have in mind?"

"I've decided I need someone technical to run the Apple iTunes project. Apple will force their design and policies if there is no one to push back."

"But wouldn't you want to hire someone from Silicon Valley or someone who understands Apple?

I hated that I had asked the question. I looked around the room to see which of my ghosts was going to lecture me for making such a stupid move. I expected Gloria or Vivian to laugh at Rose or me to give me a sympathetic look. But instead, it was Tess who showed up. She was standing by the doorway in her borrowed suit. She gave me an understanding smile.

"I've been in your shoes before. Don't let Robert know you've never negotiated. Act like you know what you're doing, and you'll close the deal."

I nodded. Tess gave me a zealous look as she continued.

"Don't spend the rest of your life working your ass off and getting nowhere just because you followed rules that you had nothing to do with setting up, okay?"

Tess ran her fingers through her new professional haircut and buttoned her borrowed suit jacket. She took a wistful look around Robert's office.

"I always wanted an office just like this."

She gave me a melancholy smile. Her eyes held mine for a moment, offering encouragement as she whispered, "Good luck. Grab your big chance, Stephanie."

Tess then waved goodbye and left Robert's office.

As misguided as she usually was on career topics, this time, Tess was right. I hadn't made the career rules I was now living by.

I had spent the last five years trying to do what was expected of me, hoping that would lead to a successful career.

But following the rules was turning me into a glorified call girl.

As likable as Vivian was, I wasn't ever going to be her. I was never going to be able to prostitute my way into feeling successful or loved the way she had in *Pretty Woman*.

Maybe there was another road I could travel.

I couldn't allow myself to hope. Not yet.

I turned my attention back to Robert, as he described the basis for his decision to discuss his job opening with me.

"Silicon Valley developers have a start-up mentality. I need to scale. The right way. And I don't want to hire anyone from Apple. It's a cult over there. I need someone who will take the time to learn about our content, who also understands the physics of scaling our distribution."

Robert had a high opinion of me, and I had no idea what he was basing this on. Dennis was not the type to rave about me, especially to other men. Any number of talented men would vie for the opportunity Robert was describing.

"But why me?"

I said this so quietly I didn't realize I had said it out loud. I blushed immediately after saying it. I felt like Beth had felt in the projection room when she had made the mistake of trying to move the lounge chair.

Robert grinned.

"Why not you? Do you have some deep dark secret I should know about?"

"It's just that you barely know me. I'm sure you've met many other men that have the skills for this job."

Robert stopped grinning, but his eyes still looked amused.

"Working for Sun, you've acquired some Silicon-Valley based technical expertise, but you also have been working in Manhattan on the broadcast end of things and have exposure to content considerations as well. I think you could hold your own with both the content and the IT folks, and you'll understand Apple's restrictions enough to push back on them or work around them if needed."

I couldn't remember the last time someone had complimented me on my technical expertise and meant it. Tears formed in the corners of my eyes.

I looked directly at Robert, determined not to let the tears out.

"Thanks for your kind words. I'm interested in hearing more about this job. It sounds like an exciting opportunity."

"Excellent. Let's discuss the details then. The job will be based out of this office. You would report to me. We can talk about salary later, but if you're the right fit for the job, I'll make sure that the offer is worth your while to make the move out here."

Robert looked at his watch.

"We only have a couple of hours before we meet everyone for dinner. Let's discuss this more tonight. I need to check with HR, finance, and legal quickly to see where we're at with the job opening. I'm pretty sure the budget has been approved, and I can start looking to fill the position."

Robert stood up. I took his lead and stood as well.

"Let's meet somewhere for a drink before dinner to discuss the role further."

Robert walked me to the door as he said this. I was supposed to meet Chris in an hour.

Fuck, Chris. This was the second time today I had wanted Chris to go fuck himself. It was a habit I was growing fond of.

"I'd love to have a drink."

"Excellent. Why don't I pick you up at your hotel at 5:00? That way we can talk in the car too. I'll order you a cab to take you back to the hotel."

CHAPTER 28

I sighed as I looked through the folded clothes in my suitcase. Thinking that I would be Dennis's escort and call girl for most of the trip, I had packed clothes better suited to a nightclub than a board room. I ruffled through my packed clothes and chose leggings and a shiny purple silk tunic. I hadn't packed any blouses that weren't low cut, but I could minimize the effect by wearing a necklace or pendant.

Once dressed, I put on my high-heeled silver sandals, grabbed my jewelry and makeup bags from my suitcase, and took them into the bathroom. I put a multi-toned set of long chains on and some bracelets to match. I then quickly applied a more dramatic eyeliner and some glittery purple eyeshadow to match my tunic and freshened my lipstick. I put the makeup, some cash, and my credit card case in my smaller evening purse and looked at my watch. If I called Chris as I headed downstairs, I would just about be at the lobby door when Robert showed up.

I dialed Chris's number as I walked down the hotel corridor towards the elevator. Chris picked up on the first ring.

"Where are you?"

"I'm upstairs headed for the elevator. I need to cancel our meeting."

There was an uncomfortable pause. Chris broke the silence. His reply was terse.

"Why?"

"The meeting today with KidsNetwork went well, and the Vice President of Strategy, New Business, and Digital Content for KidsNetwork, Robert Billings, asked me for a quick debrief before dinner. I think he's going to ask us to help him with a large streaming project."

"Do you need me to come along for support?"

I rolled my eyes as I approached the elevator. The last time Chris had "supported" me with the MediaCom account, I had ended up taking a lap dance for Dennis. I swallowed my annoyance and kept my tone even as I said:

"It would help if you'd meet with Dennis and take him out for a drink before dinner. I don't want him to feel neglected."

"Ok. I'll meet him at Spago for a drink. I have his cell number."

"Thanks, Chris."

I hung up in relief. As I reached the entrance of the hotel, I felt a humming vibration on my right hip. I pulled my phone out of my beaded purse and flipped it open to see who was calling. It was Dennis. I hit the "reject" button and sent the call to voicemail as I left the hotel lobby and walked to the car drop-off area outside.

Robert's silver Mercedes convertible pulled up. The valet held the door for me.

"Hop in!"

Robert gave me a friendly smile as he tipped the valet. I felt myself relaxing as we slowly merged onto Wiltshire Boulevard.

Every car on the road seemed to be a convertible. Traffic was stop and go. Robert honked his horn half-heartedly at a yellow Corvette that braked to a stop in front of him. The Corvette's wheels squealed as the driver revved the engine and sped up again. Robert shrugged and turned back to me, keeping one eye on the road.

"Have you ever been to Bar Marmont?"

Bar Marmont was a hipster bar and restaurant next to the Hotel Marmont and was known to be a place where celebrities went to drink and do drugs. From what I had read about it, it was the kind of place that Michael would have loved. I was determined not to hold that against it. I smiled at Robert as I replied.

"I've not been to Bar Marmont yet, but I've heard of it."

"I thought we would grab drinks there. It's an LA landmark."

Robert got out of the car and extended a hand to help me out. We headed to the entrance, which had a clichéd velvet rope and a door attendant in a black suit and shirt with a purple tie. It seemed early to have a velvet rope out. No one was trying to get into the bar or restaurant.

The door attendant gave us a curt nod. Robert grabbed the large bamboo-looking door and opened it. Once inside, I squinted to adjust to the darkness. I locked eyes with a massive portrait of Ho Chi Minh hanging over the empty maître d's station.

Robert motioned me to a hall where a bunch of Chinese lanterns were hanging. I stared at the butterflies, moths, and dragonflies glued to the ceiling. A muscular bartender slowly walked over to us. His hair was slicked back in an Elvis pompadour, and he was wearing a simple black T-shirt that showed off his heavily tattooed arms and black jeans.

"I'll have a martini."

Robert glanced around the bar as he ordered. I didn't want to spend too much time figuring out what to drink, so I also requested a martini. The bartender nodded and didn't smile. He left to make the drinks.

The bar had a happy hour crowd of what looked like movie industry middle management types. Hardly the stuff of tabloids. Bar Marmont was on Sunset Boulevard, however, so there also were a few oddly dressed characters scattered around the small room.

An older guy dressed in what looked like a suede cowboy outfit complete with chaps and spurs on his boots was sleeping at a small table in the corner, and a few aging men in leather biker jackets were at the other end of the bar talking quietly amongst themselves.

I looked again at the ceiling, focusing on the paper butterflies glued there. They were a stark contrast to the darkness of the bar, with its reddish lighting. The bar managed to feel both new and give a nod to classic noir Hollywood at the same time. I liked it.

"How's LA treating you so far?"

Robert turned to me as he asked this, looking intently into my eyes.

"Better than New York."

I answered him more honestly than I had intended to.

"Was it horrible being in one of the Towers on 9/11?"

I was startled at Robert's question. Dennis must have told him I was there that day. It was an odd way to begin a job discussion.

Robert looked at the discomfort on my face, and an embarrassed blush flushed his cheeks. He quickly continued, sparing me having to reply.

"I remember staying in my office the whole day, watching CNN and that video clip of the planes hitting the tower. I couldn't believe what my eyes were seeing. I can't imagine what being in the buildings must have felt like."

"I went numb pretty quickly that day and was on autopilot through most of it."

My voice was quiet, almost a whisper, as I answered. I was staring at the sleeping cowboy in the corner. He reminded me of the "Naked Cowboy" that spent every day entertaining tourists for tips in Times Square. I reluctantly turned to Robert, who seemed to have gotten over his embarrassment and was watching me with concern.

"The LA sunshine and a change of pace might be just what you need."

Robert stroked his goatee absently as he said this while studying my face.

Robert looked around the bar again. He then pulled a small vial out of the inner pocket of his linen jacket. Robert tapped some white powder onto his hand from the vial. He held his hand up to his nose and took a quick snort. He then pinched his nose. I had seen Michael do this and had even joined him on occasion. I could only hope that the powder was cocaine and not something worse like heroin.

"This is some good coke. Here, take a bump. It'll lift you up."

Robert tapped some powder onto his knuckle and held his hand out under my nose. I was surprised that he hadn't gone to the bathroom or somewhere private to do the coke. I looked nervously around the bar, but no one was watching us. This was LA, and this was a bar known for the excesses of its guests.

I had a quick decision to make. If I refused Robert's offer, I would alienate him, which would make my job negotiations more difficult. That's assuming I even still wanted the job. Seeing Robert snorting cocaine didn't exactly make me excited to make a cross-country move. But in LA, snorting coke was probably as ordinary as ordering a drink or taking a drag on a joint.

The coke was under my nose. I needed to either snort it or say no to it.

I half expected Tess to show up. She had kept urging me to negotiate for a better job. She had wanted me to bend the rules to succeed.

But I had already succeeded, and this is what it looked like.

If Tess had been here, she would have pointed to Robert and said earnestly.

"You have to take your chance when it comes!"

But I had no idea what my chance would even look like. For all I knew, it was here, in this dark Hollywood bar, staring back at me out of Robert's coke-glazed eyes.

Fuck it.

I was sick of trying to succeed.

Life was too much responsibility.

I closed my eyes and raised an inner goblet to my ghosts.

"L'chaim!"

To Life. I moved my face towards Robert's hand and took the snort.

The coke dripped down my throat. I pinched my nose the same way Robert had. I felt a rush of euphoria as it hit me, and I giggled. Robert grinned.

"I told you it was good stuff. It'll take your mind off New York."

I gave Robert a friendly nod, saying nothing.

A wave of well-being washed over me. I wasn't even worried that Robert hadn't mentioned the job on his team yet.

"Where are you from, Stephanie?"

Robert took a sip of his martini. He was watching me intently and seemed genuinely interested in my answer.

"Ann Arbor, Michigan."

"I'm from Cincinnati. I came out here after graduate school and a stint in Chicago and never looked back."

Robert gave me a shy smile after he said this, which made him look like the young man from Ohio that he used to be.

"Where did you go to school?"

"Northwestern. Media and Communications studies. After graduating, I took a job for a year producing the morning news at a local station in Cincinnati. I wanted to be close to my mother, who was dying of breast cancer."

"My father just died of heart failure."

I whispered this as I took another look around the bar. The sleeping cowboy had left, and the happy hour crowd had thinned out. I took a sip of my forgotten martini. My father had always wanted to see Hollywood, but I didn't think he would have liked this odd, dark bar. It wasn't the stuff of Hollywood musicals. Of course, I didn't know what my father's tastes had been for the last fifteen years. Maybe he would have loved it here.

"Were you close?"

Robert's question felt natural, like a continuation of my own thoughts about my father. I had expected a much different evening tonight. 9/11, my father, and death had all made their way into the conversation, and we hadn't even finished our first drink yet. I was curious why Robert wanted to take the discussion to such a personal level. Maybe he didn't have a job to offer me anymore.

"No. We hardly spoke."

I gave Robert a melancholy glance as I said this. I took another sip of my martini. Robert was looking at me with a personal grief that mirrored my own. His voice was quiet as he replied.

"I wasn't close to my father either. He threw me out of the house at seventeen. I was closer to my mother."

Robert seemed to be seeing his own ghosts. I watched him have his interchange with them. He shook his head as if to dispel his phantoms and focused back on me. His expression was still unguarded.

"I moved back to Chicago after she died."

"Why did you leave Chicago?"

"I couldn't stand the winters. You'll see how much better you'll feel with year-long sunshine if you move out here. Besides, I wanted to work in production, not broadcasting, and LA is the place to be for that."

I nodded, giving Robert an empathetic smile. For the first time that evening, my smile felt genuine.

Robert pulled his vial of coke out, put some on his knuckle, and quickly snorted it. He repeated the procedure for me, and I gratefully took the offered hit. Talk of my father had left me feeling out of sorts, and I wanted to be up when Robert finally brought up the job.

"That's better."

Robert whispered this as he pinched his nose and put his vial away. He then turned to me and patted my knee. It wasn't a sexual gesture like Dennis's hand on my leg had been. It was more a pat of reassurance and acceptance.

"Enough about family. Let's discuss the job. I think you're a great fit for it. I want to keep this project out of the hands of IT, and you're just the person to help me do that. And besides, I like you."

Robert said this in a low, conspiratorial tone as he leaned in towards me.

"I like you too, Robert."

I gave him a sincere smile. Robert blushed. He took a sip of his drink and shifted in his bar stool.

"Are you interested then?"

Robert pulled back so that he could look at my expression. I let him see the enthusiasm in my eyes as I nodded. I didn't have a job offer yet, but I had the promising beginnings of an offer, and that was good enough for tonight.

"Yes, I am."

"Excellent!"

Robert picked up his almost finished martini as he said this and held it up before him in a toast.

"To a promising new partnership! And friendship!"

Robert downed the last of his drink. I lifted my glass and downed the rest of my martini. We sat in comfortable silence for a few minutes. Robert pulled out his vial of coke and took another bump, and put some out on his hand for me. I snorted it and then looked at my watch.

"We need to get going to Spago. We're going to be late."

Robert considered me thoughtfully as I said this. As the waiter approached us to see if we wanted a refill, he handed the waiter his credit card without even looking at him.

"I'm not hungry at all. How about you?"

"No, why?"

"I was thinking it'd be a waste to spend time and money on a dinner that neither one of us wants. Your manager Chris is attending the dinner. He can continue a dialogue with Dennis and Derrick and anyone else who shows up."

I had no idea what Robert had in mind, but just about anything would be better than sitting next to Dennis and having him maul me and punish me at the same time while I pretended to eat.

"Give Chris a call. Let him know that I want to continue our discussion and that we'll have to miss dinner."

"Can I put you on the phone if he asks? I think hearing this from you will help smooth things over."

I pulled my cell phone out of my purse and dialed Chris's number. He picked up right away.

"Where are you? Dennis and I are already at the restaurant. We're sitting at the bar."

"Robert wants to continue our talks. It's going to lead to a big streaming project. Can you handle dinner?"

"Wouldn't Dennis's input be valuable? We'll make sure we discuss whatever Robert wants at dinner."

"Let me put Robert on. Maybe he can explain this better than I can."

I handed the phone to Robert.

"Hey Chris, can I get a raincheck on dinner? I'm having a productive conversation with Stephanie, and I don't want to interrupt the momentum."

Robert motioned me to come closer. He put the phone between us so that I could hear Chris's reply. There was a pause on the other end of the phone.

"If you feel that coming to dinner would be an interruption, I guess we'll have to take a raincheck. I was looking forward to meeting you."

"We'll connect soon. Let Dennis know that I'll debrief him later this week once Stephanie and I have finished our discussions. Enjoy your dinner at Spago. The food is great there. Try the rabbit if they have it on the menu. It's fantastic."

Robert grinned as he handed the phone back to me.

"Thanks for taking over the dinner, Chris."

I moved to hit the disconnect button after I said this. The longer I talked to Chris, the more he would try to convince me to swing by Spago with Robert. Chris managed to speak before I could finish pressing the disconnect button.

"Come join us later, even if it's just for after-dinner drinks."

Chris sounded tired. When he found out that I wasn't coming to dinner, Dennis would act up, and Chris knew this. Tough. Chris and Dennis could go fuck themselves. Or each other.

This was at least the third time that day that my thoughts had strayed into forbidden rebellion where Chris and Dennis were concerned. Maybe it was the coke, but my anarchy felt energizing.

"I'll try. Talk to you later."

I hung up before Chris could say anything more. Robert was hovering over my shoulder.

"Was Chris that disappointed? I understand that Dennis is no picnic, but Chris's job is to entertain clients."

"He wanted to meet you."

"He'll get over it. Let's get out of here. Fun awaits us!"

Robert extended his arm to help me out of my bar stool. Once standing, I shook my legs out.

"I'm going to use the ladies' room."

I wanted to splash some water on my face and pee before I got back into Robert's convertible. I had no idea where he was taking us, and I didn't want to have to worry about my bladder. My party nights with Michael had taught me to use restrooms during the transition between bars.

"I'll go get the car from valet parking and meet you out front."

The bathroom was black and silver, with chrome mirrors lining the walls. When I looked at my reflection, I was surprised at how calm and well-maintained I looked.

Having done coke, I had expected a movie cliché of frantic eyes and jitters to face me in the mirror.

I had expected my reflection to be a warning to avoid excesses.

But my image in the mirror looked focused, energized, and even excited. My "Don't do drugs" lecture was clearly not going to come from the mirror.

I thought of the scene in *Pulp Fiction* when Uma Thurman's character, Mia Wallace, did coke in the bathroom of Jack Rabbit Slim's.

"I said Goddamn!"

I said this to my reflection, trying to mimic how Uma Thurman said it in the film. I didn't quite pull it off, but I felt glamorous anyway. I reapplied my lipstick and then headed out.

CHAPTER 29

Robert was already in the Mercedes and at the front driveway.

"I know we're not that hungry, but can you handle a little bit of food? I know a great hamburger joint. It's on Santa Monica."

A burger didn't sound out of the question.

"The place I'm taking you to is one of my favorite places to grab a burger. I used to come here almost every night when I first moved to LA. There aren't many things I miss about Ohio, but one of them is the burgers. LA is not really a burger type of city."

"I guess people here think they're too fattening."

Robert nodded in reply to my comment as he put the car radio on. He had one of those new satellite radios, and the Psychedelic Furs came on. He turned to me.

"They don't know what they're missing. Do you like New Wave music? I've been on a nostalgia trip ever since I got my XM radio. And I love having no commercials."

"I love New Wave music!" I said, giving Robert a friendly smile. It was refreshing to genuinely enjoy what he enjoyed and not have to pretend.

Robert turned the volume up. "Pretty in Pink" was the song playing. It was the original version and not the remake from the movie, but it reminded me of the movie anyway. I had always envisioned myself as Molly Ringwald's character in the film, Andie. Andie was both a good student and an artsy, alternative type that worked in a vintage record store and wore hip, vintage clothes. In high school, if I were having a day when I felt particularly cool, I imagined I looked and acted like Andie.

Even though I didn't know him that well yet, Robert reminded me of the character Duckie in many ways. Duckie was Andie's loyal friend. He was honest and reliable. From our conversations so far, Robert seemed to have both these qualities.

Also, like Duckie, Robert dressed in a way reminiscent of vintage clothes, even though his clothing was expensive and new. He also had the same earnestness about him, and there was something in the way he smiled that made me trust him.

Even though *Pretty in Pink* was supposed to be set in Chicago, it was filmed in LA, and I had always felt it was about LA. I could imagine Robert acting like Duckie, visiting me at the vintage record store where I worked. I could also imagine Robert sticking up for me with Dennis and Chris the way Duckie had protected Andie in the movie from the rich kids.

"What's on your mind?"

Robert looked over at me. His glance was friendly, curious, and sincere. Just like Duckie's would have been. I smiled.

"Nothing, I was just thinking about some of my favorite movies."

"Which ones?"

"*Pretty in Pink*. I always thought it was set in LA even though it was supposed to be about Chicago."

Robert's eyes lit up.

"Me too! I love that movie. James Spader is super hot! I just want to run my fingers through that perfect blonde hair. I could watch him for twelve hours straight."

Robert's words gushed out in an excited stream. He looked over at me nervously when he realized what he had just said. I felt the tension in my shoulders relax as I took his words in. Of course.

I gave Robert a welcoming smile. He visibly relaxed and blew me a campy kiss, and then turned back to the road. The Psychedelic Furs gave way on the radio to Kajagoogoo singing "Too Shy." Robert and I both sang along to the chorus. It had been a long time since I had sung along to the radio. I didn't even care that I was out of tune.

As the song wound down, Robert asked, "Have you ever been to West Hollywood?"

He was pulling over to the right-hand lane to park. I shook my head in reply as I watched him try to parallel park his Mercedes.

"I hate parking this thing. They need to get valet parking around here."

Robert rolled his eyes as he said this and turned the ignition off. He reached into his jacket pocket and pulled out his vial of coke. He quickly snorted from the vial and held it out to me.

"Open up."

I didn't even flinch when Robert took his index finger, which had coke on it, and rubbed my gums. The gesture seemed natural somehow. I felt like I had known Robert for a long time. I tried to smile, but I wasn't sure if I had succeeded.

"I can't feel my lips."

My voice sounded strange to me as I mumbled this. Robert grinned.

"Here we are! Best burgers in town."

Robert pointed to the open door of a place called Hamburger Mary's. The restaurant had a giant statue of a woman that was painted in a skimpy, campy dress and fishnets. She was holding a giant, brightly painted hamburger.

There was a queue to get in. Robert turned to me and gave me a reassuring smile. "The line usually moves quickly."

Robert was right. We were at the front within a few minutes. When we got inside, I was surprised at the mixture of different types of decor. There was a large disco ball hanging from the ceiling. Victorian black and white velvet wallpaper covered the walls. The booths were black and red leather and had a 1950s diner look to them. Upside-down mannequin legs dressed in Christmas lights were placed on the ledges of the booths.

Inside was packed with diners, with every seat taken. There were two drag queens up near the bar. They had a mini stage set up with two microphone stands, a massive board with numbers and letters, and a contraption that shook up white plastic balls.

One of the drag queens standing on the mini stage was dressed in a blue bouffant wig and a pink dress with rhinestones all over it and a neckline that was cut to allow her very large breasts to spill out over the top of the neckline. The other drag queen was Hispanic-looking and had on a black bustier and short black spandex leggings. She wore a leather motorcycle cap over her wig and had a large belt around her waist with a glittery rhinestone buckle. The drag queen dressed in the bustier shouted into the microphone.

"Get your cards for the next game. We'll start in five minutes."

"This place invented drag queen bingo, you know."

Robert said this to me as we were taken to our table by the hostess, herself a tall drag queen with a wig of long, straight silver hair and an elegant shimmery purple silk dress with a matching bolero jacket.

"Hi, Hon. Two for Bingo?"

She blew Robert a campy kiss as she murmured this. She escorted us to a booth that faced the small bingo stage. She handed us two bingo cards and bingo marker pens and two giant, laminated menus.

"Your waitress will be right with you, Sweet Things."

She said this in a purring tone as she turned around and headed back to the hostess stand near the front entrance.

Robert pointed to the two bingo emcees near the stage.

"These two girls are legendary. You're in for a treat. Besides bingo, the burgers are what this place is known for. They're huge. Want to split one? Let's get the Mac Daddy burger. That's my favorite."

"Sure."

I looked at the menu to see what I had just agreed to eat. The MacDaddy burger was a half-pound burger with macaroni and cheese piled on top of it. It was something a stoner would order.

"I know it sounds gross, but it's so cheesy that it's irresistible."

Robert pointed to the menu as he said this. I nodded in reply. We both looked up at the stage as we heard the microphone check. The two emcees were about to start calling numbers.

A waiter approached our table. He wasn't dressed in drag but clearly was hired to appeal to the gay clientele of the restaurant. He was muscular and wore tight black jeans and a sleeveless cropped royal blue muscle T-shirt with a white hamburger logo. He had short blonde hair that had too much hair gel in it for my taste and had a great tan and perfect abs. He gave me a quick nod and then leaned in close to Robert.

"What can I get you?"

Robert gave the waiter a quick appreciative once-over.

"We'll split a MacDaddy burger and fries. Can you bring the burger out on two plates?

"Anything to drink?"

"We'll have two margaritas in the leg glasses."

"Anything you want, babe."

The waiter gave Robert a wink as he said this. He then turned around to put in our order. Robert's eyes followed him until he disappeared into the kitchen.

Once the waiter was out of sight, Robert turned back to me and asked, "Have you ever seen *A Christmas Story*?"

Of course, I had seen *A Christmas Story*. It was impossible to avoid it on Thanksgiving and Christmas at my Mother's house. It played on an endless loop on TNT, and she left it on throughout the entire day.

"Yes. Why?"

Robert was looking at me with amusement.

"Did my question surprise you?"

The bingo emcees shouted out a number before I could reply, and we both looked at our cards.

"B27. Make sure you know your alphabet, my drunken kittens, and mark the correct square on your cards. I hate do-overs."

The drag queen dressed in the bustier and spandex leggings gave an exaggerated sigh after she said this and then fanned herself with a flamenco fan. I looked at my card, and I did have B27, so I marked it.

"You'll see why I asked you about *A Christmas Story* in a minute."

Robert checked his card one more time to see if he had missed B27.

Almost on cue, the waiter came back to our table with two drinks in fishnet-covered leg glasses that were exactly like the lamp base of the iconic leg lamp in *A Christmas Story*. They were as big as a lamp base as well.

"Here you are, Sexy."

The waiter said this in a breathy tone as he met Robert's appraising stare. He looked like he was going to say something more, but Robert was too caught up in watching me take in the enormity of the leg drinks to pay attention to him.

Seeing my shocked expression as I looked at the colossal leg glass had made Robert burst into laughter.

Our small booth now had two large bingo cards and two fishnetted lamp bases filled with margaritas. I glanced over to the bingo stage, where the blonde drag queen was holding up a number that I couldn't quite see, and it all seemed hilarious to me. I started laughing.

The waiter shook his head and turned around to leave, giving up on trying to talk to Robert. He waved his hand goodbye in frustration as he left the table. For some reason, this made Robert and me laugh even harder.

It felt good to laugh.

The leg glasses were ridiculous. For one thing, they were far too tall to be able to take a drink from easily while sitting down. As Robert took his first drink from his, he turned sideways so that he could get a good grip on the leg. Seeing him sipping the giant lamp-base-sized cocktail made me want to start laughing again. Robert giggled as he took another awkward sip and then set his leg drink back down.

"Your turn Stephanie."

Robert pointed to my drink. I picked it up carefully. I turned to the side exit of the booth and put the fish-netted leg between my legs to hold it in place. I took a long drink through the straw.

I was about to turn back to Robert, but all the laughing at our table must have captured the attention of the drag queen emcees because the emcee that looked like the Tejano singer Selena, in a black bustier and motorcycle cap, was pointing to me.

"This lady has a large leg between her legs! What are you doing there, honey? Can I join you? I give good leg!"

The drag queen put her leg out seductively as she said this. There was laughter coming from quite a few tables, and all of a sudden, everyone in the bar was staring at me, struggling with my drink.

I glanced over at Robert, who was watching me. He winked.

I turned back to the drag queen and waved her to come to our table. The audience started clapping. What difference did it make if the drag queen made a few jokes at my expense? It was all in good fun.

Everyone was watching me.

"My, that's a big leg you have!"

The Selena look-alike put her hand on her chest in mock shock and gasped. She then put the mic in my face.

"What's your name, honey?"

"Stephanie. What's yours?"

I said this in a playful tone. She didn't miss a beat and answered my question with one hand on her hips and the other holding the microphone.

"If I told you I was Selena would you believe me?"

"Not unless you do a song and dance that convinces me."

I said this in a teasing tone. I heard applause and laughter around me. Robert laughed too.

"We don't have time for that now, Honey, although I'll give you a raincheck. This is bingo night, not salsa night. My name is Carmen."

Carmen patted her hair and adjusted her bustier, and continued.

"I'm working, or I would ask you for a sip of your drink Stephanie. It looks delicious. Are you enjoying Drag Queen Bingo?"

"Yes, I am. But, I'm disappointed that you won't do the Macarena for me, though."

"Oh Stephanie Baby, I would love to Cha Cha with you, but these leggings might split. Lord, what I wouldn't give for Selena's thighs! But I want you to have a good time. So, for being a good sport, the next round's on us!"

Carmen pointed both to my drink and the bar, and this elicited applause from the other tables. I raised my big leg glass in thanks.

"Let's give a big hand for Stephanie!"

Carmen went back to the stage. I took another sip of my margarita and then set the leg glass back on the table. Robert was watching me. The look in his eyes was appreciative.

Carmen read out another bingo number, but the waiter approached with our food and set the plates down before I could look at my card to see if I had a match.

"Anything else I can get for you?"

The waiter looked suggestively at Robert as he asked this. If this had not been happening right before my eyes, I would have thought it was a scene out of a bad gay movie. Robert gave the waiter a lingering look.

"We're fine for now. Perhaps later."

The waiter nodded, giving Robert a knowing smile. He pulled out his order pad and pen and scribbled what looked like his phone number on it. He handed the piece of paper to Robert.

"I'm Chad. My shift ends at midnight."

Robert put the piece of paper with the waiter's phone number in his shirt pocket. He turned back to me and the huge hamburger sitting on the table between us.

There was crusty, cheesy macaroni and cheese spilling out the sides of my half burger, along with wilted lettuce and a soggy tomato. The burger was rare, which caused beef juices to mix with the cheese. The cheese wasn't American, but a stronger smelling combo cheese of some sort. I stared at the burger skeptically.

"Take a bite, if only to line your stomach."

To emphasize his point, Robert took a big bite of his burger. This caused the macaroni and cheese to spill out the sides of the burger and land on his plate in a hot gooey lump. I followed Robert's lead and took a timid bite of my half. I was surprised that the burger tasted great. The macaroni and cheese balanced out the strong beef flavor, and it felt like I was eating Hamburger Helper, which had always been a comfort food of mine as a kid. The greasy, cheesy, beefy excess of the burger worked somehow.

My face must have shown my swift change from disgust to delight because Robert leaned over and wiped a bit of cheese that had landed on my chin.

"It's good, right? Only good things are ahead for you, Stephanie."

He said this like we were sharing a great discovery together.

"It's amazing! So cheesy. Mmmm."

I hadn't flinched at all when Robert reached over to wipe the cheese off of my chin. If Dennis had done that, I would have had to use all of my focus and energy to not let my discomfort show. But Robert's gesture felt friendly and natural. It was the gesture of a brother or a good friend. It was what Duckie would have done for Andie.

"Bingo!"

Someone in the back of the bar shouted out a win. I hadn't even been paying attention to my bingo card, and neither had Robert. We looked up at the winner in surprise. Robert took another smaller bite of his burger.

"This place reminds me of my favorite bar in Chicago, although that bar didn't have drag queen bingo. I met my first true boyfriend there. He was the bartender."

"I met my first adult boyfriend in a cafe in Ann Arbor."

"Is something wrong with the burger?"

Robert pointed to my plate and looked at me with concern. I didn't realize I had sighed out loud. There was a tear in the corner of my eye. I wiped it away with my napkin. "No, just remembering my first true love."

"Love sucks."

I nodded. He continued, putting his hand on my arm for emphasis.

"Don't let old relationships get to you. We're having a good time, right? I feel we've connected, and I'm enjoying hanging out with you."

Robert looked at me shyly. I squeezed his hand.

"Me too, Robert. I'm glad we met."

Robert blushed. He didn't pull his hand away. He then did what Duckie would do. He pulled my hand to his lips, kissed it, and then gently placed my hand back on the table.

"I told you it would all work out. You can trust me. We're going to be a great team!"

I nodded even though I didn't recall Robert ever saying that it would "all work out." Robert gave my hand one last squeeze. We stayed like that for a moment. He then pulled his hand away and reached into his coat pocket. He pulled out the vial of coke and pointed to the bathrooms.

"Want some? You deserve it."

To my surprise, I shook my head in reply to Robert's offer. I didn't want to feel a jolt right now. Robert shrugged and put the vial back in his jacket pocket.

We took a few more bites of our burgers. I looked at my watch. It was almost midnight. The night had gone by quickly. My coke buzz had worn off. All of the eating, drinking, flirting, and celebration in every corner of the packed restaurant brought home to me that I was exhausted.

Robert was watching the Bingo emcees. I looked down at my card. I hadn't listened to the last several numbers. I reached over and tapped him on the arm to get his attention. When he turned to me, I said, "I'm crashing. I'm going to grab a taxi back to the hotel."

Robert pointed to his jacket pocket where his coke was.

"Are you feeling ok? Take another pop. It'll wake you up."

I shook my head in reply. As Robert opened his mouth to protest, Chad came to the table to check on us. Robert looked at me with concern as he asked the waiter for the check.

"But you have another free round of drinks coming!"

Chad looked shocked that we would turn down free booze. Robert started to rise from his chair to help me up, but I gave his hand one last squeeze and shook my head.

"No, please. I'm going to take a cab and crash."

I motioned my head towards Chad and whispered, "Stay and cash in on the free drinks Carmen offered us."

"Are you sure?" Robert asked, scrutinizing me.

I gave him a tired smile and nodded. Robert was a good guy. I wasn't going to prevent him from getting laid tonight.

I turned to Chad and smiled politely.

"Who can help me get a cab?"

"You can catch one outside. The bouncer will flag one for you."

Chad was looking at Robert when he said this. I gave him a nod of thanks anyway and then turned to Robert.

"Thanks for a wonderful evening. It was truly special. I'll see you in the workshops tomorrow."

Robert looked confused when I said this as if everything was happening too fast. But when he looked in my eyes and saw that I seemed happy and wasn't leaving in a huff, he looked relieved.

"I had a blast. See you, tomorrow love."

"Looking forward to it."

I waved from behind me as I walked through the crowd out of the restaurant. To Chad's word, there was an available cab parked in front of the restaurant. The bouncer opened the door for me, and I gratefully climbed inside.

"Beverly Wilshire."

As the cab started towards the hotel, I leaned back in the warm, cracked vinyl of the seat and heaved a deep sigh of relief. The long day was finally ending.

CHAPTER 30

The room phone rang in a shrill, piercing tone, causing me to sit up in a sweaty panic. It was the wake-up call I had requested. 7 am. I yawned and climbed out of bed, and walked over to my window, opening the heavy gold velvet curtains. Although I had had a fun time last night, I was glad to be awake in the sunrise of a new morning.

I showered and dressed quickly and headed down to the lobby. I called Robert. He was on his way to pick me up and take me to the studio. He answered right away.

"Good morning. I'm just pulling up."

I hung up and walked out to the front of the hotel. Robert's convertible appeared within a minute or so. I hopped in. He handed me a Starbucks cappuccino that he had picked up for me on the way.

"Did you get back safely?"

"Thanks for getting coffee! I had no problems at all. Did you enjoy the rest of your night?" I said this lightly, with just the slightest hint of teasing in my tone, as I took a grateful gulp of the cappuccino.

Robert looked like he was blushing, but it could have been sunburn. The LA sun was out in full force this morning.

"I did. Chad is the ex of an ex of an old friend. I'll tell you more about him later."

I took another sip of my cappuccino and didn't press him further. I wanted to bring up the job that he had mentioned last night but wasn't sure how to broach the subject. I wasn't sure how serious he had been. The coke might have been talking.

As if hearing my thoughts, Robert turned to me.

"I have good news for you. I meant what I said last night. I talked with finance this morning and have an offer I can present to you."

"I was hoping you'd say that."

I didn't try to hide the relief in my tone. I took another sip of my cappuccino, not because I was thirsty, but more to use the cup to hide my face as I waited to hear Robert's offer.

Robert merged onto Olive and headed towards the studio. He took a sip of his coffee and then turned to me.

"I was able to secure a base of $150,000 with a signing bonus of 25k, a yearly bonus of 25%, and a relocation package. I should be able to get you some MediaCom stock options as well, but I'm still negotiating the amount."

After my promotion to account executive, my base salary was currently $125,000, and my bonus structure was 100%, based on hitting my sales target for the year. My compensation package was such that my commission went up significantly after I made my sales quota.

Robert's job offer wasn't a raise; it was a lower salary. As I listened to him, I was surprised that I wasn't disappointed in the offer.

My chances of hitting my sales quota this year as the MediaCom account executive were pretty much 100%. I would make a lot of money if I stayed with Sun Microtek, more than I had ever imagined.

I thought about Dennis and what I would have to do to earn my salary if I kept my current role. No money was worth selling myself to Dennis. Or anyone.

Robert looked over at me nervously and cleared his throat.

"What do you think?"

He must have taken my long pause as lack of interest or disappointment because he continued, his tone now pitched to close a sale.

"Your title would be Director of Content and Digital Platforms."

Robert scrutinized my face and paused as he emphasized the word "Director."

I had no idea how much rent was in LA, and I knew I would need a car here. I needed to do what a man would do in this circumstance. I didn't want Robert to see me as a lousy negotiator.

"I'd like a higher base salary to cover getting a car."

I said this as I looked out the window at all the cars on Olive Street. So many of them were expensive convertibles. It had been five years since I had owned a car. I had been a graduate student with a frugal car to match. I had never owned an expensive car like the BMWs, Audis, and Mercedes that I was seeing all around me on the drive to Burbank.

"We could probably wring another 10k out of finance. That should cover what you need." Robert gave me a look like a proud brother would give. He sounded pleased that I had negotiated.

"Sounds good, Robert."

The words popped out of my mouth before I had time to consider them. My words pretty much ended negotiations before they had begun.

My hands had been shaking the entire drive with nervous anticipation. They relaxed, and I was able to loosen my vise-like grip on my coffee. I was intensely relieved that Robert had made me a livable offer and that I had finally closed a deal I cared about.

"Are things settled then? Should we start working on a date?"

Robert must have liked what he saw on my face because his expression softened into one of relief and satisfaction.

This job offer was a great opportunity. And although Robert, a friend now, was no prince, the job made sense. Even if I ended up hating LA, at least I wouldn't be living day to day in a burial ground like I currently was in New York.

At least I would have tried to change my life.

I turned to Robert, hoping my voice conveyed proper excitement at the chance he was giving me.

"Where do I sign?"

"Excellent! When can you start?"

Robert gave me a big smile. He was pulling into the studio lot and handed his badge to the guard at the gate.

"I should be able to come out here by March, assuming that I can get all the logistics arranged."

"Don't worry about the logistics. We'll buy you out of your lease in New York and put you in corporate housing while you find a place here. I need you to start earlier than March."

"If you're going to get me out of my lease and help me find a place, I could make the move in February."

The words tumbled out of my mouth in a stream of certainty that didn't reflect how I actually felt. In fact, my words were making the decision to move out here for me.

February was a couple of weeks away.

Robert seemed satisfied with my answer. He continued as he pulled into his dedicated parking space.

"I know February's coming right up, but we can always send you back for a week to pack up your place in New York once you've started here. I'm excited to kick off this new venture. I think you're going to be a tremendous asset to the project. Congratulations Stephanie! Welcome to the team!"

Robert leaned over in the car and gave me as much of a hug as could be mustered in the small front seat. I hugged him back. It was all happening so fast.

Yet it felt right.

Now that I had made the decision, I wanted to make it public as quickly as possible. Chris would corner me today, asking how my meetings had gone with Robert last night. I wanted to avoid dealing with him. And Dennis. I took one last sip of my cappuccino and turned to Robert.

"Is the offer you just made me finalized? I mean, can I let Chris know today that I'm quitting?"

"Yes, it's approved. We just need to do a quick background check. That should only take thirty minutes or so. Why?"

"I don't want to deal with Dennis anymore."

Robert surveyed my face as I mentioned Dennis. He nodded to himself.

"I'll make an announcement during the workshops today. I'll have HR complete the paperwork this morning."

Robert came around to my side of the car and opened the door for me. We walked quietly during the short distance to the studio entrance.

"Thanks, Robert. I really appreciate all you've done." My voice cracked.

"My pleasure Stephanie."

Robert's tone was the verbal equivalent of squeezing my hand as he opened the studio door for me.

I felt like I was burning a bridge by not telling Chris I was leaving Sun Microtek before Robert announced it during the workshops. That said, I didn't care. Let Robert handle it. It was his problem now.

Robert went to his office to call HR and get the paperwork completed. I went directly to the conference room where our briefings were being held. I waited nervously for Robert to return. People started filing into the room for the briefings. Robert made it back just before Chris and Dennis arrived. He gave me a wink and a nod as he entered the room.

It was done.

Everyone grabbed coffee and bagels from the catered breakfast that had been set up in the corner. When we were seated, Robert began to make the announcement of my new job in his organization. He pointed to me and looked around the room before finally locking eyes directly with Dennis.

"I'm pleased to announce we have a new member on the team. Stephanie will be joining my organization as Director of Digital Content and Streaming. She'll be reporting directly to me and will build a team to work with Apple, as well as rolling out our own digital streaming and subscription content platform."

Robert paused and looked around the room for emphasis. There was applause and congratulations. Dennis didn't clap. He remained silent while Robert continued.

"This will be an independent, content-driven project operating out of the Burbank studios and will not involve IT."

Robert stared directly at Dennis as he said this. Dennis said nothing.

Chris looked curiously at Robert and nervously at Dennis. His eyes then settled on me. There was a mixture of admiration and anger filling Chris's eyes. He looked like he was about to ask me a question. But he quickly pulled a polite mask over his face instead, giving me a tight smile that looked more like a grimace than a friendly overture.

"Congratulations, Stephanie."

I studied Chris, not feeling the need to say anything. I was officially the customer now, and no longer owed him an explanation.

Robert moved the topic quickly to the workshop. As he went through his slides on the timing and projections for the streaming project, everyone listened politely.

Except for Dennis.

He sat with his arms crossed, an angry smirk on his face. After a few minutes, he interrupted Robert.

"How are you going to scale for multi-streams, and how are you going to handle DRM, Stephanie?"

Dennis's tone was sarcastic. He was looking directly at me. He was a recognized expert in DRM, who had written articles and a book and had given speeches about the topic. He could make my life difficult if he challenged me in front of the group. I opened my mouth, ready to admit that I needed time to figure everything out. Robert answered Dennis before I could reply.

"Stephanie will have her team look into that after we get more clarity on preliminaries."

There was a tense pause, and then Dennis shrugged.

I wanted to reply to Dennis. I wanted to look him right in the eyes and give him the same sneer he was giving me. But before I could act on my impulse and say anything to Dennis, the ghost of Phil from *Groundhog Day* came forward. He pointed to Robert.

"Something is... different."

I took a deep breath to calm myself down. Phil was right. My job was different now. I was out of Dennis's influence.

Phil looked around the room.

"Anything different is good," he added.

Phil turned back to me, a tear in the corner of his eye. "Do you know what today is?...Today is tomorrow. It happened."

Phil leaned over and kissed my forehead after he said this. He then straightened back up and wiped the tear out of his eye.

"Enjoy tomorrow, Stephanie," he whispered as he blew me a kiss and then waved goodbye. I took a sip of water as I watched him go.

Phil was right. It was finally tomorrow.

CHAPTER 31

"I've reassigned a few top-performing people under you as of your first day. Alex will be moving to a role at Paramount, so his people will be transferred to you as well. This will give you a core team to start with."

Robert grabbed a piece of salmon sashimi with his chopsticks and dipped it into his soy sauce, which had specks of wasabi floating in it.

"You're going to be great at running this team, Stephanie. I have full faith in you." He popped the salmon into his mouth.

I nervously glanced down at my hands, which were resting on the table. I quickly looked up at Robert to acknowledge his remarks. I didn't want to let him down.

"Want some more sake?" Robert held the small carafe over my cup. He didn't wait for an answer and refilled my cup. He then pointed to his cell phone in apology and took the call that was coming in.

As I took a sip of my sake, a ghost with slicked black hair and an expensive suit approached the table. It was Al Pacino's character in *Glengarry Glen Ross*, Ricky Roma.

Whenever I was at a business conference or workshop, like the one I was attending now in LA, I often thought of *Glengarry Glen Ross*, which was about the cutthroat world of commission sales. Sometimes, to psych myself up for the docket of endless sales motivation speeches that I often had to endure at these conferences, I would watch the movie.

Even though the salesmen in *Glengarry Glen Ross* sold dubious real estate and not software and services, they always reminded me of the account executives I worked with at Sun. The likeness was not a compliment.

Ricky sat down next to me. I looked at the brochure for Glengarry real estate poking out of the inner pocket of his designer Italian suit. Without wasting any time, Ricky arched his eyebrow, giving me a seductive look, as he touched my arm and began his sales pitch from the movie.

"When you die, you're gonna regret the things you don't do. You think you're queer? I'm gonna tell you somethin': we're all queer."

Ricky had a point. Maybe we really were all queer. I took a furtive look at Robert, who was struggling with his chopsticks as he tried to dip a piece of hamachi in soy sauce.

Ricky pointed to the large plate of assorted sushi that Robert and I were sharing.

"Great meals fade in reflection. Everything else gains. You know why? 'Cause it's only food. This shit we put in us keeps us going. It's only food. The great fucks you may have had, what do you remember about 'em?"

I thought about Michael. He probably could have been a great fuck, if I had ever been remotely sober when we had sex. Arthur had never been a great fuck. I took another sip of my sake as I looked at Ricky's perfectly tanned face. He was fiddling with his platinum and diamond cufflinks. When he felt me looking at him, he focused intently on me, his eyes filling with false sincerity. I could see now why he was such a successful salesperson. He had me listening to him. Ricky leaned closer towards me and continued, his voice almost a whisper.

"What I'm saying is, what is our life? Our life is lookin' forward, or it's lookin' back. That's it. That's our life."

Ricky had nailed it. I could either look forward towards LA, or I could look back at all the death and destruction that surrounded me in New York.

There wasn't any other choice.

I listened intently to Ricky's words as he continued his pitch from the movie.

"Stocks, bonds, objects of art, real estate. What are they? An opportunity. To what? To make money? Perhaps. To lose money? Perhaps. To 'indulge' and to 'learn' about ourselves? Perhaps. So fucking what? What isn't? They're an opportunity. That's all they are. They're an event."

I thought about all the objects in my apartment in New York that would now have to be sorted through as I packed to move to LA. I had worked hard as an engineer in the sales organization to afford those objects. I had eagerly gone to art galleries and flea markets to find them.

I had seen each one as an opportunity to grow, to become a sophisticated New Yorker, to indulge in all of the aesthetic pleasures that a world-class city like New York had to offer me. But purchasing those things hadn't strengthened my bond with the city or defined me as a New Yorker. The art and knick-knacks had sat in my apartment, gathering dust.

I whispered Ricky's quote to myself. "So fucking what."

Ricky pulled the brochure out of his suit pocket and set it on the table. He opened the brochure for Glengarry Highlands to the page that had the words, "Make Your Dreams Come True" in boldface.

Ricky touched my arm, reciting another line from the movie.

"Things happen to you. I'm glad I met you. I want to show you something. It may mean something to you, it may not. I don't know. I don't know anymore. . .What is that? Florida. Glengarry Highlands. Florida. Bullshit. And maybe that's true, and that's what I said. But look at this."

Ricky pointed to the glossy brochure. I stared at it. Would LA "make my dreams come true," or was I being sold a bad job and a situation in

LA that would end up being as toxic as the overpriced real estate from *Glengarry Glen Ross*?

I glanced over at Robert, who was ending the call he was on. He put his phone in his jacket pocket and added more wasabi into his little saucer of soy sauce. He must have felt me staring at him because he gave me a chummy look and pointed to the plate of sushi.

"You can have the last piece of California Roll."

Robert lifted the sushi with his chopsticks and placed it on my plate. I picked up the piece of California roll and popped it into my mouth.

"It's good, right?" Robert pointed to my mouth as he said this. I nodded and gave him the best grin I could manage while chewing.

I had no way of knowing if Robert would be a stable boss. But he was my friend already, and I liked him. Unlike my move to New York five years ago, this time, I wasn't moving to LA expecting a dream to come true. Reality would have to do.

Ricky pulled out a pack of cigarettes from his suit jacket and lit one. I had almost forgotten he was still at the table. He pulled out a contract from his suit pocket and handed me a pen. He was ready to close me. After a short pause, I turned to Ricky and shook my head.

Ricky was a closer. But I was done with closers.

When Ricky saw that he wasn't going to be able to sell me any of the Glengarry real estate, he looked at me suggestively and licked his lips, hoping to cut his losses by at least getting laid. He took a long drag of his cigarette and blew a perfect smoke ring in my direction. I again shook my head.

My life with salesmen was over. I wouldn't miss them.

Ricky shrugged. He turned away from me and looked restlessly at a blonde woman in her late thirties in a tailored grey business suit that had settled into one of the stools at the sushi bar. Ricky put the brochure back in his pocket and headed towards the woman without giving me another glance. He was on to his next sales lead.

ABC. Always Be Closing.

I picked up my sake and took a sip.

"Is your sake warm enough? Robert pointed to my cup.

"It's perfect." I took another sip after I said this and closed my eyes for a brief moment in satisfaction. I set the cup down.

Robert topped it off as he continued,

"I'm having my assistant find a place for you that will be convenient both to work and to socialize. I'm looking forward to having a friend from the Midwest. LA people can be so plastic."

"Thanks so much for all your help Robert. It means a lot to me."

I said this with more fervor than I had expected. I felt myself blushing. Robert blew me a theatrical kiss, which caused me to grin.

We made it an early night, and I returned to the hotel, crashing into my bed by 11 o'clock. As I drifted off to sleep, I could see the shadow of my fireman ghost watching over me from the balcony, his gas mask and fire extinguisher in hands, ready in case they were needed.

CHAPTER 32

The last day of the workshop went by quickly. To my relief, Dennis wasn't present. I met the new people who would be assigned to my team in February. They all seemed excited to be on the project. Time would tell whether their enthusiasm was genuine or play-acted for Robert's benefit.

I was scheduled to fly back to New York early the next morning on a six am flight, so I went back to the hotel alone after the workshops. I packed and then logged into my laptop to look at the temporary corporate housing pictures Robert's admin had emailed me. The apartment she had procured was right near the studios and had a balcony overlooking the Hollywood Hills. I stared at the pictures, trying to imagine myself standing on the balcony. But I couldn't see myself in the new apartment yet. The pictures made it look more like the scenery in a rerun of *Beverly Hills 90210* than my future home.

I ordered a chicken and avocado sandwich from room service and turned the television on, looking for a movie to watch while I ate dinner. To my surprise, the pay-per-view movie selection had a lot of classic movies to choose from. *Grease* caught my eye as I scrolled through the titles.

Grease was one of the movies that reminded me of my childhood. It was campy and mindless, just what I needed right now. I ordered the movie and sat down on my small hotel sofa to watch it. My chicken sandwich arrived, and I let the bellman in, signing for a generous tip.

As the opening credits and first scenes played, I took a bite of my sandwich and stared at the television screen, unable to focus. The intense week had caught up with me. I was exhausted. I pushed the room service tray to the end of the coffee table, away from me. The "Summer Loving" dance number started playing. I curled up on the sofa and let the movie continue without pausing it, closing my eyes, and drifting off to sleep.

The imagery in my dreams was filled with the garish colors and textures of Times Square. I was walking down 42nd Street, surrounded by the flashing lights of Broadway. There were huge animated advertisements for Bacardi Rum and the Broadway musical *Mamma Mia*. I was walking in what seemed like circles. I looked overwhelmed but excited, and the expression on my face was hopeful.

People pushed past me to get where they were going. There were too many people for me to stand still without disrupting the endless rhythm of the crowd. I had to keep moving.

I somehow ended up downtown near where the World Trade Center towers used to be. Only they were still there. I was standing in the courtyard performance space connected to Borders bookstore. There was a mixed crowd there watching a local dance troupe perform a modern dance number.

The dancers moved around the pavilion, turning into a conga line of sorts. As the dancers were rhythmically inching around the performance space, the sky turned grey and filled with smoke. The crowd started pushing towards me, screaming in terror.

Large chunks of flying debris and molten steel fell from the sky. I let myself be pushed along by the fleeing crowd. I couldn't breathe.

I looked around, trying to find a place to catch my breath. The sky was filled with smoke and dust and had darkened so much. It wasn't clear if it was day or night. I looked at the faces in the crowd. Everyone was driven by their own demons as they pushed forward blindly.

I couldn't see any familiar landmarks. There was too much dust, smoke, and chaos. I was choking. My breathing became increasingly shallow until I wasn't breathing at all anymore.

Instead of fighting my inevitable death, I relaxed into it, surrendering the best I could. I floated in my death state, carried forward on a soft summer breeze. Everything was now white, including the smoke and the dust.

At some point, my floating stopped, and I was deposited at the foot of a large white staircase. My surroundings looked just like the scene in *Grease* where Frankie Valli sings "Beauty School Dropout." White smoke surrounded me, and there was a similar staircase to nowhere, much like the one Frankie had stood on as he sang to Frenchy in the movie.

Only it wasn't Frankie Valli who was standing on the endless white staircase. It was the ghost of the fireman.

He lifted his helmet and tipped it to me. He stood tall and brave on the white staircase to nowhere. He was a statue of a god: straight, focused, and heroic. I looked intently at him. His expression was one of sympathy and understanding. My eyes searched his face. For meaning, for answers.

I opened my mouth to speak. But the fireman shook his head and put his gloved hand to his lips to quiet me. The fireman started descending the white polished stairs. His uniform was all white, the many buckles and fasteners glistening.

Quite a few angels appeared behind him. Some were suspended from the sky, hanging by theater wiring, and some were standing on the staircase to nowhere.

The angels were people who had hung out the windows of the Twin Towers. Their business clothes were shiny and white. One of the angels was the pregnant woman from the ATM kiosk I had helped. Her eight months of pregnancy looked lightened by the flowing whiteness of her angel dress. She smiled warmly and gave me a nod of recognition. Another angel was the bond trader I had sat on the bench with during my long walk home that day.

When the fireman reached the bottom of the staircase, I saw that he had a gas mask in his hands. He reached forward and, without asking my permission, placed the gas mask on my face, fastening it.

The angels of the people who were in the Twin Towers stood on the staircase behind the fireman and slowly descended it. There were angels holding "Help" signs; angels holding "missing" posters, with Xeroxed photos of themselves on them.

I took in clean oxygen from the mask that the fireman had given me. I started to come back to life. As the fireman finished the last chorus of "Beauty School Dropout," I wasn't sure if I should applaud. The music faded to silence. What was the fireman's message to me?

Should I go back to Ann Arbor? Back to New York? Back to Sun Microtek? Back to high school? Should I join the steno pool?!

Before I could ask the fireman any questions, he put his finger to his lips and picked me up. He held me in his strong arms, much as he would if I had fainted or were unconscious. Or dead.

I didn't fight him. I allowed him to carry me away.

We didn't seem to be walking towards anything. I couldn't see any landmarks. There were only white clouds. I leaned against the fireman's chest and listened to his rhythmic breathing. There was nothing but his arms carrying me and the solid strength of his reassuring chest, covered in a thick, protective glistening white uniform. I closed my eyes. I was safe.

I didn't open my eyes until the fireman's steady motion stopped. I looked around, dazed. He set me down. I was inside a building, and it wasn't white. It was dull, beat up, and beige. The fireman started walking away.

"Where are you going?" I shouted this out to him, confused.

He didn't answer. He pointed to what looked like the baggage claim area of Newark airport. I watched him as he waved goodbye. He walked away until he was just a dot on the smoky horizon.

I looked around me. I was sitting on a baggage carrel. The carrel, thankfully, wasn't moving. I stepped off it.

The fireman had delivered me back to the decision that I had already made to move to LA. But even though the fireman had not lifted me to heaven or taken me to someplace new, I was grateful to him. He had helped me survive these past four months.

I woke up confused and drenched in sweat. I looked around, disoriented. I was still in my hotel room. It was getting dark. I looked at the clock. 7 pm. I must have slept an hour or so. *Grease* had finished, and the television screen had defaulted to the pay-per-view menu and an endless loop of hotel attractions.

I turned up the air-conditioner and put the food outside my door to be cleared away. I then took a last look outside my window at the lit shops and restaurants of Rodeo Drive as I closed my email and turned off my laptop. I set my wake-up call for 4 am. It was time to finish packing and get ready for bed. I had an early flight back to New York in the morning.

CHAPTER 33

I exited the cab, paying the driver. My flight back to New York had been uneventful. It was 2 pm, and I needed coffee.

In *Glengarry Glen Ross,* the "motivational" speaker and successful salesman Blake Edwards, played by Alec Baldwin in the movie, had stated in his iconic speech that "coffee's for closers only." If Blake had said that to me even a week ago, I would have accepted his rule without hesitation.

But I was finished with the alpha-male posturing of sales. I was going to have a large cup of coffee.

Even if I wasn't a closer like Ricky Roma.

I walked to the deli next door, rolling my suitcase behind me. There were several of the staff, Pakistani guys, unpacking a delivery. I nodded to them, poured coffee into a large waxed cup, and put half-and-half and a Sweet-and-Low into it.

As I was leaving the deli, trying to balance the coffee, my purse, my laptop bag, and my suitcase, one of the workers looked up from the crate of milk he was unpacking and grinned, asking me in a Pakistani accent.

"Need help?"

I shook my head. He followed me anyway and opened the door for me. He turned around to go back to his crates, waving goodbye to me before I could say anything more.

Clichés in movies and television always painted New York as a place where people are cold and calculating, never helping others. But this wasn't what I had experienced in my five years living in the city. I often had doors held open for me or coffee poured for me without asking. The workers who I came in contact with each day extended a thousand little kindnesses my way. They were a part of the city I would definitely miss.

Once inside my apartment, I wheeled my luggage into my tiny bedroom and quickly set to unpacking. I wanted to live in at least an illusion of normalcy until I was forced to surrender to the movers.

When my clothes were unpacked, I looked at the clock on the wall above the television. It was 3:00. Even though I had only been in the apartment for an hour or so, I needed to get out and get some air. I put on my shoes, grabbed my keys and purse, and left the apartment.

The sky was grey, and it was chilly outside. I pulled the collar of my wool peacoat tighter as I walked towards the waterfront. I walked along the brownstones on Henry street, some with their holiday wreaths still on the doors even though New Years was over two weeks ago. I passed a bare tree. Its trunk still had a "missing" poster taped to it, the corners now torn, and the picture faded and weathered. There was a small remnant of an altar at the bottom of the tree. I bent down and straightened the burnt-out votive candle that had tipped over and wiped soot off the Polaroid picture that was lying face down in the frozen dirt and dead leaves.

The photo was of a Jewish man in his late thirties wearing a yarmulke and hugging a woman who had a baby wearing a powder-blue onesie in her arms. I placed the picture next to the candle, as I recited in my mind an excerpt of the familiar Hebrew "El Malei Rachamim" prayer of mourning which I had learned from my mother's Jewish grandparents and had recited at many funerals over the years. Growing up, I was taught that "El Malei Rachamim" was recited to ask God to grant the departed peace and proper rest for their soul.

"God, full of mercy, who dwells in the heights, provide a sure rest upon the Divine Presence's wings [...] The Master of Mercy will protect him forever, from behind the hiding of his wings, and will tie his soul with the rope of life.

The Everlasting is his heritage, and he shall rest peacefully upon his lying place...Amen."

I hoped fervently that the souls of all those that died in the Towers on 9/11 had found rest and peace.

I turned from the photo, giving it one last inner salute, and continued my walk to the Promenade. As I approached the riverfront, I sat down on one of the benches facing the river. Gloria was already seated there. She had on a simple grey wool coat with a fake fur collar and was smoking a cigarette as she stared out at the Manhattan skyline with its gaping hole. I sat down, saying nothing. After an indeterminate pause, Gloria turned to me.

"How was LA?"

"I'm moving there, actually."

I said this to Gloria as I would tell a close friend. My voice held a mixture of excitement and regret.

Gloria scoured my face, looking into my eyes for an explanation. She must not have found one because she shrugged, taking a drag of her cigarette and then tossing the butt to the ground and putting it out with her stiletto heel. She looked out at the East River.

"I'm leaving New York too. I'm off to Boston. I need a change. I hope to find peace there and a place for myself. Take care of yourself, Stephanie."

Gloria wrapped her wool coat tightly around her and stood up to leave. I didn't have the heart to tell her that she would die in a car crash long before she ever reached Boston. I simply waved goodbye. She waved back and then turned away from the bench and started walking down the Promenade.

I watched her go; the moment tinged with melancholy. In a manner of speaking, I was losing a close friend. I understood Gloria's quest to find a new life in Boston. My move to LA was driven by a similar need to find peace.

I hoped that my move would go better than Gloria's had.

When I couldn't see Gloria's silhouette any longer, I turned to the Manhattan skyline. I expected to see some sort of 9/11 reminder, as I had for the last several months. But although the January sky was cloudy and grey, the skyline was free of smoke and dust. I sat for a while, staring out at the river. I wanted to feel a connection to the skyline like somehow it was a permanent part of me.

But today, the skyline remained disconnected from me. The buildings that made up the horizon had existed long before me and would be there long after I moved to LA.

"Each window in each building houses someone who is in their office striving to build a better life for themselves, and succeeding."

Tess was now sitting next to me. She pointed to the Citigroup Center. I stared at the building's sloped, triangular roof. I disagreed with her statement. Many of those offices held people trapped in jobs they hated.

Tess continued.

"I start my new job at Trask Industries tomorrow. I've finally made it! Take care of yourself, Stephanie. Good luck in LA. I hope you find success."

Tess didn't turn to me when she spoke. She continued to stare at the Manhattan skyline with the same dewy-eyed optimism she had always had in *Working Girl*. She exhaled in satisfaction and then turned to me, reaching out to shake my hand. I gave her a nod goodbye as she got up from the bench and walked briskly away from the riverfront. I sat for a few more moments, staring out at the river. But the tall buildings in the skyline didn't beckon me. I saw no success for myself hidden behind their glass windows.

I got up from the bench to continue my walk. When I was on Atlantic Avenue, I took in the familiar hodge-podge of buskers, buses, and hotdog cart vendors. I passed an older, toothless man, wearing a red hoodie and spitting chewing tobacco onto the sidewalk. He had a long card table set up in front of him with an array of New York City merchandise displayed on it. There was a pile of navy baseball caps emblazoned with the New York Fire Department logo, FDNY, neatly stacked on the front of the table.

I thought of all the firemen I had seen since 9/11. They all had smudged earnest faces and a clear sense of purpose. This was especially true of my fireman ghost, who had always been there for me. Brave and strong, he had always answered my call for help.

I would never forget him.

I walked over to the table, pulled a couple of the caps off the pile, and pulled out a twenty-dollar bill. The caps were twelve dollars a piece or two for twenty. The man handed me a white plastic bag with the two caps in it, giving me a smile that showed off his gums. I put the bag around my wrist and continued my walk along Atlantic Avenue.

As I walked in the general direction of Cadman Plaza and the Borough Hall subway station, I almost bumped into a hawker who had a red vinyl apron on over his winter coat. The apron had large pockets that held maps and brochures and a stack of printed tickets. I looked behind the hawker and saw a line of tourists holding maps and patiently waiting at a large sign that said: "Uptown and Downtown Manhattan Night Tour. Drop-offs every 15 minutes".

The hawker was selling tickets to the open-top bus tours that had stops all around the city where you could hop on and hop off the bus. I had never seen tour buses in Brooklyn before. I guessed that with much of lower Manhattan closed or difficult to navigate, the double-decker tours had rerouted the buses and changed their itineraries. I looked at my watch. 5:30. It was a good time to take the night tour as the city started to light itself up.

The hawker, a man in his twenties with olive skin and black slicked-back hair, was shouting and waving his arm, which held a fist-full of brochures.

"Tour New York City! Uptown and Downtown! Unlimited Hop on Hop off! Now touring Brooklyn! Round trip only $25!"

I took a brochure from him and looked at the stops on the tour. I had no idea why I was considering taking a tour to Midtown. I debated turning around and walking back home.

But my apartment wasn't really my home any longer.

I didn't have a home at the moment.

The double-decker bus was half-filled with tourists. Maybe losing myself in the Manhattan crowds would help me feel less homeless.

I handed the hawker cash and boarded the bus. I was easily able to get a seat on the top deck, with the space next to me empty as well. I settled into the hard, plastic seat.

The bus crossed the Brooklyn Bridge and took the FDR, bypassing Ground Zero and the financial district. The first stop was Chinatown East and the Lower East Side. The tour guide was sitting near the stairs on the top deck. He had on grey double-knit slacks, a black windbreaker, and a white button-down shirt that had a mustard stain on it. His red cap was emblazoned with the logo of the bus tour company.

I only half paid attention as he recited a memorized passage in a bored voice about how immigrants had landed at Ellis Island and moved to the neighborhood one hundred years ago.

Although the guide's facts were probably correct, the Lower East Side had always been about art and music to me. As the bus drove up Bowery towards East 2nd Street, I glanced at the restaurant supply stores and Chinese groceries that lined both sides of the streets.

The bus stopped at a traffic light on Bowery, right in front of CBGBs. I was shocked that the driver didn't even mention the legendary punk and new wave club. I glanced around at the other tourists on the bus. I heard small talk in several European languages I couldn't quite decipher. No one but me was looking at CBGB's iconic red and white awning with the block lettering.

CBGBs had been a symbol of so much of what I had wanted to experience when I moved to New York. I had managed to get to a couple of shows there in the last five years, but, like so many of my encounters in the city, the experience had been anticlimactic. The bands I had seen there were just run-of-the-mill second-tier punk and alternative bands that played in many cities, including Ann Arbor.

The bar had been dirty and in poor repair. The experience had felt more like I was visiting a museum and less like I was experiencing rock and roll history being made. GBGBs had had the vibe of a bar long past its prime. After a couple of visits, I had given up trying to find meaning there.

While I would have loved for the ghosts of Patti Smith, Lou Reed, or even the B-52s to walk out of CBGBs and join me on the bus tour, Rose was the only ghost that boarded the bus. She sat down in the seat next to me. She was wearing a brown tweed skirted suit, and her hair was up in a sedate bun. I gave her a nod as I stared at the closed, graffiti-covered doors of CBGBs. I waved goodbye to the club as we resumed moving uptown.

The tour bus made its way to Soho. I looked at the stately condo buildings mixed in with the renovated loft spaces and their street-level storefronts. I had always wanted to live in a Soho loft. When I had moved to New York, I had come here with fantasies of all the romantic rooftop candle-lit dinners I would have, with stunning views of the brick buildings and graffiti-clad water towers surrounding me.

I had never made it to a NYC rooftop in the five years I had been here. The closest I had ever gotten to a romantic rooftop dinner was eating carryout alone in my Brooklyn apartment and watching episodes of *Sex and the City*, where Samantha entertained her dates and sex partners on her stunning Meatpacking District loft rooftop.

There were many things the tour guide could have pointed out in Soho. We were on Prince Street, where there were plenty of art galleries, bars, and designer clothing boutiques. But, as if reading my thoughts, the guide started talking about *Sex and the City* instead.

The bus approached a nondescript red brick building that had a rectangular, block-lettered, red and white sign that said "Fanelli Cafe." The tour guide stifled a yawn and pointed to the sign.

"And on this corner, we have the bar where Carrie and her friends first ordered a Cosmopolitan on the famous show *Sex and the City*."

Fanelli Cafe wasn't the bar that first featured the famous pink cocktail from the show. That bar was called the Odeon and was in Tribeca. I remembered this because I had argued about which bar had created the Cosmo with Michael during one of our drunken conversations about pop culture. I had been surprised at the time that he was a fan of the show.

But this tour bus couldn't go to Tribeca because that was too close to Ground Zero. So the tour guide had found a semi-suitable replacement on the itinerary to please the paying customers of the tour.

Fanelli Cafe wasn't a sophisticated martini bar. It had been around for over 130 years as a friendly neighborhood pub. I had been there a couple of times after gallery events when I first moved to the city and had been naive and eager to learn about Soho's art scene.

A group of four women in their twenties giggled from the back of the bus and pointed to the red and white "Fanelli Cafe" sign. They were overdressed for a bus tour and had high heels, disco makeup, tight-fitting silk camisoles, and leggings on. They looked like they were using the tour bus as their transportation to the nightclub district in Chelsea instead of taking a city tour.

"Can we stop here?" The women asked.

The tour driver pointed to the exit and gave them a weary nod.

After the bus idled and parked in front of Fanelli Cafe, the tour guide stepped out to take a fifteen-minute cigarette break. As we waited for him to return, I watched the street traffic, not focusing on any particular sight. After about ten minutes, Rose stood up from her seat and turned to me.

"I'm going to go take a look at that bar everyone is so interested in. It looks like something Jack would have liked."

I turned towards Rose and expected her to have the same curious and excited demeanor as the young women who had gotten out to have a Cosmo. To my surprise, Rose had a tear in her eye as she looked at the bar. She turned to me and touched my shoulder as she quoted one of her lines from *Titanic*.

"There was a man named Jack Dawson, and. . . he saved me in every way that a person can be saved. I don't even have a picture of him. He exists now only in my memory."

I watched Rose, a puzzled look on my face. She sniffled, her eyes glossy and earnest, as she continued,

"Those that died in the Towers will exist in your memory, too, Stephanie. Don't forget them."

Rose bent over and kissed my forehead. She then turned to depart the tour bus.

"I'll be staying in New York, so this is goodbye. Survive, Stephanie. Live your life."

Rose waved her final goodbye. I watched her open the door to the bar and disappear. I debated getting out of the bus and following her to tell her that she was walking into a run-of-the-mill neighborhood pub and not the glamorous bar that served cosmos in *Sex and the City*, but I decided to stay put.

Rose had her future, and I had mine.

The bus tour continued, slowly showing us the landmarks that defined the tourist version of New York. When we drove by the Flatiron building with its strange narrow shape, I felt a tap on my shoulder and turned around, thinking that perhaps Rose had rejoined the tour. But the tap had come from the woman sitting in the back of me, who was leaning forward, poised to ask me a question.

She was about my mother's age and had on wire-rimmed glasses and a giant pink knit scarf. She was holding on to the arm of a man around her age, who had a forest-green ski jacket on, and was reading the map intently. He looked up from it and gave me a friendly smile when I turned around.

"Hello, Dear. Sorry to bother you, but this is our first visit here, and we're a bit confused at what the tour guide just said. Are we in Midtown yet? I don't want to miss Times Square."

"We have about twenty blocks still before we reach Midtown."

I gave the woman a detached smile as I said this.

"Oh! Thanks so much for clearing that up. I'm Mary, and this is my husband, Bill. We're from Tulsa. What's your name, dear?"

"Stephanie."

"Where are you from, Stephanie? What brings you on this tour today by yourself?"

I wasn't sure how to answer the woman's question.

I had no idea why I was on this tour. I gave Mary a polite look as I said, "I've never been on a tour of New York before."

My answer seemed to satisfy her. She nodded. I looked at my watch. It was 7:30, and I was starting to get hungry. And tired. I barely paid attention as the bus passed Macy's and the Empire State Building.

We finally reached Times Square. As we drove past the tourist shops, chain restaurants, and flashing neon signs of Broadway, I could hear Mary behind me, taking in the cacophony of garish lights and noise.

"New York is so crowded!"

The tour bus slowed down as it approached its Times Square exit. The guide announced that we would be taking another fifteen-minute break. I got up and exited the bus to stretch my legs. We were parked in front of the faded Howard Johnson's that was on its last legs. A couple of weary-looking prostitutes were sitting in blue and orange vinyl booths near the window, the last survivors of the Times Square that had existed before the mayor had cleaned the area and made it safe for tourists. I looked at the prostitutes' heavy eyeliner, lining tired, blank eyes. They were nursing cups of coffee in the chipped white mugs with the Howard Johnson's logo on them.

My eyes wandered over to the Red Lobster restaurant, with its giant flashing lobster sign. This particular corner of Times Square always reminded me of Robert De Niro's character, Travis, in *Taxi Driver*. I could imagine him parked in his taxi in front of the restaurant. I waited for Travis's ghost to show up and quote one of his lines from the movie. But he didn't.

For all the crowds surrounding me, I was alone. And ghost-free.

I remembered my favorite quote from *Taxi Driver*, nevertheless. I whispered it to myself:

"Loneliness has followed me my whole life. Everywhere. In bars, in cars, sidewalks, stores, everywhere. There's no escape. I'm God's lonely man... The days can go on with regularity over and over, one day indistinguishable from the next. A long continuous chain. Then suddenly, there is a change."

I had been lonely for most of my time in New York.

Hopefully, I would be less lonely in LA.

The fifteen-minute break was over. Our tour guide slowly climbed back into the tour bus, and I followed him back on. When I reached the top deck, Mary and Bill were already seated. For all their eagerness to see Times Square, it didn't look like they had left the bus. I gave them a small wave of acknowledgment and sat back down.

As the bus headed towards Lincoln Center, I heard my stomach rumble. To try to distract myself, I looked out my side of the bus. We were almost at the last stop of the tour. As the bus approached 65th Street and started to pull over, I saw Holly Golightly. She was with her true love, Paul. They were holding each other and kissing, Holly's long cigarette holder dangling behind Paul's back as she kissed him with sincerity and surrender.

Holly Golightly was my sister. We were two drifters. And we were both after the same rainbow's end. But we were traveling different paths now. Holly had found her rainbow's end. Ironically, it had turned out not to be Tiffany's, but to be her New York neighbor Paul.

But I was still a drifter. I was still searching.

As I looked out the bus window at Holly and Paul embracing, I felt the rain and wet wind of the final scene of *Breakfast at Tiffany's*.

The love scene. The redemption scene.

But there was no love or redemption in New York for me. I hoped that LA would be different.

Tears started to stream down my face. I resisted the urge to wipe them away. I thought of LA. I had no idea what my life would be like there. Maybe LA would turn out to be as alienating and isolating as New York had been.

But maybe it would turn out to be home.

My thoughts were interrupted by Mary.

"Where did you say you were from again, dear?"

I turned around to face Mary and Bill fully.

"I'm from LA."

Before they could ask me any more questions, the tour guide started talking about our last stop, Lincoln Center. I took a look at the airy building with its huge lighted windows. The floodlighting surrounding the building allowed me to see, even from the bus, the warm reds, and yellows of the Chagall paintings that were on the back wall of the atrium. Of all the art I had seen in the five years since I had moved to New York, these Chagall's were some of my favorites.

Whatever had disappointed me about New York, I treasured the abundance of exquisitely beautiful public art. I saluted goodbye to them as the bus parked and idled.

My tour was over. It was time to get some dinner. I stood up and waved goodbye to Mary and Bill as I departed the bus.

Once on 65th street, I hailed a taxi and climbed into it, giving the driver the address to my apartment, where I would finish out the evening by ordering carryout and watching an iconic movie set in Los Angeles such as *China Town* or *Sunset Boulevard*.

Tomorrow I would begin to pack, initiating my move to LA, the next stop on my winding journey towards home.

Made in the USA
Las Vegas, NV
29 December 2021